The Werecat Chronicles

Sally Bosco

Cover by Lynne Hansen **http://www.LynneHansen.com**

Cover model: Alessandra Casiraghi
http://gilliann.deviantart.com

With thanks to:
Julia Starr **http://night-fate-stock.deviantart.com**
PhatPuppy **http://phatpuppy.deviantart.com**

For more information about the author, visit
http://SallyBosco.com

Also by Sally Bosco: *AltDeath.com*

Acknowledgements

I'd like to thank Lynne Hansen for creating the amazing *Werecat Chronicles* cover art and for her friendship and continual editing support. I'd also like to thank Tanya Twombly for her expert editing skills, and her daughter, Veronica Twombly, for providing excellent feedback from a teen perspective.

Chapter 1

I saw and heard more than I should.

It shouldn't be this hot; *I* shouldn't be this hot. Pushing the tangled, sweat-stained sheets away from my body, I rolled onto my stomach. The breeze that rustled the palm fronds outside my window was cool by Florida standards, yet my skin burned.

The November night with its scent of orange blossoms beckoned me. I could almost hear it whispering, "Come on. You know you want me." Unable to resist, I slid out of bed and floated down the hallway and out through the front door, still in my white cotton pajamas.

Possessed, I sprinted like an animal down Whirley Road, past massive new homes with cathedral ceilings, past small older homes connected to horse farms and past the bare skeletons of newly constructed suburban monstrosities. On autopilot, my body headed for the southwest corner's secret entrance that led through a soccer field, beneath power lines into the six hundred acre Lake Park, a huge oasis in a busy part of North Tampa. I was dimly aware of being barefoot, but it didn't concern me.

This greenway conservation area saved me from the monotony of day-to-day life and gave me access to the forest I so loved. Finally I arrived at the shelter of the dense trees that understood me, the ferns that cooled my feet. I needed relief from a heat that threatened to melt my brain.

Along with the heat came an insane sharpening of my senses. How could I possibly hear the fluttering of bats' wings, the burrowing of an armadillo? I darted through the underbrush, losing all track of time and feeling better by the moment.

Then I heard it—the jarring sound of people talking, along with the crackle of a bonfire. Who had invaded my forest? Definitely people who wanted privacy. Buried deep in this suburban jungle, they were hidden from passers-by and from the one park ranger who patrolled only the main trails.

Instinctively, I turned to go in the opposite direction. When I heard footsteps behind me, my senses jarred me into reality, and I realized what a dangerous position I'd put myself in. Was I imagining things? I stopped; the footsteps stopped. I sped up and so did they. I say "they" because it sounded like several sets of footsteps. Shit. This wasn't good.

I knew that predators pounced when their prey ran. Still, I couldn't help myself; I sped up, then broke into a sprint until I was back out onto the main trail. Then I kicked my body into some kind of overdrive and ran through a strip of scrub palmettos until I was back onto the street. I prayed for just one car to pass, but that didn't happen, so I dashed around the corner, calculating how to get back to my house. Damn, I was all turned around, so I flat out sprinted for it. Fruitless. One of the guys had gone around the other way and cut me off. I skidded to a stop. He stood there, a slight guy in his twenties with fashionably spiked up hair wearing a USF hoodie. Not exactly the kind of person you'd expect to be attacked by.

"You look like a tasty morsel," he said while licking his lips. "You looking for some fun?"

My heart just about beat out of my chest. "No. Let me by, please." I turned to run in the opposite direction, but his other two friends blocked me. They were similarly dressed indie cool. Not ghetto, not trashy, not what you'd expect.

"Please, just let me go." My pleading sounded pathetic even to me. How was this happening in my woods that used to be safe?

The three of them positioned themselves around me, like they were used to doing this. One of them moved in on me, and despite trying to weave my way around him, he wrenched my arms behind my back. It felt like he dislocated my shoulders in the process. The other tried to grab hold of my legs, but I kicked out. These thugs were not going to get me. I connected with one of them and smashed him right in the crotch. He doubled over and spit up on the sidewalk. I hoped I'd ruptured him.

That just made the other two madder though, and the one guy had my arms pinned so hard, I wasn't able to kick with the same force. The guy in the USF hoodie got hold of my legs. He was crazy strong, so much more than you'd expect from his build.

When they started lifting me, I remembered all the things I'd been told by my parents and teachers about not letting someone take you to a second location. I got a surge of adrenaline then, which made me fight back with a vengeance. I screamed for all I was worth and thrashed against them, getting one leg free which allowed me to kick one of the guys in the face. That only made him madder though and he again clamped down on my legs.

The guy who wasn't holding me slapped some duct tape over my mouth. I continued to struggle full-out, but more and more my exertion against the steel bands of their muscles drained me until my body ran out of steam and there was no fight left in me. I only hoped that they wouldn't kill me, or if they were going to kill me they'd do it fast.

That's when something astonishing happened. A dark car, low to the ground, sped up the street then came to a screeching halt. The window slid open. A man's voice, young sounding, said, "What's going on here?"

The two guys froze in mid-act of carting me off. For a split second I got the feeling that they knew him. Something about the way they stopped so suddenly.

Then the man in the car flung the door open and leapt out. "Leave her alone." He seemed like he was about to jump on one of them when they looked at each other and scattered like cockroaches, dropping me hard on the pavement. I felt like I'd shattered my tailbone. The guy I'd kicked in the nuts, who was lying in the grass, got up and limped after them.

I peeled the duct tape off my mouth and lay there panting.

"Are you okay?" He extended a hand to help me up.

That's when I recognized him—Luis, one of the cool kids from school. A track team jock, he was new to school this year. The first thing I noticed about him was his eyes—dark and warm with long lashes, they were greenish with unusual gold flecks around the perimeter of his irises. He was tall—maybe about six feet—had long black hair, a little wavy, and was dressed in black jeans and a white shirt that looked like linen. Smelling of spicy cologne, he had something special, confidence maybe.

Even though I could barely stop shaking, I took his hand, and it felt warm and reassuring as he lifted me up. "Uh, yeah, I think I'm okay. Oh my God." I felt dizzy, like I was going to fall over, but he caught me.

"You need to sit down. Are you okay with getting into my car?"

I hesitated, my mind still in a blur of pain and fear. After what I'd been through, I didn't know if I could trust him. Then I realized I was being silly. He'd saved me after all. That was reason enough to trust him, wasn't it? "Oh, sure."

I walked over to his car door and reached for the handle, but he beat me to it. "Allow me." As he said that, one of his eyes actually caught the light and twinkled. I captured that image in my mind like a snapshot. He opened the door to his car and helped me in. The seats were low, so I sunk down too fast and hit the bottom of my bruised spine in an uncomfortable way and let out a little, "Uhh."

"Oh, careful. I meant to warn you about that."

Everything happened so fast, I was still taking in the fact that I wasn't being carried off by some guys who were going to do God-knows-what to me. After I settled myself and he got into the driver's seat, I said, "Thank goodness you came along when you did. Thank you so much."

"Hey, don't mention it. I'm glad I could help. I'm Luis by the way. I've seen you at school." He extended his hand and I took it. He grasped it a little more than you'd expect a casual acquaintance to and rubbed his thumb against the inside of my wrist.

"I'm Kenley."

"Kenley." When he turned the key in the ignition, the car made a sexy purr, and I could see his smile in the glow from the dashboard. "What were you doing outside at this hour by yourself? And in your pajamas."

"Being stupid, I guess. Sometimes I get these urges late at night to go out and run, get some air and think." I wondered if maybe I'd told him too much, that he'd think I was weird.

"Yeah, I know what that's like, needing to get away to think." He looked pensive for a moment, then he snapped out of it and gazed at me. "Let me take you home."

"I just live a couple of blocks away."

"Perfect. I'll feel better seeing you safely inside."

I happened to think, it seemed odd for him to be in this neighborhood this late at night. "What were *you* doing here?"

"I have a friend who lives a couple of blocks away. I was just coming from her house."

Her house. He had a girlfriend. Mental note. My thought of him being interested in me changed then, but I exhaled, thinking more about how grateful I was to be actually safe. I shuddered at the thought of what might have happened. "Wow, it was a great coincidence that you were driving by just then."

Luis gave me an intense look, his dark eyes shining from the reflection of the street lights. "There are no coincidences, Kenley."

"No, I suppose not."

We were at my house. All too quick. We sat there for a moment.

"I don't suppose you might feel like getting together some other time?" he asked.

I shrugged. "I don't know. Maybe. Yeah, I guess so." My head swam with too much sensory input, a combination of terror and attraction that was hard for me to process.

"I'm sorry we had to meet this way, but I'm glad that we did. Meet." I could see the shadow of his slight smile in the moonlight.

"Yeah, the school is pretty big. We might never have crossed paths." And I wouldn't have thought of approaching him. "Well, I should go." I reached for the car handle.

"Wait a second." He rushed over to open my door for me. "Let me walk you inside."

"I'll be fine. Really."

"Okay. Is there someone else home? You're not going to be alone, are you?"

"My parents are on an overnight trip to buy some artwork." Why did he want to know that? Maybe I shouldn't have told him I was alone. Maybe I should be afraid of him. God, I was so jumpy I didn't trust anyone.

"Maybe you should come home with me. My parents have a big house. You can have the guest room," he said.

"I'll be fine, I'm sure. This house has a security system like Fort Knox." I grinned and turned to walk toward our front door.

"I was just worried that you'd be scared being alone after what you've been through tonight." He rummaged through his pockets and pulled out a pen and the scrap of a receipt, scribbled something and handed it to me. "Text me later and let me know you're okay. I mean, I know you've had quite a shock. You can text me any time. I'm a night owl."

"Okay. I will." God, he gave me his number.

"See you at school, then." Luis waved to me, got back into his car and started pulling away but he stopped and backed up. "You really should call the police and report those guys."

"Oh, right. Thanks!"

He waved and drove away.

The house was dark so I used my code to turn off the alarm then slithered into my room. The contradictory feelings inside my head were about to drive me insane. I'd come so close to being abducted and raped, tortured and possibly killed, all because of my own stupidity. I owed my life to Luis. Funny how someone I'd barely known before had instantly become the center of my thoughts.

I took a hot shower and noticed that pink water ran down the drain from the deep scratches in my legs and feet. How stupid was I to have run barefoot? I got into a fresh pair of pajamas, made myself some Sleepytime tea and tried to settle down. I knew I was safe inside my parents' house, yet I sat in my bed staring at the door as though those men in the park might come in and attack me. A completely irrational thought. Was this what being shell shocked was like?

I knew I should call the police, but if I called they'd come out and question me, and I didn't want to deal with it. I'd do it tomorrow.

Then I thought about how I'd said "maybe" when Luis asked me if I wanted to get together some time. What was I thinking? How dumb was I? No wonder I didn't have a boy friend. I remembered that Luis asked me to text him, so I did. **Hi Luis, I'm okay. Settling down now. How can I ever repay you?**

Almost instantly a message came back, **I'll think of something :-) just glad you're ok. sleep tight.**

Wow. He answered right away.

After that I felt a little better and drifted off to sleep wondering about the mysterious Luis.

～ぐ⿃ Chapter 2 ⿃ぐ～

When I woke, even the gray light of dawn hurt my eyes. I panicked as the events of the previous night flashed through my brain. My head felt as though a bomb had exploded inside of it and I could barely open my eyes. Did all that really happen? I found my way to the shower and let the hot jets pound into me.

The shower felt wonderful. Odd though, the deep scratches on my legs had nearly healed, leaving only fine white lines where they'd been. I let the stream of water beat against my aching head, wishing I could stay under the jets for an hour inhaling the herbal scent of the soap and shampoo, letting the steam permeate my body then crawl into bed. But no, I needed to hurry.

This was one time I was thankful my parents were away so I wouldn't have to answer any questions about where I'd been last night. They were art collectors who were always out at some gallery opening or being schmoozed by artists so they'd buy their work. They also tended to their pet snakes. Yes, it's an odd hobby, but they seemed to have a fascination with unusual, beautiful things, like their artwork collection. For the most part, they stayed out of my business.

I dashed through the living room. Artwork filled every possible surface of our house, a one-story, four-bedroom, sprawling contemporary with lots of chrome and glass. One huge room served as the main gallery for my parents' massive collection of fantasy and sci-fi art. They owned some beautiful original cover art—mainly buxom women being attacked by monsters or aliens. It kind of irked me because I thought it was exploitation, but what could I do? Anyway, though, the centerpiece was a five-foot green ghoul with popping bloodshot eyes. I kind of liked him. They also had some dusty Egyptian stuff they kept in a special case.

Fifteen minutes later I was in my green Jeep on the way to school clutching an industrial strength latté. Even the Excedrin Migraine I'd downed didn't make my throbbing brain feel any better, and because I hadn't eaten, it felt like the pills were eating through my guts. Since I was late, I had a tough time finding an empty spot and had to park on the back row near the football field. I thought I'd vomit as I rushed in to class.

Monday. First period gym class, hurdles to be exact, made me welcome death. Could there be a more cruel and unusual punishment? The only saving grace was that Michelle, my best friend, had the same class, so she'd be there to share my misery.

We sat in the bleachers watching the first of the hurdlers face humiliation.

I glanced down at a chubby black haired-girl who eyed the first barricade as though it were a medieval torture device. Her gym suit crept up the insides of her thighs and stuck to her fat. She yanked the crotch down and looked around to see if anyone had been watching. The girl backed up, shot forward like a cannon ball then fell on her face trying to clear the first hurdle. The class roared hysterically.

"Oh God, poor thing," I said. "That could be us." I'd never been all that athletic and hate-hate-hated gym class.

"I feel so bad for her. These people are horrible. Why do they have to put us through this?" Michelle shaded her eyes against the already burning sun then pulled her chin-length brunette hair back into a scrunchie. She was petite and perky in a way that I envied. My tallness had always seemed a liability to me. It made me feel gangly and awkward, and for so many years I was taller than all the boys

The chubby girl picked herself up and tried again, this time attempting to step over the hurdle, getting stuck right in the middle. Ms. Audubon, the gym teacher, had to help her off. After that she ran back toward the locker room crying.

"If that happened to me I'd kill myself," a voice behind us said.

"Yeah, I'd never eat again my whole life," another one said.

The three girls sitting behind us laughed hysterically.

"The Claw Club," I whispered to Michelle. "The cattiest bunch in town. God, I hate those girls. They think they're sooooo perfect."

"They are," Michelle said. "At least they think they are."

"Yeah, whatever." I held my stomach as it clenched up, an angry fist of pain and nausea. "I don't feel good."

"What's the matter, Kenley? You need some water?" Michelle held out her lukewarm aerobics bottle.

"No. I was up late." My spasm released for a moment.

"Partying without me?" She gave me a friendly slug on the shoulder.

"No." I paused and closed my eyes trying like hell not to vomit. "I have to tell you about what happened last night."

"What?" Michelle looked past me, distracted by another victim of the hurdles. This one had knocked one of the barricades flat.

I shook my head and doubled over from another wave of shooting pains.

"Tell me. You can't just tease me then not tell me."

"Oh no. Look." I pointed to a spot between the bleachers. "Look who's there. Luis."

"Who?"

"He's new this year."

"Yeah, so?"

"He's pretty cool, isn't he?" I bent over to minimize the icky feeling that was rising up from my stomach.

Michelle shrugged. "I suppose."

"Can I die right now? Can I just fall right between these fricking bleachers and disappear?"

"You wish."

A pain stabbed at my insides sending a wave of nausea through me that I thought would make me explode. "I gotta go. I'm going to be sick."

"Hey you can't get out of it that easy."

I headed to the girls' room, hoping and praying I wouldn't heave before I got there.

The hallway to the bathroom was dark, creepy, spinning. That same feeling of lost reality I had the previous night overtook me. The restroom door felt heavy as a coffin lid, but I mustered all my strength and heaved it open.

Once open, the sickening smell of cigarette smoke caught in my lungs and made me gag. *Please just let me make it to the toilet.* I tried to prop the door open to let the fresh air come through, but abandoned that effort as I felt my insides turn liquidy.

When I opened the door to one of the stalls, a gray cat, bigger and bushier than a house cat and with the tufted ears of a lynx, bounded out over a pile of clothes on the floor, looked up at me and screeched. As the feline glared at me with a wild look in its eyes, I noticed something glittery on top of the small stack of garments behind it.

Then the cat did something I didn't expect. It ran up to me, and even as I tried to kick it away, it sank its razor teeth into my ankle and ran out the front door.

All I needed was a bite by a rabid cat.

ᴄᴏ᷈ᴏᴷ Chapter 3 ᴷᴼᴼᴷ

I just had time to dash into the stall and be sick. Sour bile mixed with latté. Nice. And after the bile was gone, I still heaved but nothing came up. I wanted to die. Why had I gone out running last night? What was wrong with me?

After I sat there for a while with my head spinning, I crawled out of the stall and rinsed my mouth, wet some paper towels and wiped my face. As an afterthought I looked down at my ankle where the cat had bitten me. It didn't look bad, really. I put some soap on a paper towel and washed the wound. You could hardly see it. I splashed some cold water on my face and re-tied my hair into a ponytail. Once I had rested for a minute, I felt remarkably better.

I gathered myself together and went outside to face my fate.

I lowered my butt onto the scalding, metal bleacher next to Michelle. "Yow!" I inched forward so my skin wouldn't touch the metal.

"Feeling better?" Michelle asked. "You look better."

"Yeah." I sighed. "I do. You know what, though? There was a lynx in the bathroom and it ran up to me and bit me."

"A lynx? What have you been smoking? No, it's probably that big ole' gray tom cat that's always hanging around the school. It bit you?"

"Yeah."

"Better get checked out for rabies, then." Michelle squinted at the sun.

"Jeez, just what I need. Did they call my name yet?"

"They did, but I told them you were in the bathroom."

I glanced over to the space between the bleachers. "Damn, Luis is still over there. I was hoping he'd leave."

"Kenley, you're up," Ms. Audubon called out with her megaphone.

"Just kill me now," I said, making my way down to face my doom.

But I felt strangely good. My senses resonated sharp and keen, and as I stood before the hurdles, I was able to size them up in my mind with mathematical precision. I had a sense of how high I should jump, how much to raise my legs to make sure they cleared.

With every bit of my attention on the hurdles, I took a running start. As I approached the first barricade, I held my breath and sailed through the air, stretching my long legs with ease. I amazed myself by clearing the first hurdle, then the second, and before I knew it, I was in a rhythm that was fast, efficient and sleek. And I knew I looked damned good doing it, too.

I walked back around to Ms. Audubon, barely out of breath.

The gym teacher pushed back her short salt and pepper hair with one hand and looked at her stopwatch. "Well, well, I don't believe it, Miss Walsh-Bohdan. You've made the best time of any of the female hurdlers so far. Have you thought of joining the track team?"

Luis was on the track team. "Maybe. I hadn't thought about it."

"I would if I were you." Ms. Audubon blew her whistle then shouted into the megaphone. "Anyone who didn't get a turn will go first next gym class. You're dismissed."

Relieved, I looked down at the ground, turned trying to find Michelle and ran smack into somebody. Looking up I saw that it was a guy. Long black hair, big hazel eyes. He even managed to look cool in his gym outfit, a black tee shirt with a tiny white skull on one shoulder, black shorts and running shoes. And he was smiling at me.

I'd run directly into Luis.

❦ Chapter 4 ❦

At that moment, the setting of the track field surrounded by bleachers took on a surreal intensity. The grass blazed a florescent green and the breeze moved Luis's hair in slow motion, like in a movie. His hazel eyes, with their unusual gold flecks, filled the screen of my vision.

"I'm glad to see you're okay today." Luis put his hand on my shoulder and rubbed it a little. "I was worried about you last night."

His touch sent a feeling of electricity through me, like a power jolt. "I was a little queasy earlier, but now I'm fine. How can I ever thank you for last night?"

"Ah, don't think anything of it."

I kind of hoped he'd mention getting together again, but he didn't.

"Wow! You looked great out there," Luis said to me with a shy smile.

"Thanks." I glanced at him then looked away.

"Do you practice a lot?" he asked. He moved a rock around with the toe of his shoe then pushed back a stray lock of hair that dangled into his face.

"Not really." I didn't dare tell him it was the first time I'd ever run hurdles. He'd think I was a freak.

He nodded. "I understand. When you're that amazing, why should you have to practice? A nightingale doesn't have to rehearse. It simply sings." He strolled away leaving me with my mouth hanging open. Luis was new to school this year, but already he'd collected a plethora of female admirers. I'd barely noticed him before, I mean, I'd noticed that he was hot, but he seemed so out of my league. The thought that he'd even look at me was patently ridiculous.

Had it been my imagination or had he acted kind of timid around me? It couldn't be.

Michelle walked up to me. "Come on, let's hurry. We're going to be late for next period."

"Did you see that? He talked to me." I was riveted to my spot as Michelle tried to drag me in the direction of the locker room.

"What are you talking about? You're much more gorgeous than those hoes he hangs out with." She twisted a lock of my hair. "Look at your long red locks."

I kind of pulled away from her. "Oh that. I think it looks stupid. I wish it were black. Then I'd be cool."

"You need a reality check, girl."

A tall girl with blue-black hair, cut short in the back and long in the front, bumped into me nearly knocking me over. "Oh, sorry." She held her hand to her mouth and giggled. "I thought you liked bumping into people." It was Molly, the ringleader of the Claw Club.

"Yeah, don't think you're going to get his attention just 'cause you're good at hurdles." Cristen, a girl with chin-length sandy blonde hair dressed in the best Euro-trash tradition of oversized shades, black pleather mini, hot pink glittery tank and heavy gold chains with penny loafers to top it off, popped her gum and snickered. Sarah, the third member of the infamous Claw Club, a short, pixyish girl with bobbed red hair streaked with bright blue highlights gave me a smoldering look with her head down and eyes glaring up at me.

"Someone like you has no chance with him, believe me." The brunette flipped her hair behind her shoulder and headed in the direction of the locker room, trailed by Euro-trash Cristen.

"I hate those bitches." I pounded my fist on a nearby bleacher. "Come on, let's go to the bathroom. I want to look for that cat."

"The bell just rang. We don't have time. I want to go take a shower. I smell." Michelle curled up her lip as though something had died under it.

"Listen, we're not going to go into the locker room, because the three witches will be there. Besides, I need to see if I'm losing my mind."

Michelle sighed. "Ugh. Okay."

As we walked down the outdoor hallway, I poked in the bushes. "The cat has got to be in here somewhere. Maybe he went back into the bathroom."

"You're going to owe me big time. You're making me smelly *and* late for class," Michelle said.

"Let's just go look in the bathroom, then I'll be satisfied."

Once inside, we peered around. "I don't see anything." Michelle stood with her hands on her hips looking impatient. "Let's go."

Just as we turned to leave, the brunette and the redhead, Molly and Sarah, burst through the door.

"Hey listen." Molly looked directly into my eyes then down at the floor. "I'm sorry we were giving you a bad time back there."

"Yeah. Like, it wasn't very nice of us, you know?" Sarah said.

"What? You three have been making my life miserable for months, and now you're apologizing?" I started feeling so angry, all my muscles clenched up.

When Molly stepped toward me and put her hand on my arm, something inside of me snapped. I looked down at the place there her fingers coiled around my arm. "Get your hand off of me, please."

"A little touchy, aren't we?" she said, leaving her hand right in the same place as she squinted her eyes.

"Listen, we're trying to apologize here, and you're all up in our faces." Sarah scrunched her pixie nose at me.

Molly smirked. "You'd better learn to play nice or..."

"Or what?" I felt my self-control slipping away.

"Or we'll have to teach you a lesson." Molly sneered.

The anger rose up within me until I couldn't contain myself. Feeling like a coiled spring ready to pop, I made my hand into a fist and pulled it back.

Chapter 5

"What are you thinking?" Michelle grabbed my fist and shoved it back by my side.

I felt something sharp at my ankle. "Aiiikkk." I looked down to see the cat. It bit me again.

"Oh, stop it Cristen," one of the girls said then covered her mouth.

As the cat ran, I ran after it. "We have to get it so it can be tested for rabies. Help me, Michelle."

When the cat disappeared into the bushes, we lost it.

"Where'd it go?"

"I don't know. The snotty girls have made themselves scarce, too."

"What's wrong with you? They were trying to apologize." Michelle stared at me incredulously. "I've never even seen you get mad before."

"I don't know." I put my hand on my forehead attempting to regain some balance. "It's like I haven't been myself lately."

"Listen, Kenley," Michelle said, backing away. "I have to get ready for class."

"But I need to talk to you about last night."

"It'll have to be after class then in the parking lot. I need a ride to the homeless shelter to do some volunteer work." She rushed back to the locker room.

"OK." I dragged myself back to the bathroom and washed my face. I wanted to talk with Michelle, but I hated going to the homeless shelter. It made me feel crawly. If only Michelle wasn't such a goodie-goodie.

The rest of the day was okay. I didn't see Luis again, which was disappointing. I had mixed feelings about telling Michelle about last night. On one hand, I wanted to get it out—needed to tell *somebody*, but then again, she'd think I was bananas for running in the forest by myself after midnight. I leaned against the side of my Jeep and waited, hating the heat and the sun. It was November, and even though the previous evening had been cool, the temperature was in the high eighties. I longed for a drizzly November day in London or Seattle. Anywhere but this sandbox.

Finally Michelle walked toward me loaded with books and tossed them into the back seat of my Jeep. "What a day."

"Really." We sat in silence until I navigated to Dale Mabry and merged into the thick afternoon traffic. "Jeez, I've been wanting to tell you about last night."

"Sure. Go for it. I'm all ears."

"You know how I like to run late at night in the park?"

"Yeah, you're the vampire runner. Remind me again why you like to run at midnight?" Michelle was so conventional. She couldn't fathom doing anything so odd.

"You know how much I like being in the forest. It's just so quiet. At this time of year I can smell all the citrus trees, and the vegetation seems to talk to me. It's kind of healing, you know? It's the only time I can think." I knew that my explanation didn't do my night running obsession justice.

"Yeah, so? What did you do, run into some kind of pervert or something?"

"I was lying in bed feeling feverish, but in a funny way. I had to get up and go out."

"And..." Michelle made a kind of "speed it up" motion with her hand.

"And some kind of wildness in me took over, and I ran way into the woods."

"You're going to get frigging raped or murdered if you keep doing stuff like that. I swear." Michelle looked away from me, out the window and bit into her cuticle.

"No wait, there's more." I touched her forearm to get her attention. "Something drew me deep into the woods. There were people there, and I think some kind of a bonfire."

"Yeah, probably homeless people who have no better place to go. Just because this stinking city government doesn't think it's a problem." Michelle folded her arms in front of her, starting to get her anger on.

"No, Michelle. It wasn't homeless people. It was some guys, and they started following me." I shook my head.

We pulled onto the interstate, got off at the downtown exit then turned onto a side street.

"You've got to be more careful." She paused. "So if there was a bonfire, couldn't people see it from the road?"

"No, the park is five hundred acres. Do you know how big that is? The bonfire was so deep in the woods it was completely obscured from view. There's only one ranger, and he doesn't go looking around much."

I pulled into the parking lot of the homeless shelter, which was in the worst possible section of town, found some shade, turned off the motor and looked at my friend. "These three guys starting chasing me."

"Oh my God, oh my God!" Michelle started chewing on one of her fingernails.

"I got in a good crotch kick to one of them, but they were so strong they were trying to carry me off. That's when Luis came up and they all scattered."

"Luis? You mean Luis from school?" She stared at me with her mouth hanging open.

"Yeah. When I got home I was all scratched up and stuff." I wiped the sudden chill from my arms.

"Wait, wait. You're skipping the part about Luis rescuing you."

"He drove up in some kind of sports car."

"That's a Jaguar XKE." She raised her eyebrows and looked at me like I was dense.

"Whatever. He came up and they all went away, like they were afraid of him or something. I can't figure it." I shook my head.

"I'm not getting you, Kenley. You're all by yourself after midnight and you're running in the woods. Okay, what else happened?"

"Luis drove me home and he was really nice. I was a little wary, you know, because of what I'd just gone through, but he gave me his number to text him later. He kind of asked me out, too."

"What? You nearly died and he's asking you out?"

"I think I said, 'maybe.'"

"This is all too much."

"Do you think I should tell the police?"

"Uh, yeah, you should call the police. I just don't understand you. You're different than you used to be." Michelle avoided my eyes.

"How long have you known me? Just my whole life, right? Do I take drugs? Do you think I'm a lunatic?"

"No."

"Right. I've always been a completely levelheaded person. I belong to the Sierra Club, I help with coastal cleanup. I get good grades—right?"

"Right." Michelle shrugged.

"Well I'm telling you I've been getting these weird sensations: heat, a kind of super-awareness, even strength."

"Now you're really scaring me."

"I'm scaring myself. And today, clearing those hurdles when I had never ever before in my life run hurdles. I just don't know what to think, what to do." I clamped my hands on top of the steering wheel and rested my throbbing head on them.

"It's got to be a thousand degrees in this car," Michelle said. "Let's go inside."

We walked down the alley into a brick building that must have been a hundred years old. Ivy and weeds crawled up the cracked surface. One huge green chameleon stared up at us and stuck out its dewlap. Typical Florida.

We entered through the glass doors and checked in with the front desk of the Tampa Bay Homeless Shelter.

"How's everything going, Doris?" I asked.

Doris had yellow blonde hair pulled back into a ponytail showing her receding hairline and she wore a smiley face button that said, "Ask me why I'm having such a great day." Like most of the people here, she had yellowed teeth with a couple of them missing. It made me feel guilty that my parents were able to afford dentists when the people here couldn't.

"Why, hello," she slurred. "You girls are such angels helping out here. You going to do the dinner fixins?"

I forced a smile at Michelle as if to say, I don't have time to stay that long.

Michelle said, "Sure we are. We'd be happy to."

Doris handed us guest badges then brought a box of canned food to a stooped-over woman who had been waiting patiently in the next room with her four children in tow. One child wailed relentlessly in its stroller, two toddlers ran around the waiting room pulling magazines onto the floor and one girl of about ten or so looked numb and shell-shocked.

We walked down the long corridor into the kitchen. I liked the idea of helping, but the greasy kitchen smell turned my stomach. Especially today. "Can't we volunteer to do laundry some time? That has to smell better than this?"

"It doesn't always smell better."

"Oh." That put an instantly-bad olfactory detail in my brain.

"Why don't you come and help me with some of my Sierra Club activities some time? At least those are usually in the fresh outdoors." I was always trying to get Michelle to work with me on environmental stuff, but she thought that helping homeless people was much more important.

"I will. Sheesh. Right now just help me with dinner."

We took two stained but clean aprons from their hooks and put them on.

"What do we do?" I felt guilty about the fact that I just wanted to get it done and leave.

A gaunt man with a three-day growth of gray beard, apparently in charge of dinner that night, gave us instructions on how to open huge cans of beans and pour them into a pot with mammoth cans of stewed tomatoes.

I noticed a girl with a blonde ponytail wearing a blue striped shirt and torn chinos facing away from us. "Shelly?" While doing our volunteer work we'd become friends with this young girl and her mom who had met with bad circumstances.

"Hey, Kenley, Michelle. Hi!"

When she turned around I could tell she'd been crying, though she wiped back her tears with a napkin and tried to hide it.

"What's wrong?" We both walked over and hugged her.

"Oh, nothing. Nothing." She put her hand to the bridge of her nose and pressed in a way you could tell she was trying not to lose it.

"Come on now." I rubbed her back with the flat of my hand.

"It's just that..." She wiped at her face. "My mom disappeared last night, and I'm so scared."

"Oh, Shelly. Did someone call the police?" Michelle asked.

"Yeah. They don't hold much stock in it when a homeless person disappears. They think she's out getting drunk or something, but she's not."

I felt so bad for wanting to rush home to my own petty life. "Shelly, what can we do?"

"Tell the newspaper. Maybe they'll listen to you rich girls. They won't give the time of day to a homeless chick like me."

"Oh, that isn't true. And we're not rich," I said feeling embarrassed.

"Y'are compared to me. You have homes and cars."

A feeling of compassion for Shelly welled up inside of me. All she had to go through wile we complained about our middle class lives. "I'll call the Tampa Tribune and Channel 8. They're bound to listen. Maybe they can still find your mom." I tried to remember if I had any remote connections with the newspaper, maybe a friend who knew someone who worked there.

"Thank you two." For a moment she lost her composure and her face flushed before she started a kind of hyperventilating sob.

"You're so welcome, Shelly." We both hugged her.

"God, I wish we could do more." I gazed down at the dishcloth I still clutched in my left hand.

"I've been searching everywhere for my mom." She bit her bottom lip, barely getting out the words.

"How did it happen?" I asked.

"My mom went out to get some food while I stayed here and did my school work. It got later and later, and she never came home. I told the lady at the desk at night and she called the police, but they didn't do anything."

"They didn't? Why not?"

"Something about her not being missing long enough. But if somebody abducted her or something, they'd have to put out alerts to find them, wouldn't they? Like before they were able to cross state lines or something?" Her face reddened and her breath caught as she talked. "They'll never get my mom back, will they?"

"We'll do all we can, Shelly." I hugged the thin, trembling girl and looked at Michelle. We both knew that homeless people didn't have high priority with anyone.

After Shelly seemed a little better, I pulled away.

"Are you going to be okay?" Michelle asked.

"Yeah." Shelly rubbed her eyes looking like she was trying to hold it together.

"You have to stay safe yourself, Shelly. Don't be out at night alone," Michelle said.

"I won't."

We both felt horrible leaving her, but we had to get back to making dinner.

Right after kitchen duty, I called the police, the newspaper and the TV station. Having no luck on the phone, I drove to those places trying to find an actual human to talk to, but all I could do was leave messages. I filled out a report at the police station, but I hadn't gotten all of the details from Shelly, so I didn't know how much good that did.

While I was there, I filled out a report on how I'd been attacked in the woods, but then when I put the time, which had been about two a.m., I felt stupid, like I'd asked for it being out alone that late.

They said they'd look into Shelly's mom's disappearance. Great. I owed Shelly an explanation about why the police hadn't acted on looking for her mom, and I'd have one for her, I vowed it. I'd make them do some kind of investigation.

I drove home after midnight exhausted and frustrated but too wound up to sleep, but I fought the urge to go running. A restless and troubled night for me.

∽⟨Ꝛ⟩≫ Chapter 6 ≪⟨Ꝛ⟩∽

The next morning I dragged myself to school. I looked in the car mirror. Even my hair looked tired and straighter than usual. I'd put some super hold gel on it to make the strands look separated and messy, but still it hung listless. My blue eyes seemed drained of their light. These late hours were catching up with me.

North Tampa High was a relatively new, small school, full of upper middle class kids from the Carrollwood area. When the district started to grow, the local politicians realized they needed another school, and due to the demographics and financial support, they'd made it really nice. Because of the small size, it should have been easy for me to find the one particular person I wanted to see. You'd think.

I looked for Luis in the hallway, but there was no sign of him.

In homeroom Michelle said, "You look beat."

"I was up late chasing around to newspapers and TV stations trying to get them to cover Shelly's mom's disappearance. Do you know what it takes to get a live person to talk to at that hour? I went to the cops, too, but all I could do was fill out a form. There's a waiting period to be able to report a missing person so I didn't have much luck there. After all that I couldn't sleep."

"Yeah. Poor Shelly. I feel terrible." Michelle clutched at her chest as though she felt an inner pain.

"I have study hall first period so at least I can chill."

The bell rang.

My first period study hall was in a large utility room that was sometimes used for smaller assemblies or club meetings. It had rows of library tables with a podium and screen for projection on one side and a row of windows overlooking the track and field area on the other. I peered outside intently to see if Luis might be running. No sign of him.

I opened up my chemistry book and took yet another stab at learning the periodic tables. Out of the corner of my eye I saw someone sit down next to me and didn't take much notice. The person was on the window side of the room, so the backlighting kind of obscured him.

As I continued studying, I heard the person shift around in his seat and looked up. My heart jumped into my throat. Luis sat there with a grin on his face.

"Hey, you don't belong in here," I said playfully.

"I know." He waved a piece of paper. "I have a special pass."

Damn, he looked good. Dressed entirely in black, his long hair hung loose framing his striking café au lait face. With his high cheekbones and large hazel eyes, he could have been a model for a European fashion designer.

"So, why are you in here?"

"To see you." His jovial expression turned serious. Serious and hot.

I could feel the red creeping up from my neck. And I knew with my fair skin the blush looked very obvious.

"I wanted to ask you if you were interested in joining the track team. With that display you put on yesterday running the hurdles, your talents are going to waste if you don't join the team."

"Oh. Sure. I'd be interested." I looked back down at my book feeling kind of foolish. His interest wasn't personal after all. He just wanted me to join the freaking track team.

"I didn't come to see you just for that. But it was a good excuse." His eyes gleamed.

"Well then." I struggled for something to say. "I've watched you run. You are amazing." It was true. He ran faster than any of the other kids and always looked liked he wasn't breaking a sweat.

"It comes easily to me for some reason. The same way it does to you." He gave me a penetrating gaze making me think his statement had some deeper meaning.

"It's only recently, though...that I've become good at track."

"Hmmm. I see. I'll bet you're good at a lot of things." He said this with very little expression, which made me wonder if he was serious or flirting, then he gave a hint of a smile.

Just then the overzealous student monitor wandered over to our table. Typical computer nerd with those skinny black glasses they all wore. She said, "Study hall is for studying, not talking."

"We have some important business to discuss about the track team," Luis said.

"I'm sure you do, but this is not the place." She straightened up and walked away looking pleased with herself.

"Future warden in a women's prison," Luis joked. "Anyway, go see Coach O'Brien about joining the team. We can use you. I'll see you later."

I watched him walk away, his black jeans clinging to his beautiful butt. Needless to say, the periodic tables eluded my attention after that.

At lunchtime I made a sweep of the cafeteria to see what was going on. Luis sat at the Claw Club table with Molly, Cristen and Sarah. The girls were at their fashionista-best, most notably Cristen in white shredded jeans, grey hoodie and skull scarf, Molly wore a black leather pencil skirt, white wife beater, and black gladiator ankle boots. Luis was laughing, apparently telling some kind of story they all found so amusing. I slipped out before he saw me. I must have been tripping thinking that he'd be interested in me when he had all of that right at his fingertips.

I caught Michelle in the hall. "Let's eat outside, okay?"

"Sure, it's a nice day."

We grabbed some quick burgers and chips and sat at a picnic table under a stately oak tree. The pleasant breeze made the constant sunlight bearable. In the fall it actually turned nice in Florida. Due to the isolated location of the school, the air had a clean scent.

"Why did you really want to come outside?" As usual, Michelle could see right through me.

I told her the story of Luis coming to find me in study hall. "And I wanted to come out here because Luis was in there with all those girls." Who else but Michelle could I possibly spill my insecurities to?

"Kenley." She looked me in the eye. "I'm going to tell you one more time, and I want you to listen. Those girls are all bling and fluff. They couldn't carry on an intelligent conversation if their lives depended on it."

"Intelligent conversation isn't exactly what guys want, is it? They want hot babes." I looked down at the greasy residue of my chips, not wanting them any more.

"Well, he's obviously interested in you. And Kenley, look at yourself. You're gorgeous, you just don't know it. How many times do I have to tell you? Look at your long red hair, big blue eyes and great figure? What are you thinking, girl? You're elegant, and they're trashy."

"Thanks, Michelle." Even if it wasn't exactly true, my friend had made me feel better.

"Did you get those college applications out in the mail?" she asked.

"Yeah, two of them, University of Florida and Florida State. I'm glad I got that going before all this weirdness started. What about you?"

"I applied to USF, but that's right here in Tampa, and I think I'd rather go away. I'm not really sure if I want to major in Social Work or PE." She pulled off the lid of her yogurt, inserted her plastic spoon and stirred. And I'm not sure I want to go to a commuter school, especially one that looks like a golf course."

"I can't see you as a gym teacher. Social work is your life. I mean, you really have a feeling for all that stuff. You're not selfish like I am. You truly want to help people. I guess I have that feeling for animals and the environment, but what you do for people, like homeless people and everything, is awesome." I hugged her, even though it might have seemed geeky to an onlooker. There weren't many people outside anyway.

"Yeah, but social work doesn't pay much. Maybe I should be an attorney."

Suddenly the thought of being separated from her gave me this incredible pang of loneliness. "Michelle, let's go to the same school. I can't stand the thought of losing you." I felt a swell of emotion realizing just how much she meant to me.

"You wouldn't be losing me." She looked down at her uneaten food then up at me. "We'd always stay in touch."

"Yeah, I suppose, but it wouldn't be the same." Though I didn't want anything to change, I knew that it was inevitable. Kind of sucked, but that was the way life worked, it seemed.

After school it was my turn to hold the meeting of the Sierra Club. We usually met in the chemistry lab once a month, this time to plan a cleanup of the Hillsborough River. The northern part where people frequently rafted had become littered and dirty. I was vice president, but since the president was kind of a slacker, I got stuck doing most of the work. I didn't mind since it was for a good cause.

Today, however, I just didn't want to deal with it. I had so much going on I thought of blowing it off. Only a handful of people ever attended these things anyway. If I didn't show, after ten minutes they'd get the idea and leave. I stood in the hallway and hesitated, the proverbial angel on one shoulder and devil on the other. I could so easily blow it off. No, I should go. My dorky sense of responsibility overcame me and I headed toward the meeting.

The ten kids in attendance all looked as though they were beat from spending the day in class. Most slumped in their seats discussing video games or lazily text messaging absent friends. Oh damn. One boy who had a crush on me and didn't miss a meeting was sitting right up front. He was kind of chunky and had buzzed-off sandy hair. As I entered, he hitched up his pants to try to tuck in his muffin top, but it didn't work. You could still see a thick ridge of chub rolling out from beneath his green S.P.C.A. tee shirt. He smiled at me in a way that made me feel guilty.

I wanted to start right away so I could get it all over with and go home that much sooner. I mean, I loved the environment and wildlife and everything, but I hated meetings. "I'm calling this meeting to order. As you know, our quarterly project is the cleanup of the Hillsborough River. I'll start by reading the minutes from last month's meeting." Fascinating stuff. I was even boring myself.

The door opened again, someone late for the meeting, no doubt. As I read from last month's minutes, I looked up and nearly choked. Looking so cool, dressed entirely in black in a sea of khaki-clad granolas, stood Luis.

⚜ Chapter 7 ⚜

What in the world was he doing here? I smiled at him and paraphrased the rest of the minutes, kind of stumbling at one point. Suddenly I was hugely self-conscious. All I ever wore were jeans and tee shirts, not stuff that was all fashiony like Molly and Cristen. I felt so lame, and what I had to say was so stupid. "Does anyone have any questions or suggestions?"

Crickets from the crowd.

Then Luis spoke up. "Have you checked into using 'Green Tag' credits to fund alternative power suppliers? The National Renewable Energy Laboratory has designated hydroelectric and solar power as renewable power source. Florida has a lot of sun."

I was completely amazed. Luis actually knew something about this, almost like he'd researched it online; he'd put some time into something I cared about. It couldn't be. "Can anyone answer Luis?"

No response. "I'd certainly like to look into it," I said. "It's something we could promote. Do you have a URL?" Even though everything I said sounded pretty dull and unimaginative to me, Luis gazed at me with an intensity that was hard to read. Maybe he actually did care a lot about this stuff.

"I can look it up. I'll get together with you later."

Luis wanted to get together with me later. I did an instant reality check with myself to see if I was misreading his signals. "Yeah, I'd like that." Then I had a sudden fright. If he got to know me at all, he'd realize how boring I was.

After I adjourned the meeting, everyone filed out except for Luis and the kid who had a crush on me. Luis momentarily looked at him, like he was maybe thinking that he was my boyfriend. Oh no. The guy (admittedly I couldn't remember his name) kept making conversation. *Wha, wha, wha.* All I could think about was how could I shake him without being rude.

"You're doing something quite amazing here," Luis said, interrupting the boy's diatribe.

"Really?"

"Yeah, you're rallying all of these kids to do something. That's major, you know? What else would they be doing? Sitting home, surfing the net, gaming. Worthless stuff. But you...you've got them caring about something."

"Thank you. No one has ever said that to me before."

The three of us started to walk out into the hallway. The boy made a subtle move to get between Luis and me then said, "Oh, Kenley, I tell you all the time how much we appreciate you."

Luis looked at me then at the other kid and took my arm. "Kenley, can I talk to you in private for a minute?"

"Um. Sure," I said. Luis actually took matters into his own hands and made the situation go the way he wanted it to. That was impressive. It also scared me in a way I couldn't describe.

My unwanted admirer left us soon after that. I felt bad, but not too bad.

Luis walked me out to my car. I had to make sure my feet were touching the floor.

"That was really nice of you to show up at our meeting," I said, walking slowly to stretch out our time together.

"It's one of my interests. I love wilderness and I'm appalled at the way the world leaders do so little to protect it. My dad's a big environmentalist, too." He grinned. "Now maybe you'll join the track team."

"I will do that."

We arrived at my car much sooner than I would have liked. To alleviate the awkward pause while we stood there, I opened the door and chucked my book bag inside. "What did you want to talk to me about?"

"I was just trying to get you away from Brian. I sensed you wanted rescuing."

Luis knew the kid's name and I didn't. "You were right. I did."

Luis parted his lips and took a breath, as though he was about to say something.

I stood there expectantly.

But then he pursed his lips together and looked at something beyond me, so I think the moment, whatever it might have been, had passed.

"Goodbye, Kenley." He nodded his head. "I'll see you tomorrow."

"Goodnight." I waved after him.

From that point on, I couldn't think about anything but Luis. Everything I saw made me wonder how he'd react to it. I held imaginary conversations with him in my head. As I walked, I pretended he was walking along side of me, and I thought of what I'd say to him.

I called Michelle and told her how Luis had shown up at our Sierra Club meeting.

"Careful of him," she said. "I've heard he's a heartbreaker."

I shouldn't have called her; I should have kept our little moment to myself. "Do you know if he's going out with anyone in particular?"

"I don't know. Maybe Molly. They hang out together, but they could be just friends. It's hard to tell."

"Yeah, I'll be careful. Thanks for being such a good friend, Michelle." I said goodbye and hung up. Then I dozed and thought about Luis—hazy, languid dreams of kissing in summer meadows, or talking for hours in the moonlit forest.

That night I felt the familiar burning heat sensations that somehow always grew more intense in the evenings. I was tingly and antsy, and it took all of my self-control not to go out running in the woods again. I didn't want to find get myself in trouble again. And now that I knew those evil guys were out there, I wanted to go out even less. So I lay in my bed and sweltered, tossed, got up and took a cold shower, got into bed again and thought of Luis.

Sure, I'd be careful of Luis. Yeah, right.

⋘❦ Chapter 8 ❦⋙

After two uneventful hours at school, I rushed to my third period Chemistry lab and found Luis standing out in the hall waiting for me.

"Hi." His long black hair was pulled back into a ponytail except for several gelled strands that hung over his face. He pushed these behind one ear, showing the silver and black bracelets that adorned his wrist. He smiled at me, glancing down at the floor then back up, almost like he was insecure, but how could that be possible?

"Hi," I said.

"Have you been practicing your hurdles lately?"

"Oh, no." I laughed. "I haven't even gotten to the track. I skipped gym class today."

His presence actually made the room look brighter. I supposed it was because my irises dilated to let in more light. What was wrong with me? I was so insanely gone over him and I hardly knew him.

Luis's eyes grew intense. "I see a lot in you, Kenley. Not just the stuff about running hurdles. There's so much more to you than that. I can sense it. I think we have a lot in common."

"I think we do, too." When I looked into his eyes it sent me into another dimension. Everyone else on the planet could have disappeared and I wouldn't have cared.

Luis hesitated. "Say, um, how about going out with me on Thursday? We can catch a flick or something."

Wait, let me think about this for a second. "Oh. Sure."

"Great. I know where you live. I'll pick you up at seven." As an afterthought he said, "Hey don't let the Whiz ruin your day." He squeezed my hand very quickly and ran off.

"I won't." By the Whiz he meant Mr. Wizofsky, the chemistry teacher. I waved after him and when I was sure he was out of sight, I touched the spot on my hand he'd squeezed. How could a chemistry teacher possibly ruin my day now? Luis had asked me to go out with him.

But something haunted me. Yeah, he was interested in me, sure, but why. And how could I keep his interest when he had all the glam Claw Club girls vying for his attention?

I practically levitated through my next classes. Then came lunch. Michelle stopped just short of the lunch line, looked me up and down, tilted her head and narrowed her eyes. "You're different."

"That's what I've been trying to tell you."

"Hey, would you two move?" Two redneck guys with baseball caps on backwards shoved ahead of us, making Michelle bump into me.

Michelle felt my forehead. "Jeeez, you're hot. You're burning up."

"I'm changing, and I don't think it's entirely bad."

Michelle backed away. "I think you need to go to the nurse. A high fever can cause brain damage, you know."

"Never mind the brain damage." I grasped my friend by both shoulders. "Michelle. Luis asked me to go out with him."

"What? That's incredible."

I started bouncing up and down like a dork, then Michelle joined me, but realizing where we were, we stopped and tried to act nonchalant.

"Come on. Let's get some lunch," Michelle pulled me toward the food line.

"I'm starving," I said, feeling the grinding need in my stomach.

"Aren't you supposed to lose your appetite when you're in love?" She looked at me with her head tilted.

"Not me."

Michelle grabbed a piece of thick crust pepperoni pizza, while I ordered two burgers.

Molly brushed past us, taking a bottled water and dinner salad. At first she had her mouth pursed with her upper lip curled and I thought she was going to make a comment about my burger consumption, then her face brightened as though someone had turned on a hundred watt bulb.

"Oh, Kenley, Michelle, come and sit with us today," Molly, all in black, purred. She winked at Michelle.

"Huh?" Michelle moved her head forward on her neck.

"She said, come and sit with us."

"Say, you girls look fabu today," the blonde Cristen chimed in. She wore a brown leather skirt with a chain belt denim jacket and short leather boots.

I shrugged. "Okay." This was really odd. Since they knew everything about Luis's activities, shouldn't they have been jealous of me having a date with him? Maybe they didn't know.

We took our red plastic lunch trays and followed Molly over to the special table, the one near the window overlooking the courtyard, palm trees and fountain.

"Wow," Michelle whispered to me. "We're privileged." She cleared her throat. "I'm just not sure I want to be."

"Be nice. They're making the effort," I said, hoping they wouldn't hear.

"Yeah. They want something."

"You're so cynical."

Cristen's boyfriend, Josh, was already sitting at the table. A hip-looking guy with short prickly hair, in jeans and a green hoodie, he carried a brown and orange bag that looked like an old-fashioned airline bag or bowling bag. He always waited around for her like a puppy dog. He wasn't a geek, but he always had his nose buried in a classic novel. Today it was *Moby Dick*. When Cristen walked over, he gazed up at her expectantly.

Cristen ignored him and sat on the other end of the table next to me. "There are a couple of parties this weekend. Orlando's parents are going to be away all weekend, so we're going over there on Saturday. They have a Tudor mansion with a pool. We'll have a fabu time."

"Yes, you're all invited. Partaé!" Orlando, who had a Mohawk and tattoos on each arm sat down next to Sarah and put his arm around her tenderly. He just didn't seem to fit in with them, and he looked a tad overweight in his black tee shirt and black leather pants with red pinstripes. But whatever. Sarah liked him.

"That's great, you guys. Thanks for inviting me." I scrunched down in my seat feeling unworthy.

"You're both invited, Ken and Michelle," Sarah said as she sucked on the straw of her fountain drink.

Then Luis strode over looking amazing in a white linen shirt and jeans. He stood by the side of the table and stared directly at me. Directly into my eyes.

I couldn't tear my gaze away from his amazing, hazel eyes that practically glowed. "Are you going to join us?" I asked.

The Claw Club girls stopped talking and watched both of us. Molly's nose flared a little, but she continued smiling.

"Oh, no. I was just on my way out. I'll see you later." Luis winked at me.

"Okay." Brilliant conversation, Kenley.

He turned and glided out the door.

I tried not to let my mouth hang open as I watched him.

After school, I sat in my car with the air conditioning running, waiting to see if by some chance Luis would be out to talk with me. He said he'd see me later, and I wondered if that meant after school. Apparently not.

I decided to go to the Tampa Bay Homeless Shelter and check up on Shelly. Damn! I'd forgotten to follow up on my phone calls to the media about Shelly's mom.

"Man! How can you stand those girls?" Michelle stood at the sink of the homeless shelter peeling a huge stack of potatoes. "You could help, you know." Again, the greasy smell of the kitchen almost did me in, but I breathed through my mouth and tried not to think about it.

"Oh, yeah." I tied my hair back, washed my hands, picked up another peeler and went to work. "I know they're shallow, but it's so much fun being in the cool group. I've been a loser-geek my whole life."

"Oh, hardly." Michelle dumped her stack of potatoes into a huge pot.

"I've always been on the fringes. Anyway, it's not like they're the jocks and cheerleaders. They're all interesting." I worked on peeling a potato, holding it over the cutting board and slicing carefully.

"The only one you're interested in is Luis." Michelle curled her lip a little, obviously disgusted with me.

"Yeah. Obviously. I know you said to be cautious." The potato slipped out of my hand like a wet otter and landed in the sink.

"I'm suspicious of any guy who has groupies like he does."

"They're not groupies. They have boyfriends, and other friends." I brushed a stray hair out of my eyes with the back of my hand.

"Whatever. Kenley, I can't be friends with you any more if you're going to hang out with those witches. They probably talk about us behind our backs."

"Come on. Don't be like that." I dropped my potato and peeler on the cutting board and glanced around the kitchen. "Have you seen Shelly lately?"

"Yeah. She's none too pleased with you." Michelle gave me a scathing look.

"I know. I forgot to follow up with the Trib."

"You promised you were going to get media coverage for her mom's disappearance and you didn't do anything. You're so selfish. All you think about is Luis." Michelle looked really angry now, the red creeping into her face.

Ouch. It was true, but it hurt. "I called all the newspapers and TV stations. What else could I do? I filled out a report with the cops, too."

"Whatever you did or didn't do, there hasn't been one story about the disappearance."

"I know. I suck. I should have followed up." At that moment I hated me.

"You don't care about anything except Luis and the Claw Club."

"That isn't..." I turned to see Shelly walk in. She looked thinner and paler than usual. A washed out denim dress hung from her stooped shoulders, and her face had a desolate look.

I rushed over to hug her. "Shelly, I'm sorry."

The girl's arms hung limp at her side. "It's fine. I didn't expect anything; I've learned not to. There's no hope of finding my mom now."

"I let you down. I'm so sorry. I called and visited the Tampa Trib, Channel 8 News, and the police, but I didn't follow up."

"It's not just you. It's everybody. I don't know what will happen to me now with my mother gone. I s'pose I'll go into foster care." She collapsed onto an old wooden chair at the side of the kitchen.

Foster care brought to mind abusive stepparents. Not a good thing. "Can't you keep staying here?" I asked.

"No, I'm a minor. I have to have a guardian." She looked down at her hands with their raw, bitten nails. "You know there have been others, don't you?"

"No. What do you mean?" I asked.

"Other homeless people have been disappearing. It's been happening for months now. It's just that nobody cares about us homeless people. We don't count."

"I know I let you down, but I'm going to go to the Tampa Tribune right now. I'll make them listen."

Michelle gave me this "you just want to get out of helping with dinner" look, but I went anyway.

I drove straight over to the Tampa Tribune offices, but when I got there, it was like a locked box. The receptionist out front absolutely wouldn't let me in. "Please? I have a very important story that needs to be covered. A possible serial killer."

"Do you have an appointment with anyone?" She looked over her reading glasses at me.

"No, but it's imperative that I see someone."

"Hang on. Our staff reporters are too busy, but I have a freelancer who might talk to you. He just happens to be here now." She dialed the phone. "Andy, I have someone out here who says she has an important story. Yeah. All right. Thanks." She hung up the phone. "He'll be right out."

Fifteen minutes later, a short thirty-something guy wearing cut-offs and a muscle shirt held out his hand to me. "Hi, I'm Andy."

"Andy. Hi! I'm Kenley." I stuck out my hand and he shook it with a firm grip and looked directly into my eyes. I knew that was a good sign. "I know your time is valuable."

"No it isn't." He laughed. "What's up?"

We sat down on the brown leather waiting room chairs.

"Anyway, um. I do volunteer work at the Tampa Bay Homeless Shelter, you know, the center for homeless families? And it seems that there have been some disappearances that no one is talking about because they're homeless people. One in particular, the mother of one of our friends."

Andy pulled out a netbook and took some notes. "Interesting. How long has this been going on?"

"From what I've heard it's a couple of months now. I hate it, because it's as though society doesn't think these people are worth bothering with. They're throw-away people."

"Huh. Can you give me any names?" Andy narrowed his eyes.

"Yes. Shelly Jackson. Her mom disappeared two days ago. One thing, though. I don't know how receptive the center will be to a reporter coming in and asking questions."

"Maybe I can pose as a homeless person and get in." He raised his eyebrows.

I shook my head. "No good. This place only takes families."

"I'll figure out something then." He pressed his hand to his mouth, thinking then grinned. "This could be Pulitzer material. Is the government refusing to protect people because they're homeless—the most vulnerable and helpless people in society? Hmmm."

"Yeah. They shouldn't be allowed to get away with it, right?" This was good. He was seeing my point of view.

"Absolutely. I'm disgusted with these wimps who call themselves journalists not covering the difficult stories. Just because it might endanger their jobs, you know?"

"I do. I sympathize, but a serial killer on the loose? Come on, why would they want to overlook that?"

"Sometimes the City doesn't want people to panic."

"But they should warn people." My head felt heavy and my limbs ached.

"I'll do my best to ask questions and get stuff stirred up." He looked over his notes on the small screen. "Is there anything else you can tell me?"

"No, just that Shelly's mom went out to get food in the early evening and never returned. She didn't have a habit of running off, either."

"Sad story." He looked down momentarily and sighed.

"Can you just promise to do something? Write an article and get some media attention?" My eyes drooped as I was talking with him, but it made me feel good that I was doing something about this.

"I will do that, fair lady. And what was your name?"

"Oh, uh. Kenley. Kenley Walsh-Bohdan."

His big fingers fumbled to type it into the tiny smaller than normal keyboard. "If you think of anything else, e-mail me or call me." He handed me a business card. "Where can I reach you?"

I gave him a fake number. I don't know why. I just didn't want him bugging me. Andy could have his Pulitzer all to himself.

We shook hands, and he seemed like he wanted to keep talking, but I told him it was a school night and I needed to get home.

The next day I combed the Tampa Tribune for an article but found nothing. I probably couldn't expect to see anything that fast. And even though I was concerned, very concerned, about Shelly, I had something huge on my mind. The big night had arrived. Date night with Luis. Yeah, shallow of me, I know.

I tried on a short denim skirt, heels and a tank top. No, too trashy. I tried on jeans, but they made my butt look flat. I finally settled on a short purple and black plaid skirt, fishnets, a black tee and buckle boots. I put some gel in my hair and messed it up just a little. Perfect.

I thanked whatever deity would listen that my parents were in Orlando for the Autumn Harvest Arts Festival. Luis wouldn't have to get the third degree in a straight-backed chair with a spotlight and all of that.

At about ten after seven, there was a knock at the door. I held my breath and opened it.

Luis stood there looking fabulous all in black, but something was wrong.

Standing next to him with her arm threaded through his as though she owned him was Molly.

⸎ Chapter 9 ⸎

Standing behind Molly, Cristen led dog-collared Josh along on a leash. Sarah babbled in back of them singing a funny song she'd seen on an Internet feed, doing a little dance while Orlando watched her.

"Luis." I tried to look as though I wasn't perplexed and disappointed.

He leaned forward and kissed me on the cheek. "Kenley, you look so beautiful tonight. You can't even imagine."

"Thanks." I cleared my throat. "Is this a group date?"

"We're all going to see the new movie, *Already Dead*." He shrugged and looked around awkwardly.

"Oh. Okay." My big plans for date night with Luis crumbled before my eyes.

He pulled me aside and squeezed one of my hands. "Kenley, I'm so sorry about this. I couldn't shake the group tonight, even though I tried. I can make them all go away if you want. I hate to disappoint you."

"No, that's fine. It'll be fun." I grabbed my jacket. "Let's go."

Luis held the door of his white Jaguar open for me. I caught my toe on the floor mat and tripped a little getting in. Luis caught my arm, then he kind of squeezed my hand as though to say, *Just relax, Kenley. It's okay*. I was so freaking nervous just being around him, I could hardly act normal.

Once inside I noticed that the interior was spotless and it had that new car smell. Only one personal item adorned his dashboard: a bronze engraving of an eye with a curlicue coming out of the bottom.

"What's that," I asked. "It's Egyptian, isn't it?"

"Oh yeah, It's the eye of Horus. It's good luck." Luis shrugged and turned the key in the ignition, causing the motor to give a sexy purr. He smiled at me and shifted gears.

Once we started driving with the convertible top down, and I felt the wind blow through my hair, I stretched my arms out and relaxed.

"Kenley, I'm sorry about tonight. I mean everyone tagging along. I didn't plan it. It just kind of happened." He shouted to be able to be heard above the din of the air rushing past us.

"It's perfectly fine. I don't mind a bit." The air felt pleasantly cool and I caught a whiff of fresh cut lawn as we left my neighborhood.

He flashed me an awesome smile and put his hand over mine. "That's what I like about you. You're low key and adaptable. I've had my fill of drama queens, if you know what I mean."

"I do," I said, trying hard not to smile as much as I wanted to.

As we pulled up to the huge, new Cineplex that housed sixteen movie screens, I hoped somebody I knew from school would see us. The film we were going to see, *Already Dead,* was playing in fifteen minutes. Luis bought me a ticket as the rest of the Claw Club stood around talking and laughing.

Cristen ignored Josh, even though he looked as though he desperately wanted her attention. While she talked with Molly, every once in a while Josh tugged on her sleeve like a puppy wanting to be petted. She even shoved his face away one time. It shocked me that any girl could treat her boyfriend that badly and have him still hang around.

Molly and Cristen looked entirely absorbed in each other. Josh finally gave up on Cristen and started singing a quirky Internet jingle, "The Potato Song," with Sarah while Orlando looked away with a pensive expression on his face. Then Cristen made Josh buy all of us popcorn.

The fake butter smell from the popcorn was making me hungry. But then I was pretty much always hungry these days.

Orlando, with his straight up Mohawk, walked over to me as Luis hit the restroom. "You're looking awfully serious tonight, Ken Doll."

"Oh, I do? I don't feel serious." Actually I was trying hard not to have a goofy grin on my face.

"Yeah." He pulled up on his Mohawk to make sure it was standing straight. "Don't let Mr. L get to you. I mean, don't start thinking he's all that, cause he's not. Okay?" His dark eyes showed an intensity that I could only interpret as concern for me. This genuinely touched me. These kids weren't all just selfish like Molly and Cristen.

"Yeah. I know. I'm not going too crazy over him." I glanced over toward the glaring neon of the snack counter as Molly and Cristen ordered Josh around.

"The *hell* you're not," Orlando fake-frowned and shook his head slowly. "You know, we're all with you, even though some of us—well, some of the girls—can act pretty lame. We're on your side."

That comment struck me as odd. "Anyway..." I wanted to change the subject. "I love your nose ring."

"Thanks." He touched it for a second as though remembering it was there. "I could do one for you."

"Ah, no, that's okay. It looks good on you, though."

"It's all bullshit, basically. Let's go in and see the freaking movie already." Orlando started chanting, "Zombies, zombies, zombies." Orlando seemed to think that everything was bullshit, or at least the extraneous things.

Luis came back over, laughed at Orlando's antics and took my hand. Orlando may have said not to take Luis seriously, but they all followed him like lemmings over a ninety-foot cliff. I wondered just what kind of hold he had over them.

We entered the nearly-empty theater and sat down. Molly, Cristen and Josh parked themselves a few rows away from us and immediately started eating popcorn and whispering. The rest talked and laughed too loudly.

When the movie started, Luis took my hand. "Don't worry,' he said. "We'll get to be alone together later. Even though you're being a good sport, I could see you were kind of bummed out about my bringing everyone along. I'm kind of bummed, too." The fact that he repeated this again made me think it was bothering him.

"Not at all. I like your friends." I squeezed his hand.

"Good, because you're one of us now." He dug his fingernails into my palm, giving me a tingly sensation.

Already Dead had a few "got cha" scares where I had to grab Luis's knee, which always made for good date moments.

After the film, everyone wanted to go to a rave in the woods. I wasn't so sure.

"You guys go ahead," Luis said. "Maybe we'll catch up with you later."

"Come on. You know you want to go." Molly brushed her hand on Luis's shoulder and pouted with her full, candy apple lips.

"No, like I said, maybe later." As he slid her hand off his jacket, her expression immediately melted, and she snatched her hand away.

Molly looked at me then at him and her eyes narrowed. "Come on, Cristen. Let's go."

The kids scattered to various cars, and Luis and I walked toward his Jaguar. I noticed the full moon silhouetted against a lone palm tree, and felt the warm Tampa breeze blow through my hair.

"Where are we going?" I asked as he opened the door for me. Truly, I would have gone anywhere with him.

"You'll see." He turned and grinned at me then lowered the convertible top. We took off and soon the wind scrambled my hair. He turned on his stereo, and we listened to some haunting cathedral rock. What could be better, driving down the street with Luis, the wind in my hair and infinite possibilities for the evening ahead of us? I felt so alive.

Then Luis turned onto my street.

"What are you doing? Taking me home?" He may as well have stabbed me.

"It's late and it's a school night. I don't want you to get into trouble with your folks."

"Are you going to dump me and go to the rave?" I wished I hadn't said that last part. It made me sound so needy.

"No way," he said as he parked on my street but away from my house.

"What, then?" At that point my emotions were a jumbled mess.

He smiled. "I thought we could go for a walk. This is a nice neighborhood, and you're right next to the forest."

"Are you crazy? I'm not going near that place."

"Listen, I know how much you love the forest and now there's nothing to be afraid of. Those guys have been caught."

"How do you know?"

"Because I personally followed up with the police. Your attackers are behind bars. They have so many other crimes they've committed, the police didn't even need you to put them in jail. It's safe now. There's nobody around who's going to hurt you."

"Wow, you followed up?"

"I know how you love the forest, and I couldn't stand the thought of you're not being able to walk around there any more. Mostly, I wanted to make sure you were safe."

"Oh, Luis, thanks." I felt guilty for not following up myself.

"I wanted to make sure you could still go to your favorite place."

We got out of the car and walked down Whirley road into Lake Park. The clean scent of pine trees along with the sweet smell of decaying foliage flooded my brain and transported me to another world. One in which I was more in touch with my animal feelings.

"Do you like being outdoors at night?" he asked.

"I crave being outdoors at night." I hugged myself and kind of whirled around.

We walked past the equestrian trail, north onto a less-traveled side path.

"Tell me about yourself," he said. "What do you want to do with your life?"

"I love being in nature, and I feel compelled to protect it. One thing that makes me really angry is the way people have abused the environment for so many years.

They have totally messed up this planet, and it's unforgiveable."

"Yeah, that's one of my things, too. People just don't care, and corporations are greedy and only care about making a profit."

"I was amazed when you showed up at our Sierra Club meeting." I looked at his profile in the moonlight and smiled to myself. Funny how you could love the silhouette of someone's face.

"It was my pleasure. So, what else have you done regarding that?"

"I applied to University of Florida to major in environmental studies. I just hope they accept me and that I can make a difference somehow. To think that all this beauty..." I motioned to the majestic pine trees. "...is being clear-cut, pillaged, drilled on for oil by greedy corporations. Our water is polluted. There's an island of floating debris twice the size of Texas in the Pacific. It makes me sick. I know I talk about this stuff too much."

"Not at all. I feel the same way."

Then that magic date moment happened. He took my hand and it felt as though we were a real couple. Suddenly all of my senses were focused on those few inches of flesh where our hands intersected. The feel of his strong, smooth hand sent a tingly glow through my whole body. My heartbeat and breathing sped up.

"What about you?" I asked trying not to grin too obviously.

"I love running track, but that's just to build my physical strength and agility. I feel the urgency to work for conservation, too. It runs through my whole family, actually. My dad's very active in environmental matters."

"Really? What a coincidence."

"That's part of the reason I was attracted to you, you know. Well, outside of the obvious." He squeezed my hand. "I read in the school paper how you helped to organize the coastal cleanup. That's very impressive."

"It's not much at all." I felt the heat creeping up my neck in the darkness, and I knew I must have a horrible blush going.

"I have to confess something." He paused as though struggling to find the right words. "I didn't object to the group going tonight because I was a little shy about being alone with you, like I might say the wrong thing and scare you off. Stupid, huh?"

Wow! It floored me that Luis could be intimidated by me. "That's the way I felt about you."

Luis stopped and faced me, taking both of my hands in his. "Kenley, even though we've only known each other for a short time we have a strong bond. I mean...I can feel what you feel. I've been through what you're experiencing."

God, was it that obvious I was going through an uber-awkward stage? That I was sweltering half the time and super sensitive? "You know, I can't help it. I must be having some kind of late growth spurt—delayed hormones." I was mortified; I was tall enough as it was. Why couldn't I be normal?

"You have no reason to be self-conscious. Don't you wonder about the way you're changing? How your senses are sharpening? You're feverish." He felt my forehead. "Burning up."

I could see the care in his eyes as he let his hand linger on my forehead. This person whom everyone thought was so self-centered was showing genuine concern for me. "What are you trying to say?"

"Look at the way you jumped hurdles, and you admitted that you never practiced." He took his hand from my forehead and let it drift over to the top of my shoulder. Something like an energy surge flowed through him into my skin.

"Yes, I can't help it and I don't know what's happening to me. I admit it," I said.

"I can show you why you're all heated up." He put his face close to mine. "Do you trust me?"

"Not really." I laughed then grew serious as I looked at his dark, inviting face, his hazel eyes, straight nose and tan lips. I stroked his long hair that had just a hint of curl. He always smelled so good, like spicy cologne and hair products.

He moved even closer toward me then stopped. Didn't he want to kiss me? What was the matter? I stared into his eyes for a good long time trying to read him. He held fast, and his lips, his eyes shining in the moonlight melted me.

I couldn't resist him; I drew my lips toward him and kissed him. The smoothness, the infinite pleasure of those lips made my world spin into a vortex. I had never felt this way about anyone before. We kissed some more, and this time he moaned, just softly.

For a moment I stopped to catch my breath and swayed a little. He steadied me. "Let's walk," he suggested.

I only wanted to kiss him some more, but I didn't mind walking. I supposed it was a good thing to cool down. "It's a beautiful night. Look at the moon. My mom calls that a cookie moon when it's in a crescent like that," I said.

"Lovely." He traced his finger along my jaw. "But not as lovely as you."

At this point I felt as though I had some kind of drug in my veins—opium maybe, I had no idea. No, it was better than any drug could ever have been, a true adrenaline high.

"The scent of the orange blossoms is so much stronger than usual. And there's jasmine, too." I inhaled deeply, the scents of the forest flooded my brain added to my euphoria.

"I love it," he whispered.

As we walked toward where the boy scouts camped out in the summer, an eerie tingling coursed through my body. We were all alone in the woods now. Not another living soul could hear us.

Luis stopped me, and put his hands on my shoulders. "Kenley, are you ready to find out why you're going through these changes?"

My heart beat like mad. Loose connections formed in my brain, threatening to end the idyllic quality of this night. "I don't know."

"Just keep in mind that I really care about you and I only want what's best for you." His eyes, shiny in the moonlight, fringed by his long dark lashes clearly showed all his concern for me, and I had no doubt of his sincerity.

Then I came to the realization that he was being nice to me because he wanted me to do something. Something kinky or strange. The good intensity I had felt turned into uncertainty. I should have known he hadn't just wanted me for me. "Luis, I'm scared. Tell me what's going on."

He took a deep breath and said very carefully, "Have you ever heard of shape-shifters?"

I didn't like where this was going. "Yes, werewolves. American Indians shape shift into their totem animals, don't they? But what does that have to do with me?"

"You're a member of a race that's been around for thousands of years. You originated from the Egyptian Cat Goddesses—beautiful, lethal and possibly immortal."

I felt the blood drain from my head. "No. There's no such thing. Only in novels and legends."

His eyes bore into mine like laser beams. "Yes there is. You're part of that heritage."

"What? What are you talking about? I thought you were going to tell me something real." But deep down inside I knew. I knew that what he was saying was real.

"I'm dead serious. This is real; more real than anything you've ever known before. I'm talking about people who shape-shift. Kenley, think about what you've been going through the past few months. You can hear things other people can't. You're capable of superhuman feats."

"No." I strained to wrap my mind around that concept. Impossible. That was something out of movies and novels.

"I know you don't believe me right now, but you will."

As we walked further, something turned over in my brain, allowing me to at least entertain the thought. "I think I'm losing my mind."

"Kenley." He put his arm around me as we walked. "Don't be afraid. It's awesome, really it is."

"This can't be real. It's not possible." I had the creeping realization that he'd sought me out somehow, for his own purposes. Why did he just happen to be there that night when I was being attacked in the woods? The pieces started to fall together. I stopped dead. "I hear something."

"What do you hear?"

I tilted my head. "People." I held out my hand, touching the air. "And I feel heat, too." I looked at his classic features in the moonlight. His profile could have been that of a

Renaissance statue. The sheer beauty of him, the strangeness of the situation, made the surreal seem possible.

The scent of burning pine filled my head.

We walked a little further, and soon I saw a bonfire with figures milling around it and smelled the wood-singed scent that reminded me of fireplaces on a crisp winter day.

"Is this the rave?" I asked, knowing full well it was not. "I can make out Molly and Cristen. Josh."

"No, this isn't a rave. Tonight this is just for you. It's you're werecat birthday, and we're going to help you change."

⚘ Chapter 10 ⚘

"What the hell's a werecat?" None of this made any sense to me.

"A werecat is a person who shape-shifts into cat form. It's passed down from your parents. You're in the royal like, Kenley. That's why I knew about you." *He* came after *me*. I thought about the implications.

"I can't handle this. It's stuff for books and movies. It's not real." I started to pull away from him, confused, scared, devastated. He didn't want me, he wanted something *from* me.

"You'll find out tonight that it is real. And for you it will be as natural as a waterfall." Luis's grip on my hand made me want to run far away and never see any of them again. "You have to understand, this is already inside of you. You were born with it. You're a werecat, Kenley, just like I am." Like a dancer pulling his partner in close for a tandem step, he reeled me in. Hugged me. Kissed my face softly.

I was done for then. I felt as though I was in some kind of fog or thrall. Not that I was being led to do anything against my will. I knew in the core of my being that this night was inevitable. This was something I had to experience in order to break my crazed mood, stop the insane fire within me. I needed it to regain my mind, bring my fever to a head so I could be normal again. No, that wasn't entirely accurate. I knew I'd never be normal again.

Luis kissed me sweetly on the cheek.

The Claw Club members milled around the fire joined by many others, probably about twenty in total. All young people, some I'd seen at school, some I knew I'd never set eyes on before.

"Who are all these people?"

"They're your family now, your werecat brothers and sisters. And you're the center of attention."

Apprehension seized me like bony fingers around my neck, and I started to back away. "Are you going to tie me up or something?"

"No, not at all. It's nothing like that. This is your special turning ceremony. Your party. Kenley, this is your night." He put his back toward the other people, faced me and whispered, "Don't be afraid. I'm right here and I won't let anything happen to you."

"You mean you're going to turn me, like being turned into a vampire? I don't want that." What was this going to do to my future? My college plans. None of this made sense.

"You can't escape it. It's going to happen to you one way or the other," Luis said softly as he held out his hands to me.

"What are you going to turn me into?" My head swam in crazy confusion. Were they going to drug me and make me believe in the hallucination?

"It's not certain what kind of cat you'll be. The ceremony will tell us that."

"Ceremony?" I backed away again. "No, no, no."

"You have to understand. I'm not going to turn you. Kenley, you *are* a werecat. It's in your genetics. I'm going to help you through your first turning to stop all the insanity you're feeling. Like it or not, you're going to have to face your true nature."

My head felt like a helium-filled balloon that would take off and float away at any moment. I didn't say anything, just searched his face trying to understand. I didn't didn't didn't want to believe it. But in my heart I knew it was true.

"It's really important to me that you understand...I feel bad..." he hesitated, "like you think I lured you here to do this. But this is inevitable for you, Kenley. At some point you're going to have to deal with it." His eyes fixed on me with an intensity that threatened to set me on fire.

"I know that, Luis. Somehow I know." I did.

"Let the girls get you ready now, okay?"

"Okay," I said quietly. I needed to face my fate.

Molly and Cristen came over and each took one of my hands. Orlando came over, too. "Remember when I said it's all bullshit? Well, it is. Don't take any of this too seriously."

So that's what Orlando had meant when he'd said that they were all on my side.

"Oh, don't listen to him," Molly said. Her lips looked like red, shiny, candy apples. "He thinks everything is bogus. This is possibly the most meaningful thing that will ever happen to you in your lifetime. You're going to become a true member of the Claw Club now."

"Yeah!" Shouting and whooping arose from the group.

"Here, undress and put this on." Cristen pushed a cream-colored, silky robe in my direction.

"What do you mean *undress*? You want me to take off my clothes?" I couldn't possibly do that. There was no way.

"No, you're going to put on this robe. You can't be constricted when you make the change. Just do it, girly. Take this mask, too." Sarah handed me a beautiful gold cat mask with a curlicue design all over it. It felt heavy, like real metal. "So you won't feel so self-conscious the first time."

Sarah untied her blouse and threw it up in the air, revealing small breasts with little rose bud nipples. Then she put on one of the sheer robes.

I had never taken off my clothes in front of people before. Luis approached me and put the gold cat mask on me. It covered the top part of my face but left my mouth and jaw uncovered. Once on my face, it had a metallic scent and felt heavy.

Still looking at me, he slowly unbuttoned his shirt.

"There's a reason for taking off your clothes. Once you make the change, you might get all tangled up in the material. Zippers caught in fur are not very much fun."

My heart beat so furiously I thought I'd pass out. I looked at him and unbuttoned my blouse, still wearing my bra. When he saw that I looked uncomfortable, he walked me behind a tree. "You can get changed over here where no one will see you."

I unzipped my skirt, pealed it down, removed my shirt and put on the flowing garment. What was I doing? What was I thinking? How far would I go for Luis? I only knew that I wanted to—had to—please him. I had a sense that our destinies were entwined.

Luis called to me, "Are you ready yet? But don't let me rush you. Take your time."

"No, I can't." Clutching the top of my robe up around my chin, I started to panic. I had no idea what they were going to do to me. "I have to go."

Luis came around the corner wearing the silky garment and put his hand on my shoulder. The gentle pressure stopped me as certainly as if it had been steel. "Kenley, your parents completely neglected telling you about your roots." He sighed. "You have to realize that this is something you'll face sooner or later, and we're just helping you. We're not changing you, because the cat blood is already inside of you. We're just bringing you to fulfillment."

"What do you mean the cat blood is inside of me?" Yes, of course I knew but at the same time I didn't know.

"Just that. You're in the werecat line."

I was still having trouble with the whole werecat thing. "How can that be? My parents are regular people."

"They're not regular people; they can't be. They were lax about informing you about the ways of being a werecat, just as my father indoctrinated me in a way that was very brutal. I don't want you to have to go through that. We'll talk about everything later as much as you want. Right now, drink some of this." He reached for a goblet behind him. "It'll relax you."

"What is it?"

"Just wine. It's more ceremonial than anything." He took a big gulp himself.

I reached for the goblet with the tiger on one side and took a tentative sip. It was white and sweet. Not bad. I drank some more.

He moved closer to me.

I hesitated then felt the magnetic pull of his body to mine.

He put his arms around me and said, "Kenley, remember, I'd never let anything bad happen to you. I'm here to protect you."

The cool air blew up and under the material, tingling against my skin. I had the sense that everyone busied themselves trying not to look, but stole secret glances at us.

Luis held me at arm's length. The beauty of his face, his big hazel eyes, straight nose and full pale lips made me want to weep. He otherwise didn't touch me. I kind of wished he would, because my skin sizzled, ached for his caress. What madness possessed me that allowed me to be in just this sheer piece of clothing with a group of people in the woods?

He put on his cat mask—black spots dotted golden fur in a patterned design, the nose devoid of spots and the muzzle white, outlined in black around the nose and mouth.

"What kind of cat is that?"

"Jaguar," he said through the mask.

"Like your car." Kind of funny in an ironic way. I adjusted my own mask.

Luis led me to the fire. The heat of it threatened to singe my skin. The others were dancing around it. I took a few tentative steps, and once I got into the rhythm of it I felt like a perfect witch dancing in the moonlight around the camp fire. Wearing the cat mask helped.

I danced until I was nearly worn out. It reminded me of the girl in the "Rite of Spring" in which she danced until her death as a human sacrifice for the gods. I tried to shake that feeling. When I was nearly worn out, Luis pulled on my hand. "Come on. Now you're ready to get in touch with your inner cat."

We ran away from the group, past the palm-like palmetto scrub bushes, the bayonet-sharp yucca plants, down paths; we jumped over fallen trees.

When Luis pulled off his robe and mask as we ran, I followed suit. I felt so incredibly free at that moment, and I started to have the assurance that everything we were doing was right somehow.

"It's time. Imagine your arms lengthening, your legs shortening, your hips growing slim. Tiny hairs sprout from the ears on top of your head."

I tried to feel it, but I couldn't. I still wasn't sure I entirely believed. "I don't think I can do it."

"Yes, you can. Feel what it's like to be prowling in the moonlight. You are the master of all life. You're changing. I can see it."

The core of my being vibrated, and a strong throbbing traveled out to my limbs. Some kind of a chemical reaction flooded my brain. My heart fluttered in quick hummingbird pulses until I couldn't breathe.

"Easy," Luis said. "Deep breaths."

"I don't know if I can do this." I knew I'd faint soon.

"You can't stop it now." Luis grasped my forearm, holding me up.

A popping and bubbling worked beneath my skin, so subtle at first I wondered if it was my imagination. But soon there was no mistaking the rumbling beneath my flesh until I felt like a volcano about to explode. I made an embarrassing gasping sound. Surely I'd die. But just as I thought that, a rabbit running through the underbrush captured my attention and I zoomed in on it with eagle eyes, blocking out everything else.

The human part of my brain interceded enough to know that the feline was taking over, and as much as my senses had been heightened before, they now increased a thousand fold. A palmetto bug scurrying over the grass sounded like a horse, the nearby fox like an elephant. I swore I could hear people talking in houses that must have been at least a mile away. All the noise pounded inside my head until I thought it would drive me insane.

When I clasped my hands over my ears, they felt different, so I extended my fingers in front of my face. My stubs of fingers had claws on the ends. I gasped again and tried to scream, but my vocal apparatus had changed.

Luis held me. "Don't worry. It's going to be okay." He pulled my hand to the top of my head. "Feel your ears, you look cute."

I explored the top of my head and shrieked when I felt velvety cat ears with their down-like fur.

The change, it seemed, worked from the extremities in. My ribcage and hips began contracting until my internal organs felt a throbbing pressure followed by sharp pains. I wrapped my arms around my stomach.

"It only hurts like this the first time. Try to relax," Luis said.

Deep breaths, deep breaths. Something compelled me to drop to all fours, and I was able to settle into my new skin. I looked down at myself and saw the dark brown rosettes that to the untrained eye made a completely black color. I was a panther, big, dark and beautiful. But just as I started checking out my hands and feet, a noise took my complete attention, and I zeroed in on an armadillo foraging for food in the grass. My entire being wanted to chase it. I looked over to watch Luis; he changed so quickly I nearly missed it. Luis wasn't Luis anymore, but a full-grown cat.

He bumped up against me. *Run with me.*

At that moment, instinct took over. I sprinted on all fours, my mind a jumble of feline instincts. I understood on a very deep level that the primary motive of a cat was to hunt. Everything else supported that. That was why they didn't care so much about trying to communicate or pleasing anyone else but themselves. I suddenly understood the feline attitude of selfishness.

I was a panther. And I owned the night.

~~✿~ Chapter 11 ~✿~~

We slowed down. Luis put his forehead up against mine then nuzzled me and rubbed against the length of my body. He circled around the other way and pressed his nose to mine. *Kenley, you are a panther. So regal and beautiful. And rare. You take my breath away.* He snuggled his nose into my neck. *Kind of nice, isn't it?*

Wonderful and amazing. I realized that we were communicating through telepathy. We didn't actually speak but understood each other none-the-less. My senses on overload, I heard every night bird singing, every bug scurrying through the grass, every leaf rustling. *But how do you block out all of the noise?*

I can't explain it, but you'll learn. Things will dull back out for you after a while. He licked my face.

I giggled inwardly, able to smile only in a limited way with my cat face. *And I can see everything. I swear I can see an owl miles away.*

Yes, you can. His eyes drew me toward him. I could tell they were Luis' eyes, but they were larger and glowing. Even in his cat body, Luis was stunning.

Scents so powerful they practically had solid form, leapt out at me. Orange blossoms. The sweet scent of decayed foliage. I swore I could smell the mushroom-like scent of a field mouse miles away. And my body... I took a moment to examine my paws, turned one over to see the cute pads on the bottoms. How different it felt to be in this flesh, so muscular and swift.

Your body is a magnificent one. He put his nose to mine and gave me the closest thing to a cat kiss, which was kind of like a little lick on the lips. It tickled and felt wonderful.

Come on, now. Luis prodded me with his nose. *We have to hunt.*

Hunt?

Yes, we'll find some wild game.

Luis led me in chasing a wild pheasant. I followed along behind and couldn't resist the impulse to play with it a little, bat it with my big paws. But even in cat form I took no delight in being cruel, so I pounced on it and quickly ripped out its throat. I lapped at the sweet blood then tore into the flesh. Nothing had ever tasted so good as this fresh kill. I devoured nearly the whole bird while Luis looked on. He didn't have even one bite. I offered him some, but he shook his head. *This kill is all for you.*

But then the human part that still existed within me made me stop and look down at the violated creature that was living its own life until I cruelly took it. A gag reflex formed deep within my throat, and I had to concentrate to keep down what I'd just eaten.

Luis must have noticed my discomfort. Kenley, this is the natural cycle of the food chain. These animals are born knowing that they're part of the whole system. You mustn't feel guilty or bad for eating them.

But I do. I do. I was never a big meat eater.

Like the Native Americans do, honor them for the life force they give you. His eyes glowed with an inner conviction.

That makes me feel better. Thanks, Luis. He snuggled me with his velvety muzzle. The scent of him, like spring rain and fresh earth and clean musk all rolled together, put me into a kind of thrall.

We found our way back to the gathering, but now the bonfire lay dormant and everyone had gone home. I changed back effortlessly just by thinking about it. It amazed me how everything was so instinctive.

I found my clothes and dressed. It was nearly sunrise. "My parents are going to kill me," I said.

"They're probably sleeping soundly in their beds. They're cats, too, you know? We like to get a lot of sleep."

"They couldn't be werecats." I sat down on an overturned log while I pulled on my boots. "They're not cool enough."

"You're not adopted, are you?" He sat down next to me.

"No." I struggled with one of my laces that had a knot in it.

"Then they're part cat. They have to be. Maybe they're in denial." Luis picked up my foot and worked the knot out of my shoelace for me then re-tied it. "There." He helped me up.

I half didn't believe him. I'd known them all my life; how could they be shape-shifters? You couldn't just hide that kind of thing. But this night had taken everything I'd known of reality and turned it upside down.

"Do they keep any kind of small animals?" he asked.

I thought about the snakes, the one thing that didn't fit in with their personalities. "They keep live mice to feed their snakes."

"There you go. They keep animals with the smallest amount of life force to keep themselves alive but barely feed their inner werecats." Luis took my arm, and exhausted, we walked back toward my house.

"Did you somehow plan to find me in the woods that night and rescue me?" I asked.

"No, but I have some sixth sense when it comes to you."

"But you didn't know me then."

He hesitated, searching for the right words. "No but even then I was...picking up on your essence somehow. I could never stand to see you hurt." He stopped, turned me toward him, wrapped his arms around me and rested his chin on top of my head.

He felt amazing to me, but there was something I had to ask him, so I pulled away. "Luis. What about all those other girls in the Claw Club?"

He looked surprised that I'd asked. "They mean absolutely nothing to me. Kenley, you're *it* to me."

His words comforted me, but still I had more questions. "Do you turn people? I'm confused. What was that bobcat that bit me in the school bathroom? Is that somehow related?"

"A bobcat? No, that was Cristen. She was probably pissed off at you and being mean. Or she was smoking in the bathroom and changed so she wouldn't get caught. She does that a lot. Anyway, her biting you didn't do anything. You were ready for the change."

"But why? There's so much I don't understand."

"You're of the royal line." He held my hand as we continued walking down the street toward my house.

"What royal line? Could this be more confusing? To think I'm a regular kid then find out I'm from some lineage of shape-shifters?"

"It'll all come clearer to you as time goes on. You're one of the few of your kind left."

He said *your* kind, not *our* kind. "I am?" We stopped in front of my house. "So, you can turn people?"

"Yes, my father has instructed us to increase our numbers."

"Your father..." It didn't occur to me that Luis also had a shape shifting father.

"Yes, he's the leader of..." He paused. "A different family lineage of werecats."

Lead weights pulled on my eyes, and I could hardly hold up my head. "I'm exhausted. You'll have to explain it to me later." We'd reached the front of my house.

"Good night, Kenley." He looked into my eyes. "I'm so glad I found you—that we found each other."

"So am I."

"Good night." He kissed me softly on the lips, massaging the back of my head, then turned and backed away as though he couldn't stop looking at me. He waited until I was safely inside the house then zoomed off in his Jaguar.

"Okay, young lady. Where have you been?"

I peeked at my mother through slitted eyes. Mom, who always had to look perfect, wore a designer sweat suit with rhinestones around the neck. She had bobbed blonde hair, a French-tipped manicure and applied subtle makeup that enhanced her face, so she looked like a perennial thirty-something.

"What, Mom?" I viewed her differently now. A werecat—my parents were werecats.

"*You* know what. You were out all night. Tell me where you were and what you were doing." Mom stood with her hands on her hips, bent forward in a confrontational pose.

"I was out with friends. We went to a movie then sat around talking. No biggie."

"You sat around talking until six a.m.?" Mom crossed her arms in front of her, the red creeping up her neck into her face.

I tried to walk past her to the stairs, but she barred my way.

"You're not going anywhere until you explain."

Then Dad walked in stretching and rubbing the sleep out of his eyes. He had short brown hair and also appeared young for his age. I couldn't look at my dad the same way either. I pictured ears sprouting on top of his head, a furry mouth poking out from in front of his face. I couldn't shake these images of them from my mind.

"Kenley, you could have been hurt or killed. We didn't know. I've been worried sick about you. Besides, it's a school night. How are you going to be able to keep up your grades to get into a good college?"

"I'm sorry. I know it was selfish of me. I just lost track of the time."

He looked down at his slippered feet and continued. "We never wanted to have to be disciplinarians with you. It's not our style."

They never wanted me in the first place. Dad didn't say it, but I knew it was true.

Mom nodded. "That's right. We don't want you to do anything you'll regret, like getting into drugs or hooking up with the wrong sort of people or—God forbid—getting arrested."

"Listen, guys. I was just out with friends. Mom, you always said you wished you had a popular daughter. I have more friends now. It's what you wanted, isn't it?"

"I..." Mom played with the ends of her hair. She had an oblong face with big eyes and a turned up nose. "I didn't mean that you should hang around with the wrong crowd and stay out all night."

"Mom, Dad, it's nothing. You don't have to worry. I'll come home early from now on. I promise."

"That's my little kitten," Dad said. Now his pet name for me struck me as ironic. Of course they had to know about our family background. Why hadn't they ever told me?

"We just want what's best for you, you know." Mom bent over and hugged me.

I honestly did feel bad, like I'd let them down. "I know. I won't disappoint you."

"You're grounded for a month and after that you'll be home by 11:00 on school nights, 12:00 on weekends." Mom stood with her hands on her hips. There was no discussing it.

I knew I needed to confront them about their werecatism, but I didn't want to deal with it then. Besides, if I told them I'd had my first transformation, they'd be watching my every move.

Even though I didn't have time to go to bed, I didn't feel half bad. I took a shower and stopped and got a latté and a breakfast sandwich on the way to school. Food tasted so good to me. I worried I'd put on a zillion pounds. But no, I knew those calories were burning off at quadruple speed.

It was Friday morning. TGIF. I really needed the weekend to chill and think about things. I hung out in the hall just in case Luis wanted to talk to me. But it was another boy who sought me out instead.

⤳❦ Chapter 12 ❦⤳

As I headed toward my homeroom, I felt a tap on my shoulder. Edgier than normal that day, I spun around. "What?"

A tall, slim boy with spiked, sandy brown hair said, "I'm sorry. I didn't mean to startle you." He extended his hand toward me apologetically.

"You just surprised me. No biggie." I held my books tight in to my chest.

"You're Kenley, right?" The boy wore a lose chambray shirt, chinos and Doc Martens. I instantly sized him up to be smart and friendly, maybe a little too friendly.

"That's me." I scowled. Not because I didn't like him, but because I wondered what he wanted. This seemed kind of random.

"I need to talk to you." He had a serious look on his face.

"Why? What's this about?"

"I know this sounds crazy, but..." He raked one hand through his gelled hair. "I have reason to believe you're in some serious danger."

I looked at him and blinked my eyes. "Excuse me?"

He whispered. "You're in danger. Listen, you probably think I'm crazy."

"Umm." He was creeping me out. I was also terrified he knew something about last night. I turned, wanting to get away from him. "I have to get to homeroom now."

"Can I talk to you later?"

Not answering his question, I hurried into room 102, slammed the door and leaned up against it, breathing hard.

"What's with you?" Michelle said from her seat in the back row.

"Oh my God. This freak just came up to me and said something strange to me." I sat down next to her.

"Freak? What do you mean, freak?"

"I shouldn't say freak. He was a normal guy, pretty nice-looking, actually. But he told me I was in danger."

"Do you think it might have something to do with this?" Michelle held out a copy of the Tampa Tribune. The headline read, "Serial Killer Targeting the Homeless."

I skimmed it quickly. The bell was about to ring.

A girl barely sixteen is sitting on the steps of the Tampa Bay Homeless Shelter with her head in her hands sobbing. She wipes her eyes with the ragged end of her shirt. "People are missing. Every couple of nights another one of the people I know ends up gone. Sometimes kids, sometimes their moms. And no one cares, because we don't matter. They think a homeless person might've gone out and gotten drunk or something, but that isn't true. I know these people. They wouldn't just disappear, because the Tampa Bay Homeless Shelter has given them the most hope they've had in a long time. And now..." The girl grew teary-eyed again. "A couple of days ago my mom turned up missing. Now I have nowhere to go. I'll end up in a foster home."

"Your name's in here," Michelle said.

I skimmed down the page, dreading what I'd find.

And how did I find out about this? A courageous young woman named Kenley Walsh-Bohdan, a volunteer at the Tampa Bay Homeless Center, sought me out and asked me to write an article because these disappearances weren't getting attention from the police force or the local media.

"Oh, oh." I could feel the blood draining from my head. The killers wouldn't like this.

"So that guy might be wanting to tell you about something connected to these murders."

"You think?"

"Ah, yeah." Michelle looked at me and nodded as though to say *obviously*. "What else could it be?"

"I guess the secret admirer theory is out." I felt stupid for even having thought that.

"I think you should prolly find him and see what he wants."

The bell rang, and Michelle dashed off. I left for first period feeling as though I had a family of bats in my stomach eating it from the inside out.

After running another successful length of hurdles in gym class, I talked to Coach O'Brien, the track coach, about joining the team. I was just talking, not making any kind of commitment, as I had way too much to think about as it was.

"Luis Malik suggested I come and talk with you about joining the track team." I blotted my sweaty face with my towel.

Coach O'Brien had sun-cracked skin that looked as though he'd been out in the elements for about a thousand years. "Luis, huh? That boy's an amazing runner."

"He definitely is."

"And you are?" He put down his clipboard.

"Kenley Walsh-Bohdan."

The Coach extended his hand and I shook it. "Pleased to meet you Kenley."

"So what about the team?"

"The season has already started, but by the looks of your talents, I think we can make a spot for you. Why don't you show up for practice next Monday after school."

"You mean I don't have to try out?"

"Naaa." He waved his hand. "I've already seen what you can do."

I thanked him and left, not even totally sure I wanted to be on the team. I knew that in my mind I felt it was a connection with Luis, but what could be more of a connection than what we'd experienced the previous night?

Luis didn't seem to be at school. At lunchtime, the regular pack welcomed us to their table but when I casually asked where Luis was Molly just shrugged. "Probably taking a mental health day. I dunno."

The afternoon dragged on and at long last the final bell rang.

Since Michelle had driven her mom's car that day, she went to the homeless shelter alone.

When I went out to the parking lot and walked down the aisle where I'd parked my car, I found the boy who had confronted me that morning leaning against my Jeep. Not that I was completely surprised to see him, but how did he know that was my car? It creeped me out.

I stopped right where I stood, not wanting to get any closer to him. "Are you stalking me? That's illegal, you know." I took out my phone hoping it looked like I was calling the cops.

"Kenley, I'm sorry. You must think I'm some kind of creep or something. I assure you, I'm not."

I didn't say anything.

"I'm Brendan Fournier. I'm new to this school." He extended his hand.

Still wary, I hesitated for a moment. As I shook his hand I noticed that he had a clean scent like fresh soap. "Hi Brendan." In sizing him up, I started to think I'd overreacted. He seemed like a nice guy, and there were plenty of people coming and going in the parking lot so we weren't alone. "Where did you move from?"

"I'm from all over, actually. My parents move a lot."

"Are they military?

"Military?" He laughed. "Sometimes I wish they were that normal. No, I come from a family of cryptozoologists."

"Crypto-what?"

"Cryptozoologists. People who follow paranormal phenomenon. I have seen a lot of the world, though. My parents have dragged my little sister and me from Egypt to Seattle to Malaysia and right here to Tampa, Florida."

What he said should have made me nervous, considering my werecat-ism and all, but there was something about him I liked. He had a friendly face with dimples when he laughed. He didn't act at all slick; he was real. A regular guy.

I thought about Michelle telling me I should find out what he knew, and I thought it might be better to get away from school to find out. I still wanted to be in a public place, though. "How about going to the Starlight Coffee House where we can talk?"

"Sure. Thanks." He looked surprised I'd suggested it.

"Do you have some way to get there?" I was hoping I wouldn't have to drive him.

"Oh yeah. I have my trusty Sadie here." He pulled a metallic green scooter from behind one of the other cars.

"Is that a scooter?" I asked trying not to giggle. The fact that I could have been scared of a guy who drove a moped was patently ridiculous.

"Hey, Sadie's not just a scooter, she's a Vespa. I'll have you know she's a really cool scooter, like the kind they drive in those old Italian movies."

"Right. See you there." Okay. I *had* to like the guy after that.

Brendan ordered some green tea, and I ordered a skinny latté. He paid for both. The green tea added to the Vespa made him certifiably harmless in my book.

As we waited, two twenty-something girls behind the counter loudly complained about the political situation in the country and the fact that she wasn't eligible for any financial aid for school. All of their sentences rose at the end like questions. "I've always supported myself? No one has ever had to help me? But like when I apply for financial aid? I'm completely passed over?"

I loved the way the Starlight Coffee House smelled, a combination of coffee beans and patchouli incense. Plus, it was independent, not part of an evil corporate chain.

Brendan and I sat at a table for two by the window. I liked his bright blue eyes, and the fact that they were slightly wide-set gave him a friendly, honest look.

I took the cover off my latté and stirred the foam. "Tell me about your parents."

"Oh." He rubbed both of his palms into his eyes. "Where do I start? My parents are journalists. They write for magazines like *Dark Journey* and for web pages like *CryptozoolgyNow.com*. We've chased mummy's curses, yeti and chupacabra. We originally came to Florida to look for yeti, you know, abominable snowmen, but in the swamps. My parents turned up something even more interesting, though."

"Really? What?"

"I'll come to that in a minute. Tell me something about yourself." He stirred his green tea and took a sip, which made me wince, because to me green tea smelled like cat pee.

"There's not much to tell. I was born in Connecticut and we moved here when I was twelve."

"What do you like to do?"

"I'm really into environmentalism. I've organized coastal cleanups, and I'm vice president of the Sierra Club for North Tampa High. Oh, and I do like to run at night. I might join the track team."

He nodded his head, seeming to understand. "It invigorates you, right?"

"Yeah."

"I love running, too. Whoever called it the runner's high wasn't fooling around." His hand started to creep closer to mine on the table, which I did not want.

I sat back in my chair and folded my arms across my chest. "Now tell me why you said I was in danger."

"You're probably not going to believe me." He sat up straight, pulled his hand back and put it on his lap.

"Try me." I hoped I was conveying my no nonsense mood.

"There's some very unusual activity going on in this area." He removed his tea bag and put it in the lid of his cup.

"Did you see my name in the Tribune newspaper article?"

"Yeah." He raised his eyebrows. "That was a rather unfortunate thing."

"Why? I mean I think I know why, but I want your interpretation."

"I'll get to that." Brendan stretched out his long legs and took another sip of his green tea. "Surely you've heard that this area has a lot of paranormal activity."

"You mean like the Tampa Triangle?"

"Yes but the kind of activity in this area is like nothing we've ever seen before. Ms. Walsh-Bohdan, have you ever heard of werecats?"

⚜ Chapter 13 ⚜

Suddenly I grew kind of afraid of this Vespa-driving nerd. Maybe I'd underestimated him. Obviously his main goal was to expose us. "Werecats? Uh. What's that?"

"In simplest terms they are people who have the ability to change into cats at will. It's a phenomenon that's been reported all over the world. The Malaysian werecats are famous. Have you heard of them?"

"Tell me more." I was very aware of the fact that I needed to be cautious around Brendan.

"You haven't heard of them, then?" He looked into my eyes a little too deeply. Still, his gaze was so endearing, something about the softness of his eyes.

"Ye-a-h," I said, drawing the word out, trying to make it seem like I was searching some deep, dark recess of my memory. "I think I may have heard something about them before. Like on some show about myths or something. Don't really remember much, though. Tell me about them."

He hesitated, sizing me up. "From what I can gather, there are two factions of werecats: There are the good ones who pretty much go about their own business. They all have to kill and eat live creatures, but the good ones eat small animals. They may keep rabbits or mice for that purpose. But then there are the bad ones." He hesitated again, still gauging my reaction. "They kill and eat people."

I felt the blood drain away from my face. I took deep breaths in order to stay calm and not faint.

Brendan was scrutinizing me in a way that wouldn't seem too obvious. He had intelligent eyes, and I knew he didn't miss a thing. Unlike most guys, he caught all the subtext. He continued. "There has been an upsurge in werecat activity in the Tampa Bay area."

"You've got a pretty wild imagination there, Brendan. I like urban legends as much as the next person, but, uh...maybe you should write a horror novel about all this stuff. You say *your parents* are into all this woo woo fantasy?" I drank some more of my latté trying to appear casual.

"It's not fantasy. My parents are hooked into all of the paranormal happenings on whole planet. Sometimes I wish they weren't." He raked one hand through his sandy blonde hair and looked away.

"And how does this relate to me?"

"I suspect that the disappearances you brought to the attention of the reporter from the *Trib* are connected to the werecat activity."

Now I stared at him as intently as he did me, but I still wanted to seem like I didn't believe him. "What do all these so called..." I made air quotes. "...information sources tell you about the local werecat activity?"

"My parents have been making a study of them for the past ten years. There are whole societies dedicated to pursuing these creatures. Do a web search for 'Alien Big Cats' sometimes."

"And what? You think they're going to come after me because I busted them?" Damn! That was all I needed. A deep oppressive fear settled into my chest.

"Possibly, but I'm going to tell you something else and you've got to believe me.

"We'll see about that." I poked around in my purse to keep my hands busy as I braced myself against what he was going to say.

"Luis, the person you've been hanging around with lately, is involved with them."

My heart stopped for a second. "Have you been spying on me?"

He turned his head to the side while still looking at me and narrowed his eyes almost imperceptibly. "No, not at all. It's just that you can't believe how obsessed my parents are with this stuff. I've been living and breathing it my whole life."

"Your parents know that I'm friends with Luis?" I pulled back in my chair getting more uncomfortable by the second.

"No, but they're watching *his* family."

"So you're saying that he and his parents are werecats?" I scowled and made a small *pfft* sound then laughed. "Yeah, right."

"Yes, right."

"And you expect me to believe this? That's absolutely ridiculous." Now Brendan's motive was clear to me. He liked me and was jealous of Luis, so he was trying to make Luis sound bad. "I've got to go."

I started to get up, but he caught my wrist. I looked down at it. "Let go of me."

"Sorry." He released his grip, but his expression grew more solemn. "You're not taking this seriously. I don't know why you think I'm telling you this. It isn't for my own health."

"I know you mean well, but it's just kind of ridiculous, okay?"

I stormed out the door and got into my car.

When I arrived home, I realized my cell phone was still turned off from being in class. I flipped it on and saw that I had a text message from Luis. My pulse pounded just from seeing his name on my phone. God, I was really hopeless. I read the message—**Want to hang out tonight? Call me.**

I fell back on my bed clutching the cell phone to my chest. I'd give it an hour or so before I called him back so he wouldn't think I was too anxious.

About an hour later I called him and we set our rendezvous time for nine.

Since my parents were at some art show, I planned on getting home before they did so they wouldn't know I'd gone out. I was ready ahead of time and stood at the window peeking out from behind the blinds. He pulled up in his sexy white Jaguar and easily climbed out of the convertible without opening the door.

When I heard the knock, I counted to ten then answered it.

He stood there with his long hair hanging in front of his face in strands wearing a white gauzy Indian shirt and dark jeans. Delicious. Good enough to eat. And he had a big smile on his face.

I hugged him, inhaling his spicy cologne and looked around behind him. "Hey, no Claw Club?" I grinned.

"We don't go everywhere together."

"No, just nearly."

"No parents? I was expecting to have to answer questions." He glanced around my living room at the rows of books, art and artifacts from my parents' travels. "Looks as though they're pretty interesting people."

"Yeah, they like to travel. They're always out volunteering or something. I think they're at some art collector friend's house tonight."

"They must be pretty cool."

"Ugh, they're embarrassing. Horrible and materialistic. Where are we going?"

He took my hand and led me to his car. "Hop in. You'll see"

He parked on a side street in downtown Tampa and we walked across Ashley to the riverfront district that was the home to the Straz Performing Arts Center, Tampa Museum of Art and the Hillsborough River walk. The scent of water from the Hillsborough River floated through the air reminding me of evening walks along the beach.

We hurried toward a big open square building that had walls almost composed entirely of glass. "You're not going to believe this. It's so cool."

Inside the building, there were about fifty full-sized sculptures of fanciful creatures, all done in latex to make them look super real. A fairy in a green gossamer dress wearing a huge bluebell hat sat on a bench as though she were waiting for a commuter train. Her face was so life-like, I thought she might breathe or blink her eyes at any moment.

I put out one finger to touch her then pulled it back.

"It's all right. They don't mind if you touch them," Luis said, stroking the fairy's cheek carefully with one finger.

I pressed the girl's cheek just lightly. It felt weirdly life-like.

Dragons in various poses, a werewolf, little gray aliens and leprechauns stood or hung from stair banisters, or sat in office chairs. "I've never seen anything like this before. To have artwork so integrated into a building..."

"But wait, there's more." He took my hand and pulled me outside.

The sculptures spilled into an adjoining park. A unicorn grazing in the grass emerged from between the marble blocks that comprised part of the lawn. "I love this place, this little garden tucked away in between all the concrete. I can't believe I didn't know this was here." I inhaled deeply of the sweet night foliage scent and gazed up at the stars.

Hidden benches, fountains and the generally overgrown look of the garden provided a great place for a lover's tryst. A tangled fragrant garden. Perfect.

"I love this place, too," Luis said. "The city cut down half of it to make a parking lot. They'll keep ruining all the wilderness, all the natural places until they're stopped."

It was awesome that Luis was focused on my one big passion in life—conservation. "I feel the same way."

"I love the fact that you care about these things. Like I said before, my father has some conservation plans of his own. Are you interested in helping?"

"Definitely. Let me know."

His face lit up? "You're on. I want to show you something."

We walked back to a small, cylindrical structure—a mini-coliseum of sorts right on the Hillsborough River. Luis walked me up to the middle of the small stone bleachers then stood dead center and said, "Hello, Kenley." His voice magnified as though by loudspeaker.

"I wonder if they did that in the ancient Greek theaters?"

"No doubt they did." He ran back towards me and pulled me down to ground level. "Tonight I have a surprise for you."

We walked through a small slit in the side of the building. I gasped and put my hands up to my face.

A full-grown werecat stood on its hind legs.

⁓⧉ Chapter 14 ⧉⁓

Caught in the change between human and cat, the werecat looked like a beast from hell. It stood erect, but the furry face sprouted cat ears. The muzzle had not yet pushed out, rather the killer fangs stuck out of the still-human mouth. It stood with its hands poised in the air, clawing an invisible foe, talons that could rip an opponent to hell sprouted from human hands.

For maybe two seconds I thought it was alive, then I realized it was obviously one of the statues. How could I have not known that?

"There's a secret about this artist, Emile DeContrares. He's one of us. He's a werecat."

A dizzy feeling rushed through my brain, and I tilted to one side, almost falling down. For the second time that day, adrenaline flooded my body. The first had been good, when I received Luis' message, but this one...

"What's the matter?" He caught me and walked me over to the stone stadium seating that lined the small structure.

"That sculpture is horrible. It shows the worst of us."

"What, that he's changing?" Luis held me as we looked at the thing. The salty breeze kicked up and blew my hair into my eyes.

"No. The inherently violent nature. I'm not like that. Luis, I don't know about this life. I don't think I can do it." I pressed my face against his shoulder.

"Kenley." He rubbed my back to warm me in the chill November air. "We're cats, and as such we have unique personalities. Think of your own house cat. We're independent. We love comfort and luxury. But most of all, we're hunters. Even with a house cat, if you leave him inside, he'll stalk lizards in the sunroom, or he'll pounce on imaginary prey. It's in our nature. We can't fight it."

We walked back into the little coliseum structure and sat down on one of the stone bleacher seats. I settled into his arms, his words sounding better to me now. "What if I can't kill my food all the time? I felt bad killing that pheasant in the woods the other night."

"You can't think that way. It's the natural order of things. If you don't get fresh blood, you'll die."

I pushed away and stared at him. "If I don't want to slaughter animals I'll die? What if I want to be a vegetarian?"

"You can't be a vegetarian. Did you know that if you don't give a housecat meat it'll go blind?"

"But I don't have to go make a fresh kill and give it to my housecat."

"No, but somebody had to. The animal had to die by someone's hand."

I must have looked pained, because he said, "Kenley, please don't worry about it. Your instinct, your hunger, will make you eat." He pulled me back toward him.

His warmth felt so good. It felt so perfect being with him in the open air just then. "Luis, tell me about your parents."

"My parents are divorced. My father can be kind of driven sometimes and my mom couldn't take it. She lives up north."

"What does he do?"

"He's an attorney."

I laughed, but felt as though I shouldn't have. "A werecat attorney. Kind of fits."

"I know. I've heard all the jokes about blood sucking. But you'd be surprised. There are werecats in every profession and some in high government positions. Anyway, he does a lot of pro-bono, free, work for the Hispanic community. He's seen as a very good guy."

"What do *you* think of him?" I asked.

"He's okay. I mean, he doesn't try to control my brother and me, but he's a stubborn bastard. When I was a kid, he and my mom used to get into some knock-down-drag-out fights. He never hit her, but he came close, and he tried to control her. She's a hot-blooded South American woman— from Columbia—and he'd never let her win an argument, always had to have the upper hand. That's what tore them apart." A sea of emotions played just below the surface of his face. I could tell he was trying not to look like the whole thing upset him.

"Was it really hard on you when they got divorced?" I asked.

"It completely shattered my world. I thought it was my fault. If I had acted better, not gotten into the kind of trouble that kids get into, maybe things would have been different."

"Yeah, kids always blame themselves, but you know now that you had nothing to do with it, right?"

"Yes." He answered as though he was maybe not so sure.

"How do you get along now?"

"He's trying to get me into the family business."

"Being an attorney?"

"No, being a werecat. You'll see."

My butt was nearly numb from sitting on the hard concrete, but I didn't want to say anything and ruin the moment. It felt so good being close to him. Not to mention being without the whole Claw Club entourage. "How did the Claw Club start?"

"Molly, Cristen, Sarah and I found ourselves here. Our parents all moved here from various places, and we started hanging out together. Molly actually gave the group its name. Since then we've grown."

"So you turned them?"

"No, they're all from were-families. Some of them are mixed 'were' and human. Molly's parents are both werecats."

Molly must have been a pure blood, too. I felt jealous. I thought about what Brendan had said about Tampa being a hotbed of werecat activity. All of the Claw Club's families had moved here, converged on Tampa for some reason. "Do you turn people who weren't born into it?"

"Sometimes. Let's get up. My butt's falling asleep."

I had to wiggle my leg a couple of times in order to get the feeling back into it.

We walked through the park some more. Because city budgets had been cut, it looked like a tangled garden with vines growing here and there. Part of the lawn was made to look like a giant checkerboard of grass alternating with large squares of marble.

Luis led me over to a bench and straddled it, facing me, and pulled me close to him. His shiny eyes reminded me of the high gloss of cats' eyes. Though we sat under a tree, they caught the glint from somewhere, probably a streetlight across the way or maybe the moon. With his coco lips and strong jaw line, he was beautiful, no doubt about it. And now he had a hunger in his eyes, but the hunger was for me. I smiled inside.

He brought the smooth silk of his lips toward me and kissed me. The sheer heaven, the rightness of that kiss made me feel my body open up to him. There could be no question that we belonged together. He kissed my cheeks, nose, eyelids and neck, playfully biting into it.

Facing each other, he brought my legs up over his until I could feel myself pressing into him. I rocked back and forth, wanting him.

"It's great the way no one bothers you in this place," he said.

I could only kiss him some more, wishing the moment would never end. I wanted to become him.

"What are you thinking?" he asked.

I gazed up into the sky and said without thinking, "Just wondering about the whole werecat thing."

He kissed me on the nose. "Don't think too much. That's my recommendation."

"Easy for you to say."

"Kenley." He looked up at the moon for a moment and then his face turned grave. "It's not easy for me to say this, but I have feelings for you I've never had for anyone else. You are so incredibly special. And I want to help you. I don't want you to have to go through what I went through."

"Do you mean what happened with your parents?"

He pulled away a little, and I thought I'd said something wrong, but I noticed that a police officer doing his rounds had walked up behind us.

"Isn't it little late for you kids to be out?" A strong cigarette smell lingered around him.

"Sorry, officer," Luis said.

We untangled ourselves from each other and walked back to Luis's car.

"I guess you'd better take me home. My parents grounded me for the night we stayed out all night."

"Oh, sorry about that. I don't want you to get into any more trouble than you're already in. I'll take you right home."

"They tend to forget in a couple of days, though. They're too busy to notice what I do."

We walked, hand-in-hand, through the magical garden and back to his car. The conversation flowed easily between us as he drove. "I think we should go on vacation some time," he said.

"Yeah, but I don't know what my parents will have to say about that."

He tapped the top of his head with his wrist. "D'oh. Parents. I forgot." He glanced at me and grinned. "But look, you won't be seventeen forever. After you graduate in June they won't have that much say over you, will they?"

It floored me that he was thinking that far in advance about us, like there was really an "us." The thought made me tingle with happiness.

Luis stopped his car just before my house. "Night, Kenley. I always have an amazing time with you."

What could I say? "You're pretty amazing yourself."

"Want to come over to my parents' house tomorrow? They're away."

Wow! An invitation to his house with no parents home. That was a step forward in seriousness. But could I get away from *my* parents? I'd find a way. "That would be great!"

"Okay, I'll pick you up at eight." He caressed my cheek with his soft hand and kissed me again. The honeyed feel of his lips transported me to another world and made me want him so much, but I knew I had to go so I took one last look at his warm eyes and tore myself away.

As I walked into my house I wondered to myself, how could I live that violent werecat life of having to kill and eat my food? It seemed wrong somehow. Then I pictured Luis's eyes as he kissed me in the moonlight, and those fears receded into the background.

Just past eleven. I'd made it home before my parents. I went to my bedroom and changed into cotton jammies. When I heard them come in, I gave them a few minutes to settle in. I was going to ask them; *had* to ask them.

They sat in the den watching a documentary about Salvador Dali. My parents ate up everything about artists, especially quirky dead ones.

I vowed to ask Luis about the werecat/homeless-person-killer connection soon. I'd wanted to do it tonight but never found the right opportunity. Since I hadn't done that, I wasn't going to bomb out on confronting my parents. I mulled over in my mind the fact that if they knew I was fulfilling my werecat destiny they'd watch me even more closely. But no, I decided I needed to confront them.

I emerged from the bedroom trying to look sleepy as though I'd been in all night, but I was sure I couldn't pull it off, I was too hyped. My heart spasmed in my chest. I jumped right in so I wouldn't lose my nerve. "Why didn't you tell me?" I felt myself hyperventilating, practically on the verge of tears.

"Oh, for heaven's sake, Kenley." Mom paused the movie looking annoyed at the interruption. "Tell you what?"

"That we're werecats."

᳇᳇᳇ Chapter 15 ᳇᳇᳇

Dad dropped his freshly made Cape Cod all over the white carpeting, making it look like an abstract-expressionist painting. "Um...Mimi?" His head whipped around toward Mom as though waiting for her to tell him what to say.

She reached over her recliner and took Dad's hand then she said. "It's okay, Bruce. Honey, we knew you were going to ask us about this one day."

That floored me. If I'd been a gambling person I would have bet money they'd deny the whole thing.

"Have you...?" Dad glanced toward me and hesitated.

Mom completed his sentence. "Been feeling anything strange lately?"

"Yeah." I rubbed the back of my head, trying not to cry. "I've been feeling strange for months now, and I thought I was losing my mind."

"Oh, no. Now we're going to have to deal with this." The corners of Mom's mouth turned down and her teeth clenched together. "We were hoping it would skip you like it did your cousin Lucy."

At that instant my hurt turned to anger. I bent down and pounded my fist on the coffee table. "You knew about this all along, and you let me suffer?"

"You're two years late in turning," Mom said as though it were my fault. "So we thought it had skipped you. We watched you very closely when you were fifteen, which is the normal turning time. When you didn't show any signs of inheriting the werecatism, we were relieved. We said, thank God she doesn't carry the gene."

"What? And then you just forgot all about it? You forgot about me? You stopped caring if I knew about my heritage?

Why?" I was so angry I had a hard time making a coherent sentence.

"No, we never stopped caring. The truth is that even though you're experiencing this change, you don't have to live the werecat life; you can live like a normal person, just like your father and I do, just like *you* have for the first seventeen years of your life."

"What do you mean? I can never be normal. Normal isn't within the realm of possibility for someone who turns into a giant cat." I stood facing Dad on the couch and Mom in the recliner.

When I said the thing about the giant cat, she flinched as though I'd wounded her. "No, but there are ways to minimize the hold it has over your life," Mom said.

"And you never thought to mention any of this to me?"

"I wish we'd told you. I wanted to," Dad said.

"Yes, your father wanted to tell you, and I didn't. I guess I didn't want to spoil your innocence if you weren't going to be affected."

"Innocence. Huh! You didn't do such a great job of explaining sex to me either. Did you have the same rationale there, too?" I stomped back and forth across the room, furious with them.

"Have you...made the change?" Dad slid forward in his chair, asking the question he'd tried to ask me before. Before Mom finished his sentence for him.

"Yes, and I was tortured over it, thanks to you." Tears welled up in my eyes. "Your parents are supposed to prepare you for these things."

"We thought...well...I thought that you'd come to us if you started experiencing any of the physical signs," Mom said, looking a little softer and amenable now as though she'd melted inside, just a little.

"Go to my parents with what I thought was my adolescent angst? Why would I do that?" I shouted, which wasn't like me. "The truth is you just don't care about me at all."

"That's not true, Kitten. We love you more than anything," Dad said.

"If you loved me, why didn't you tell me we're werecats?" I couldn't control the tears any more so I let them flow down from my eyes.

"We screwed up, Kitten." Dad had tears in his eyes, too.

"Okay," Since I felt like I was about to pass out, I sat down next to Dad on the couch. "Just level with me now. So you guys are both werecats, right? How come you never change?"

"We suppress it." Dad looked at Mom who had an expression of irritation on her face. "Like we do a lot of things. We have to eat some fresh meat. That's why we keep the snakes. We eat the mice."

"You eat live mice? Gross." I felt like I was going to vomit.

"Yes. They're small and have a low life energy level, so it keeps our werecat-ism to a minimum while allowing us to survive," Dad said, ready to level with me.

Just like Luis had said...

I looked over at mom who sat quietly, wrapping her beige cashmere afghan more and more tightly around herself. "I didn't want to have to deal with this."

"I know you didn't want me." That sounded kind of mean to my own ears even as I said it. I knew it would get to my mom, though.

Mom wiped her eyes with a crumpled up tissue, sniffled and blinked, trying to get a grip. "Well, it's true that we didn't want you. We wanted to have a free lifestyle so we could travel whenever we wanted to."

That one statement made me feel as though she'd cut me with a knife. Water started to leak out of the sides of my eyes even though I squeezed them as tightly as I could. Dad got up and hugged me, which made me cry all the more. They'd never been very physically demonstrative parents.

Her expression softened. "But once we had you..." She almost broke down into tears. Almost but not quite. "...we loved you so much."

I felt kind of a lump in my throat when she said this, so I got up and hugged her then when Dad sat down on the couch, I sat next to him. "Explain to me now all the stuff you kept from me all these years." I sniffled and wiped my eyes with a tissue. "How about starting out by telling me about our family and why you're in such denial about the whole thing. You are werecats, aren't you?"

"Yes," Dad said. "We're werecats, but we wanted to break with that lifestyle. Our positions demanded certain duties of us. We're in the royal line of the Favrés and as such, we were going to have to perform royal duties."

"What are Favrés?" I asked.

"It's the royal line of werecats that, legend has it, descended from the Egyptian Cat Goddess, Bastet."

"Royalty? Like the British royal family?"

"Very near to that, but much grander," Dad continued with a hint of pride.

Mom leaned forward and started to talk. "Let me tell her, Bruce," she said to Dad. "The werecats—our family anyway—are matriarchal. The lineage is passed down through the mother. My family was...is, in the royal line. Then I fell in love with your father, even though he wouldn't have been accepted into the family. He wasn't from a royal lineage, you see."

"The reason we rejected this life is that, for one thing, we didn't want to be part of the whole royalty thing. It carried too many responsibilities," Dad said.

"Responsibilities? Like what?"

"The Favrés, that's our branch of the werecat family, has a leader in each country. From time-to-time they have to get together and decide various political issues for all cats." Mom waved her hand. "Neither of us wanted any part of that. The cat leaders are so impossible when they get together. They couldn't cooperate to save their skins, which it does come down to sometimes. We're not very political; we just want to live for ourselves."

"Yeah, talk about egos. They all think they're master of all they survey. You know how even house cats are," Dad said. "They're not crazy about other cats. Your mom's mom was just about impossible."

Mom shot him a scathing look. "Nothing in the family ever gets decided and everyone ends up going back to their own lairs to lick their wounds."

"Who's the leader now in the states?" I asked.

"That's just it." Mom said. "There is none. We're hiding out so they won't find us and make us be leaders. That's the main reason we left. Another reason we've split with our werecat heritage is that when you're a full, active werecat, you're at the mercy of your instincts. You might be in the middle of the mall and feel like changing, and there you are. You either have to fight it or run away." Mom shook her head.

"And the temptation to go running wild at night is more than most people can stand. If we killed and ate bigger animals, we'd be out hunting every night. It perpetuates itself. You eat the bigger animals, and you have to go out chasing them to keep up your energy," Dad said.

I pressed my hand to my right temple, and rubbed, trying to work out the shooting pain that had developed there. "Oh my God. I can't believe all of this."

Mom looked at me sternly. "You have a serious decision to make, Kenley: whether you want to suppress it the way we do or embrace the lifestyle."

I debated telling them about Luis, then decided to. "Mom, Dad, I've met someone."

Mom's mouth dropped open. "Oh, Kenley, you're going to have a rough time getting along with a regular human."

"That's just it. He's a werecat, too."

ᚂᚉᚉᚋ Chapter 16 ᚉᚋᚉᚋ

"You mean you've met one of our kind? How *dare* you do this without asking us," Mom said, the red creeping up into her face like the mercury on a thermometer that was about to burst.

"I didn't even know what 'us' was until a couple of days ago." I found myself nearly shouting again. "What am I supposed to do? Ask you before I get a boyfriend?"

Mom spoke in an ominously low and quiet tone. "I forbid you from getting involved with a werecat. It'll skew you in the wrong direction. Get some other interests."

"So, you don't want me to have a normal boyfriend and you don't want me to have a werecat boyfriend. Why don't you just send me to a convent?" I was trying to be nice, but I couldn't hold in my frustration with them.

Dad spoke up. "Kitten, you know how it is with us parents. We never think anyone is good enough for our little girls. We just want you to be happy, that's all."

"What's his name?" Mom asked.

"None of your business, and if you think I'm going to let you tell me who I can and cannot go out with, you're crazy. I'm going to bed." I jerked up off the couch and started to bolt.

"Wait a minute..." Mom put out her hand.

"No." I sprinted down the hallway and slammed my bedroom door.

I had to talk to Michelle, so I dialed her number. It rang a long time, then a groggy voice answered. "Hullo."

"Michelle, I'm so glad you answered. I really need to talk."

"Come on. It's midnight, and it's a school night."

"You never used to mind." I had a sinking feeling that I'd been inconsiderate.

"Why don't you call up Molly or one of those other obnoxious Claw Club girls you seem to be so infatuated with lately?" Click.

Wow. Michelle hated me. I supposed I *was* going over the edge with the whole thing. Michelle was mad at me and she didn't even know about my nasty little secret. I half wanted to tell her. Maybe that would change things between us for the worse, though.

I decided to go to bed, hoping I'd dream about Luis.

On Saturday morning I caught up on my rest. After having had practically no sleep and a lot of trauma the previous week, it was glorious to luxuriate in bed.

Soon my sense of duty got the better of me. I went to the Tampa Bay Homeless Shelter and visited Shelly. She was still inconsolable about her mom, so I paid a visit to the director of the facility and asked what would happen to her. She assured me she'd be placed in a good local home. I don't know if she was just telling me that to make me feel good or what. I know I shouldn't have, but I felt kind of responsible.

Next I called Andy, the reporter from the Tampa Tribune, to see if he'd gotten any response to the article.

"Response? Where have you been? The city is up in arms. You'd think Godzilla was attacking downtown Tampa. They've got cops and National Guard out all over the place."

"That's good. Hey, Andy, can you do me a favor and keep my name out of any future articles? I'm just a little worried about them coming after me, you know?"

"You? How about them coming after me?" He sounded indignant.

"You're a reporter. My situation is a little different."

"I will do that for you. I promise."

"Thanks, Andy. And here's my number in case you need anything. I think I gave you the wrong one last time." I gave him my real digits.

"Thanks, babe," he said.

"No, thank you for getting this crazy situation some attention. And good luck on that Pulitzer."

I was really Miss "To Do List" that day, getting all those things done.

By then it was time to get ready for my date with Luis.

I took a hot bath, loofahed my skin, perfumed myself in all the right places and gave myself a ballet pink manicure.

All that was left were the clothes. Of course I had nothing to wear. But I chose a blue top with matching blue sweater in case it got cold, jeans and strappy sandals. It had just turned a little cool in Tampa for November. I added a choker with a blue stone and matching earrings. I was set.

"Kenley, you look so beautiful," Luis said as he entered the door to our house.

"So do you." That was no lie. Every time I saw him I was amazed that he was attracted to me.

"Wow! Can I look at your parents' artwork? We didn't have time when I was here before." He headed straight for our green monster in the gallery room just like everyone else does. "This guy is cool." After giving a cursory look at all the Frazetta babes, he drifted back to the cases in the living room.

"That's their Egyptian stuff," I said.

"Since your parents are gone, may I snoop around at their artifacts?" He bent to look into a case filled with Egyptian bowls and knives.

"Be my guest. There's a lot of old dusty stuff in here."

Through the case, he examined one brown bowl with hieroglyphics painted on the side. "Kenley, do you have any idea how old that bowl is?" He tried to open the case, but it was locked.

"I don't know. Mom and Dad love that stuff, but I didn't think it had any particular value. Why?"

"The bowl is easily from 2,000 BC, the time of Menthuhotpe II's rule." He gazed at it fascinated.

"I didn't realize you knew so much about Egyptian history." I crouched next to him and examined the pieces.

"Those relics have been there my whole life and I've never taken much notice of them."

"My dad made us learn some Egyptology so we'd know about our distant heritage." Luis's eyes remained transfixed on the bowl.

"But you're South American?"

"Yes, Columbian. Werecats come from all over, you know, but the origin is Egypt."

"Very interesting."

"And this knife." He stared intently at a knife made from a purple sliver of stone with a cat's head sitting on top. "This may be significant. I'm pretty sure the figure is Bastet, Egyptian Cat Goddess of peace. I'll have to look it up." He gazed back at the knife again. "I've rambled on too long. Let's go."

Suddenly the door opened. Ready to do battle, Mom stood with her hands on her hips. "Who's this and what do you think you're doing? Going out? You're grounded, young lady." Her eyes narrowed as she stared Luis down. "And you are?"

"I'm Luis Malik. Pleased to meet you." He extended his hand, which Dad shook and Mom didn't.

"I want you out of here right now. You're a bad influence on my daughter."

Dad looked embarrassed by Mom's outburst but he knew better than to say anything.

I quickly made the universal "call me" sign to Luis as he hurried out the door.

At midnight Mom and Dad were safely ensconced in their room. That was the great thing about our house. Because of the split plan, Mom and Dad's room was on the opposite side of the house. They had a complete video system, small fridge and microwave in there, so they could be happy in their own little cocoon. And they hardly knew what I did, ever.

So, I took full advantage of the situation and snuck out my bedroom window. I hoped they'd never catch on to the fact that I'd disabled the extensive security system they had on the house to protect their artwork. Just for my bedroom window, though. The alarm on the rest of the house remained intact.

Luis whisked me away in his sexy Jaguar convertible.

We zoomed up Dale Mabry Highway and turned onto a side road into an area of estates called Somerset. Massive houses with perfectly manicured gardens sat on acres of land. Some houses had the usual assortment of palm trees, but most had northern-looking yards with miles of golf-course-green lawns and old oak trees. Carpets of petunias, zinnias and impatiens edged the lawns. It must have taken an army of gardeners to maintain these places.

Luis pulled up to a house that looked as though Frank Lloyd Wright had gotten together with Renaissance architect Filippo Brunelleschi to create a modern marvel. It sounded weird, but it looked amazing. The two-story, tan building had brick archways built into its windows and doors. The decorative lights that shown up into the trees reflected on the windows making them look like eyes staring out at me. A dome befitting a Florentine cathedral spanned the back of the house. Quite amazing.

When he extended his hand to help me out of the car, I took it and stepped out gracefully, trying not to look awestruck. It was indeed a splendid place. He opened the two massive oak doors and led me into a marble entryway that held a flowing staircase straight out of a classic Hollywood movie. I gazed up at an odd chandelier made from multi-colored hand-blown glass.

"It's from Venice," he said. "We brought it from our old house."

"You lived in Venice?"

"Um hum. For a little while," he said nonchalantly.

"This place is amazing."

"Yeah, actually, it's the biggest house we've ever had. Come on out and see the backyard." We walked through a sunroom filled with Moroccan-looking dark wicker furniture and tons of plants: palms, orchids and birds of paradise.

"This place looks like an arboretum."

"Growing orchids and violets is Dad's hobby. It calms his nerves."

"It's high pressure being a werecat attorney, huh?"

"You could say that. Let's go out to the garden." He took my hand and brought me out to the most amazing backyard I'd ever seen. A two-story waterfall splashed into a freeform pool that contained the bluest water on earth. I guessed it looked so blue from the lights shining up from the depths of the pool.

Luis picked up a remote control and turned off the lights. "Want to go in?"

"Um, well, I didn't bring a bathing suit."

"You don't need a bathing suit." He cocked his head and looked at me sideways with a devilish grin.

"No?"

"Not at all. We have tons of them for guests."

"That's great." I was kind of relieved that he didn't want to skinny dip. On the one hand, I wanted more than anything to be naked in the pool with Luis. On the other hand, I knew this guy could get any girl he wanted, and I didn't want to be a one-night stand to him. I wanted it to mean more.

He disappeared for a moment and returned to open the door to a cabana adjoining the pool. "Here you are. Take your pick of styles."

"Thanks!" I entered the cabana and closed the door. It was a sumptuous room with a bed made up with fiesta-colored sheets, red leather couch and matching chairs. A full bath with whirlpool adjoined the bedroom. "Wow." I perused the styles. String bikinis—I didn't think so. On the other hand the one-piecers looked too geriatric. I settled on a bright blue bikini that had a full bottom rather than a T-back. I regarded myself in the mirror. Not bad, the bra pushed me up nicely and the blue accented my eyes. The top wrapped and tied in a strange way, so I did my best to fasten it. Once the outfit was completed, I emerged from the cabana all smiles.

"You look amazing." Luis held his hand out to me and I grasped it.

Luis kissed my hand, and put it back down. He pulled his top over his head causing his long hair to spill down over his shoulders. The moonlight gleamed off his smooth tan skin showing his just-right muscles. He started to remove his jeans, smiling obliquely as though he perhaps didn't have anything on under them. But he fooled me and had gray swim trunks on underneath.

It was pretty dark except for the moonlight. "Let's go!" I jumped into the pool, bracing for chill water. "Hey, it's warm."

"It's heated. Surprise!"

He rushed in after me, wrapped his hands under my shoulders, and pulled me toward the waterfall. "This is fun, you'll love it."

"No, I don't want to get my hair wet." I fake-struggled with him.

He placed me under the gentle part of the spray and kissed me lightly on the neck. I moaned. I'd never felt a more delicious sensation in my life. Could I die right now?

He reached down into the water and tickled me. I pulled away and flipped over to back-stroke away from him, and as I did, I heard something rip and watched helplessly as my top got caught up in the maelstrom of the waterfall.

"Luis! Can you get that for me?"

"Hang on." He dove under the water, then popped back up holding the run-away top.

But just as I thought I was having the greatest night of my life, the lights burst on, burning a purple spot in my retinas.

"Hey, who's there?" Luis asked with one hand up shading his face from the glare.

A voice bellowed from the darkness. "Just what do you think you're doing? Get out of that pool right now."

Chapter 17

"Enrique, cut the crap. Turn those lights out." Luis sounded angrier than I'd ever heard him before.

Feeling exposed and more naked than naked, I submerged myself and crossed my arms in front of my chest.

The man clicked his tongue. "What would Dad say if he could see you?"

"He'd say have some freaking manners and turn the lights out." Luis turned toward me. "You'll have to excuse my brother. He's a complete lout."

After my eyes became accustomed to the brightness, I took a good look at the intruder. He had close-cropped black hair and a face that resembled an older harder version of Luis's. His bulky muscles made him look almost squat, despite his height. He wore a black tee shirt and jeans.

"Enrique," I said. "Pleased to meet you." I'd have extended my hand had if it hadn't been for my unfortunate state of dress.

"Likewise, *Seniorita*," Enrique said.

"Now would you leave please?" Luis shouted, just about to lose his patience.

"Dad might be coming home soon."

"You're full of bullshit, Enrique. He's in Boston on business. Now turn off the lights."

"Don't say I didn't warn you." He flicked out the lights and sauntered into the house.

I wondered if he was still watching us from inside the house. "That was kind of creepy," I said wrapping my arms more tightly around myself.

"Kind of ruined the mood, huh?"

"Yeah."

"I'll get you a towel." Luis effortlessly hoisted himself up onto the side of the pool.

After I dried off in the cabana and got dressed, we sat on a stone bench underneath a willow tree in the garden. I leaned back and inhaled the sweet aroma of gardenia and enjoyed the multi-colored flowers that were softly lit by a row of low solar-powered lamps. The whole garden seemed to be enveloped by a soft mist. And to be enjoying this with Luis. Unreal. "Enrique is your older brother, I take it?"

"Yeah. We've never gotten along. He's into all the macho bullshit stuff like football. It's surprising he didn't join the Marines. I'm the oddball who took up the loner sport of running track."

"How does your father feel about you?"

"He thinks I'm wimpy and indecisive just because I'm not a jerk like my brother. The two of them are so much alike." He turned to face me. "But enough about me. I've been talking about myself all night. Let's talk about you. What's your fondest dream?"

I had to think. "I love nature, and I want to do something to make people realize that our forests and wildlife need to be protected, but I don't have a real calling."

"But that is a calling."

"Yeah, but it's not specific."

"Maybe I can help you figure it out. Help you find your purpose in life."

"You'd do that?"

"Sure I would." He leaned in and kissed my neck. I threw my head back and gazed up at the branches of the swaying willow tree silhouetted against a perfect full moon.

"Will you let me tell you a secret?" he asked as he kissed me lightly on the lips.

"Yeah, what?"

"I am absolutely crazy about you." His eyes sparkled as he talked.

"I feel the same way about you, but the whole thing scares me."

He took my hand and rubbed it, in a very reassuring way. I felt so secure with Luis. "Understandably so. You'd be a fool if it didn't. This has been a lot for you to take in. I know that. I'll help you with it. I went through it, too, you know."

"What can I help *you* with?" I pushed back his damp hair from his face.

"You can help me feel less lonely."

"You lonely? With Molly and Cristen and Sarah at your beck-and-call?"

He waved his hand. "They're nothing to me. But you..." He kissed my hand again. "You surpass everyone and everything. I'm so thankful for the day I met you."

What could I possibly say to that?

He stood and took my hand, pulling me up. "Come on. I'm taking you home. I don't want you to get in trouble with your folks."

Climbing back in through my bedroom window proved to be no problem, but I couldn't sleep with that inexplicable call of the wild that beckoned me. I tossed and turned and slipped into a fitful sleep at the gray light of morning seeped in through the curtains.

In what seemed like only a few minutes later, I got a surprise in the form of a tapping on my bedroom window.

⮞⥤ Chapter 18 ⥢⮜

Tap, tap. Tap, tap. At first I thought I was dreaming. I rubbed the sleep from my eyes and looked around. A soft *Tap, tap. Tap, tap* echoed from the window pane. Since it was daylight, it didn't occur to me to be frightened, so I opened my frosted window a crack and saw a large pair of hazel eyes and streaming black hair. "Luis." My pulse gave a little surge.

"Want a ride to school?" His usual dark brooding looks had been replaced with an infectious grin that showed a dimple on the left side of his face I'd never noticed before.

Oh my God, I panicked. I looked like hell. No makeup, hair all over the place, morning breath. "Uh...yeah. Give me fifteen minutes?" I was probably pushing my luck. He probably didn't want to wait.

"Sure. I'll go get us some lattés."

"That would be so wonderful." How did I get a boyfriend who was so considerate and perfect? I rushed through my morning shower, makeup and hair prep, hoping beyond hope that I could get myself to look awesome in time, and that everyone at school would see me getting out of his sleek white Jag.

I dressed, trying for a casual messed up look and rushed out the front door. There sat Luis with the convertible top down, holding out my favorite, a latté. "Soy, just the way you like it."

"My favorite. Thanks!" The fact that he remembered my soy touched me in some deep internal place. I sank down into his white leather seat, took a sip of the fragrant brew and sighed. Heaven, just heaven.

He gave me a little kiss. "Nothing's too good for my girl," he said as he peeled out onto the street.

We didn't talk a whole lot on the way to school. It was too noisy with the top down, but when we pulled into the main parking lot, Molly and Cristen were just walking into class.

Molly looked at Luis with squinted eyes, her nose flaring in the way it did when she was upset. But she quickly corrected her expression into a smile. She and Cristen waved, all light-hearted and cheery. Both girls looked like they'd stepped out of the pages of *W*. Molly wore black leather micro mini skirt, ballet flats, and short sleeved silky see-through shirt with camisole underneath, and Cristen wore shredded jeans, gray beret, grey hoodie and scarf. How did those girls manage to wear new outfits to school every day?

I had kind of an odd feeling in the back of my mind that I didn't want to acknowledge but the small voice in my head nagged at me. Maybe he was parading me in front of Molly on purpose, like maybe to make her jealous.

We walked in through the main double doors where the principal stood like a welcoming committee. He did this every so often to take note of who was on time and who was late. *We* were on time. Not what you'd think of as a typical high school principal, he was muscular with thick hands, he looked like he should have been in a plaid flannel shirt rather than in a nondescript gray business suit. He must have been thirty-five or forty.

"Good morning, Mr. Trask," Luis said, the perfect model of an obedient kid, the kind of obedient kid who could get away with murder and no one would suspect him.

Mr. Trask nodded. "Good job on that half mile, Mr. Malik," the principal said as he clasped Luis's shoulder. He looked at Luis then at me, but his gaze lasted a couple of beats longer than normal.

"What was that about?" I asked Luis when we'd gotten clear of him.

"What? Him looking at you? I don't think he meant anything in particular. You just look beautiful today, that's all." He took my hand as we walked up the stairs toward my home room.

I wondered why Luis was walking me to my home room when he never had before.

We passed by Molly and Cristen. Those girls seemed to be everywhere. Luis didn't even say anything to them, just walked on past them seemingly oblivious. "What would you like to do tonight," he asked me, all nonchalant.

He was asking me out again tonight, like we were really an item now. "Anything you'd like to do. I need to do some homework first."

He turned to look at me with a slight grin. "You're kidding, right?"

"Actually, no."

"What a normal high school senior can do in two hours, you can do in five minutes. We have a superior intellect, and now that you're officially one of us, so do you." He leaned in toward me and tapped the center of my chest as he said this.

"Wow, really?"

"Have you tried studying lately?"

"No."

"You'll be amazed."

We were at my homeroom. Michelle wasn't waiting for me, which made me feel kind of bad.

I smiled at him and thought about backing away but found it incredibly hard to do. "Well, I'd better go."

Luis kind of winked at me then turned and left.

He wanted to do something tonight. Oh my. This was just too good to be true.

Michelle was sitting in the back row, but she didn't look at me when I entered the room. It made me feel really uncomfortable and creepy. My best friend had turned against me, and it was completely my fault. Still, my elation at Luis's invitation trumped my sadness at Michelle's dissing me.

When the bell rang, I tried to catch her. "Michelle," I called after her and barely touched her shoulder, but she ignored me and walked on.

What a roller coaster of feelings I had: happiness because of what was developing between Luis and me and sadness because I'd lost the only person who had stuck by me through everything, Michelle. I thought about Brendan's warning that I should be careful of Luis. I momentarily wondered what kind of boyfriend would make my best friend turn against me, but he hadn't done that, I had.

I decided that for the moment, I'd push all of it to the back of my mind...all of it except my euphoric feelings for Luis. He was the first guy I'd really liked who reciprocated my feelings. I wished more than anything I had parents I could talk to about these things.

The day went by in a blur. Web Design II, Physics, Trig. Luis was right, I could absorb ideas, facts and formulas about a hundred times faster and more efficiently than I ever had before. These new abilities had been coming on so subtly I'd hardly recognized them, but once Luis pointed that out to me, I was able to focus my thoughts.

When lunch time came, I was momentarily at a loss as to what to do. Should I go to the lunchroom and have an awkward moment with Michelle or maybe hang outdoors? To my surprise, Luis found me and took me out to lunch.

As we pulled out of the parking lot, I noticed that the sky looked a little dark and the air felt heavy and electric with that clean pre-rain ozone scent. "I hope it doesn't pour on us," I said

Luis looked up at the sky. "We should be finished by then. Come on."

We ordered sandwiches at a small kiosk set up for business-lunchers who were in a hurry and wanted to grab something fast. Then we sat outside at a picnic table in a little park near school. He seemed like he wanted to talk more than he wanted to eat.

"You know, Kenley, I've never met anyone like you before. I've never felt I could be totally myself with anyone. All of those Claw Club girls...they actually want me to be something that I'm not. They want the popular kid who's good to be seen with, the life of the party, and I'm so not that. I'm just a quiet guy. I just want to keep to myself and do whatever work I end up doing quietly and for the good of mankind."

"I feel the same way about you. I feel so lucky to have found you. It's as though we fit together in every way." We sat across the picnic table looking into each other's eyes. Though I never could have imagined it before, I didn't feel awkward saying these things to him.

Then he came around to my side of the picnic table and sat next to me. His eyes were kind of shiny as he talked. "I think I'm making some major decisions because of you. Like maybe not going along with my father's wishes for my life."

"Your dad seems like a pretty good guy. Didn't you say he was into conservation and everything?" I noticed that the storm clouds had gathered and looked considerably more ominous.

"Yes, but not into conservation the way you and I are. He has selfish motives. To him everything is for money and power." Luis looked up at the sky but didn't react to the growing darkness.

I contemplated that for a moment. "I think I know what you mean, like someone who does the right things for the wrong reasons."

He put his arm around me and squeezed a little. "You do understand, huh? But you have no idea of the magnitude. Someday I'll tell you all about it in great detail."

I looked at my phone. It was getting late. "Hey, I don't want to spoil the moment, but I think we should get back."

"Don't worry, we'll have lots of other moments. Like tonight." His face brightened up.

At that moment the heavens opened up and it started to pour. Not a nice gentle rain like you might find in Seattle, big sploochy drips that turned into driving nails two second later, just like someone had turned on a shower.

Luis grabbed my hand and we dashed to the car. He hurriedly popped up the top, but not before we'd both become drenched right down to our underwear. Florida rains were like that.

As I sluiced the water off my arms and Luis rung out his hair we both started laughing uncontrollably. "Oh my God, I'm sopping wet. How can we go back to class like this?"

"We could skip and go to my house." He raised his eyebrows and looked at me expectantly.

"I can't. I've got a physics test right after lunch."

"Come on."

"No, I can't."

"Okay, just as well. I have track today after class." He started up the car and blasted the heat. "See? You're a good influence on me."

As we sat there drying off, he leaned over and kissed me. In a way that was unhurried, tender, wonderful really. "Want to watch me run track after school? You need to be practicing, too. Miss Werecat."

"Sure, I'd love to."

He worked the gearshift into reverse and slowly backed out.

I was a little bit late for physics, and got a dirty look from Mr. W, but I aced the test. It was so easy. Luis had been right. It was like the other eighty percent of my brain had opened up to me, like I'd gotten a RAM increase.

After school as I hung around the track, I wasn't there two minutes when I saw Brendan hurrying over toward me. He was the last person I wanted to see while I was waiting for Luis. "Hi Brendan," I said, not able to escape him.

"Hey. Listen, I know I'm not the person you want to see right now, but..." He hesitated for a moment to catch his breath. "You have to watch out for Luis."

"Brendan, I'm fine. I know what I'm doing." Just go away, please?

"No, you don't."

"Yes, I do." I started walking away from him and he followed me. He was obviously jealous.

"Why won't you listen to me?" He spread his fingers apart, palms up and shook his head at me.

"I'll call you later, okay?"

"You won't."

"I will. I promise."

"Wait. Here's my number." He scrawled something on a scrap of paper. "I'm not doing this for my health, you know."

"I know. I have to go." I hated being so mean to him, but I didn't want him around at the moment. I pushed the paper with his phone number into my pocket.

"I know when I'm not wanted, but call me." He trudged toward the parking lot.

"I will, Brendan." I walked away from him and saw Luis just coming out of the school building. I didn't think he'd noticed that I was talking with Brendan.

Luis sauntered toward me in his cool black track outfit, not at all in a hurry.

"Are you ready for practice?" I asked knowing full-well that he was. Luis actually held the US record for the fastest half mile by a high school student.

"I kind of hold myself back so they won't suspect anything," he admitted as he bent forward to stretch his legs, then put one leg back into a lunge.

"Must be tough being so great," I teased.

He looked pretend hurt then swatted me playfully. "Careful girl. I'll get my claws out. Meow." We both laughed.

The rest of the team came around. I sat on one of the bleachers and killed some time until they got around to running. There were three other guys with Luis, and when the coach gave the signal, they were off. I could tell that Luis was holding back just keeping barely behind the other runners. When they got toward the end he pulled ahead easily, and ran through the marker with his hands up in the air. Then he bent over pretending to be winded, but I knew very well he hadn't even broken a sweat.

If I were the other guys, I'd get so discouraged because Luis always won. How could he not win? After they'd gone a few more rounds, Luis walked over to me. "We're done. Do you want to get going?"

"Yeah. I have to go home to do a few things."

"Sure. I'll take you home." We walked to his car, Luis in the same black tee shirt with the little skull on the arm and shorts to match. I wondered why the coach let him dress differently than the other kids. Probably because he was so freaking awesome.

As he drove me to my house, I couldn't stop thinking about how cool he looked, even in his gym outfit. He had well defined, but not bulky, arms and powerful runner's legs. Sleek as a jaguar.

"I'll see you in an hour," he said nonchalantly, looking sexy in his shades, sitting in his hot little white convertible.

"Well, I..." I thought about the stuff I needed to do: homework, projects, maybe call Michelle and try to make amends.

"I have a really nice surprise for you."

I hesitated.

"It's a good one. You'll really like it."

I put my hands on my hips. "Well, okay. I suppose."

"Cool."

He drove off and I stood there watching as his car turned into a little white speck on the road. I must have done something right to have him in my life.

I wasted no time in showering and getting ready. The dampness from the afternoon rain still clung to my clothes, and I couldn't wait to get the musty smell off of me. One hour didn't afford me the time to work on any of the stuff I needed to, but who cared, right?

Luis returned in one hour on the dot. I saw him driving up and hurried out to the car to meet him. Even though my parents had grounded me, they generally forgot about it in a few days. They were out on another art collecting expedition anyway.

"You look amazing, as always," he said as he opened the door for me. I'd never get over the thrill of getting into Luis' white Jag. It smelled like new leather along with Luis's spicy-clean cologne. The scent actually caused a physical excitement in me.

His hand brushed my leg as he put the gear shift into drive, causing a little shiver to go through me. I couldn't take my eyes off the polished wood handle of the gear shift. It looked so smooth and pale, I wanted to put my hand on it and feel it but didn't.

"I'm glad you could come out with me this afternoon."

"Hey, it's my pleasure."

He stared straight ahead at the road and hesitated for a moment, then said, "Who's that guy you've been hanging out with? Kind of tall with sandy hair."

"That's Brendan. He just moved here and he doesn't know anybody so he kind of glommed onto me." At first I was worried that he'd think Brendan meant something to me, then it occurred to me—Luis was jealous! How about that? I could barely hide the elated expression that threatened to creep onto my face.

"Do you know anything about him, like anything about his parents or anything?" I could tell he was trying to sound really casual about the whole thing.

"No, I've barely spoken to him." Why had I just lied to Luis? I wanted to tell him the truth, but then it would seem like I was covering something up, so I let it go at that.

"We have to be careful about who we associate with. No big deal. I'm just saying..."

"Yeah, I know. I'm careful."

"I don't want you to think I'm jealous or anything."

"Oh no, I wouldn't think that." I grinned a little to myself but wondered if that was his real reason for taking me out this afternoon, to pump me about Brendan. "He doesn't mean anything to me, you know."

"I know. I just worry about you, I guess."

I could handle that.

We swooped down I-275, got off at the Lois Avenue exit and ended up at the last place I would have expected him to take me, the International Mall.

I couldn't imagine why he'd brought me here. Maybe he was taking me to the Cheesecake Factory.

He valet parked the car, which seemed like an extravagance to me, not that I didn't enjoy it. I secretly gloated as a group of girls eyed Luis getting out of the car. We stepped onto the sidewalk and passed by shops and outdoor bistros that had been created to look like a Mediterranean street scene, in other words, Disney faux-Eurpoean all the way. A red clay fountain at the end bubbled its cool liquid that reflected the waning sun. Even though it was fall, the heat seeped out of the pavement, magnifying the scent of the garlic and tomato sauce that wafted out of the Villa D'Italia. Being with Luis I could almost buy the fantasy.

He took my hand as we strolled past the Cosmo-drinking singles as if to say, *See? I'm with Kenley and I'm proud of it.* I could practically feel a physical opening of my heart.

"These places are such meat markets, aren't they? All the pretty people come to show themselves off," he said.

As if he wasn't one of them. "Yeah, pretty lame, huh? So, why are we here?"

"You'll see." He put his other hand over mine and rubbed it as we passed through the automatic double doors into the mall proper.

I'm one of the highly unusual members of the female gender who does not like malls. I'd rather go in, get whatever I'm after and get the hell out of there, rather than lingering about and making a day of it the way some packs of girls do.

It was obvious that Luis was heading somewhere with a purpose. We came to a dead stop right outside of the Betsy Johnson shop. Betsy Johnson...that icon of trendy-quirky high fashion clothes. I'd looked at these clothes before, coveted them even, but never wanted to ask my folks for the bucks to purchase them. Besides, where would I wear this party stuff? "Why are we stopping here?"

"Because I want to buy you some stuff. Some clothes." His face brightened like he was so proud of himself, like he was giving me a million dollars.

But I felt as though he'd slapped me. Obviously I dressed so badly that he was embarrassed to be seen with me. I tried to control myself but the tears welled up in my eyes. I'd never be good enough for him, never be the fashionistas that Molly and Cristen were.

He started to pull me into the shop, but I resisted. "Come on, let's go in. I can't wait to..." Then he looked into my face. "What's the matter?" His expression told me he couldn't fathom what I was thinking.

I felt like a five-year-old who'd had her cookies taken away and couldn't control herself. "Damn," I muttered under my breath.

"What?"

"It's nothing." I shook my head taking deep breaths, a little more under control now.

"No, tell me please." He gently guided me over to a nearby bench, not seeming to care that people were staring. "I want to know. I've hurt you in some way."

I didn't say a thing as he searched my face. "Come on," he said. Then a kind of recognition washed over his face. "I've insulted you, haven't I?"

I felt foolish then. "I'm sorry. I know I don't dress all that well."

He sighed and rubbed his hand over mine. "No, I love the way you dress. I just wanted to do something nice for you."

"Oh, Luis. I feel like an idiot. Let's go back into the shop."

"You're sure?"

"Yeah, I don't know what I was thinking. I guess I'm insecure."

"No, you're sensitive and I love that about you." He hugged me and the herbal scent of his hair along with the silky feel of having my face pressed into it made me feel entirely better.

After that we had fun with me trying stuff on and Luis encouraging me to buy more and more. I could handle a boyfriend like this. I could completely handle it.

We walked out to the curb with our bags and bags of purchases and waited for the car. "God that was fun. Now what?"

"I've got nothing in particular in mind. Let's talk."

"Okay." I was all too happy to do that.

He parked next to the woods by my house. Because the top was still down, the scent of pine trees and the sound of crickets and frogs enveloped us as though we were in our own fairy tale world.

"Tonight was really great, you know? I'm sorry I got all weird on you."

He had his head rested against the seat facing me, his eyes hooded. "Don't even give it another thought. That's what makes you *you*...the way you react to things." He took my hand and fidgeted slightly in his seat.

My breath sped up, and I felt myself gradually losing control. I shifted my body to face him, also laying my head against the headrest. We sat there for a long time not speaking.

I swear if he didn't kiss me soon I was going to pounce on him. My body felt open to him in a way I'd never experienced before.

He pulled me toward him just slowly and put one hand around my ribcage. He didn't kiss me yet, but let our faces remain close together. Gradually, slowly, he pressed his soft lips against mine. I'd never felt such a powerful rush of sheer lust in my life. I never would have believed anything could have felt so good.

He pulled away. I noticed he looked a little pale, woozy even.

"What?"

"Listen, I don't want you to think I bought you stuff so I could...you know."

"I don't think that. Not for one minute."

He started the car. "I'm taking you home, and tomorrow we can figure out where we can go so you can wear all your new cool stuff."

I grinned. He was so unlike any other teenage boy in the known universe. "Deal."

We drove to my house, Luis opened my door for me, gave me a comparatively chaste kiss and bid me goodnight.

I floated into my bedroom not quite knowing what to think. One thing was for sure. I couldn't sleep.

Besides, I needed to feed.

⚜ Chapter 19 ⚜

A run would do me good, get rid of all my weird feelings.

I checked on Mom and Dad. They were in their room and safely back in their own little protected world. I shivered at the gristly thought of them eating live mice.

Still in my pajamas, I crept out my window, carefully closed it and bolted down the street, feeling as though I could fly. At full speed, my feet pounded the road, past the ranch houses with their careful gardens into the wilder outskirts of the neighborhood. Palm trees, Poincianas with purple flowers, palmettos with their spike leaves spilled onto the landscape. The sweet scent of decomposed foliage grew stronger and mingled with the light aroma of citrus blossoms.

I knew enough to hide my clothes under a neighbor's fake rock so I could find them later. As I sprinted down the street, my body tightened into a coil of wild impulses. Hunger twisted my stomach like a meat grinder.

I entered the park through my usual secret entrance in the southwest corner. Maybe I could get lucky and find a wild rabbit. As the change came on, I felt afraid. Luis had been with me for my first change. What if I didn't know what to do? What if I couldn't change back? My arms lengthened and claws sprung from my fingers. I felt fur sprouting all over my body, and ears popping out on top of my head. I worried that I hadn't gone deep enough into the woods, that people might see me. No. Looking around, I realized that I was pretty well concealed by underbrush.

I held my hand up and realized that my fingers had turned to a padded paw with killer talons on the end. The weirdness of that made me gasp. I felt my face. Ouch, I scratched myself. My nose still felt human. Finally the skin on my face tightened and my muzzle popped out with the sound of crunching cartilage. I dropped to all fours, my heart pounding so hard I could feel it in my hands and feet.

I observed the change in my thinking. My animal senses became so much stronger—no, they became everything. My need to hunt and eat overpowered any kind of rational thought I might have had.

Padding into the woods, I easily sought out a groundhog, brought it down with one swipe of my paw and ripped into its still warm flesh. I lapped at its fresh sweet blood, letting my wild instincts entirely take over. I ate the carcass right down to its skeleton, licking and crunching on some its bones, sucking out the tasty middle.

I was so at one with my feline brain at that moment, I couldn't ignore my strong instinct to take a nap. So I nestled right down into a mossy spot and slept.

After a brief nap, I set out for home, my stomach pleasantly full.

On the outskirts of the forest, I smelled something—a strong flesh-like scent that stirred my hunger. I followed it, padding back out onto the street. Did I care that I was completely out in the open? Not at all. I could wipe out anyone who might bother me.

My curiosity overtook all of my other instincts at this point, and resisting became completely impossible.

Rounding the corner, I halted, stretched out my neck and stared.

I heard a meaty, ripping sound and smelled the unmistakable scent of blood.

Off to the side of the street.

Hidden partially behind a hedge.

A shadowy figure crouched on the lawn of the happy suburban house with its manicured boxwood hedges and chintz curtains.

I should have run, but my curiosity got the better of me. So I flattened myself to the ground and crept up toward the scent of flesh.

Still crouching, I saw a big cat in the process of gnawing a carcass. Even on the dark street, my super-sharp eyes began picking up the details.

I hoped with every fiber of my being that it wasn't what I thought it was. Then I saw it.

One white tennis shoe and the shreds of an acid-washed blue jeaned leg stuck out from behind the bushes.

The cat tore strips of flesh and slurped at the resulting fluids. As I shifted my perspective, I watched the cat as he disemboweled a human, probably one of the house's inhabitants.

My breath caught in my throat as I backed away.

A tail stuck out the other side of the hedge. It had a tawny brown base with yellow spots.

It couldn't be.

Yes it was.

In my own neighborhood.

A werecat attack.

I wanted to leave, knew I must leave, but couldn't tear myself away from the sight of such carnage.

Even in my cat state, the sight of human blood oozing into the grass made my stomach heave. I heard a wet, slurping sound as I watched the big cat tear a chunk out of the man's bare thigh and lick up the blood. He gobbled the flesh and, having heard me, peered out from behind the bushes and stared up with laser beam eyes, the strands of bloody muscle hanging from his mouth.

Without thinking, I turned and bolted down the street, so fast the pads of my feet barely touched the ground.

Would he come after me because I'd seen him?

I found the fake rock where I'd dropped my clothes, pulled them out with my teeth and sat, panting. My pulse raced too hard to be able to concentrate on transforming back to human.

I heard the cat gliding along the road toward me. A human never could have heard him with footsteps light as sparrows, but I could. I had to get out of there. My life depended on it.

The steps drew nearer and changed from the thrumming of four padded feet on the ground to the slapping of two skin ones—hard like a man's footsteps.

As the human rounded the corner, I prayed he'd spare me.

The running slowed. The man stopped directly in front of me with a magnificent naked body and hair swirled around his head as though he'd been in a cyclone.

No. No. No. My brain seethed. Still in panther form, I backed away as my stomach rasped with nausea.

It was Luis.

Chapter 20

"It's not what you think. I can explain," Luis said. He stood there completely naked.

One short hour ago I would have wanted to wrap myself around him. Now he repulsed me. His declaration reminded me of a man who'd been caught sleeping with another woman, yet still denied the whole thing.

The despair that filled me made my black furred body feel heavy, so heavy I had to sink down into the ground. I rested my head on my paws, and soon I felt the change coming on involuntarily. As my body took on a human shape, I lay shivering.

"Are those your clothes?" He motioned toward the heap I'd pulled out.

I nodded.

He removed the pajama top from the pile and draped it over me, rubbing my shoulder, then helped me on with the bottoms.

I pulled away but felt too weak to actually flee. Instead, I lay in the grass coughing.

"Honestly, it's not what you think. I was driving home after dropping you off and my instincts screamed at me so loudly I had to stop and check out the situation. I caught him beating his wife to a bloody pulp. He'd have killed her if I hadn't come along."

"That's an excuse. I don't believe you and I don't understand. Why eat a human? It's cannibalism." When I looked up and saw a trace of blood around his mouth and on his hands, I crawled closer to the bushes and vomited up the wild game I'd just eaten. I wiped my mouth with some leaves.

Luis tried to hold me, but I pushed him away.

"Kenley. I can explain all of this. I love you."

Get a grip, Kenley. "Don't tell me that now." I closed my eyes trying not to be sick again.

"Let's get you into my car." He carried me back to his Jaguar, deposited me on the seat and started the car. Even though I'd been so warm as of late, at that moment I was freezing. Turning on the heat, he rubbed my icy hands between his warm ones. He pulled some clothes out from behind the seat and put them on his own naked body.

"Drive me home right now."

He drove around for a bit to warm up the car then parked in a secluded spot.

"I said 'take me home,' not park." When I tried to open the door, he held my arm.

"Let me tell you about my background, my family."

"Don't bother." I grasped the handle, about to turn it and jump out, but he leaned over me and caught my hand again.

"Just listen, please. If you listen to me now, after tonight, I'll never talk to you again if you don't want me to. Just hear me out," he pleaded.

"Whatever you say won't matter." I crossed my arms.

"We are a family of werecats, just like yours, but there's a difference. Your side is the Favrés, the peace-loving side of the family. Descended from Bastet, Egyptian Cat Goddess of Peace, you eat small animals, you keep to yourselves and your longevity is about a thousand years."

I whipped my head around and looked at him. "I didn't know that." That explained why my parents didn't seem to age.

"Yes, it's true. My side of the family is called Rogues. We're descended from Sekhmet, Egyptian Cat Goddess of War. As such, it's our lot in life to eat human flesh, and we are immortal." He turned to look at me in the darkened car.

I dug my nails into his leather seat until it tore. "I can't believe this." I'd let myself get involved with a monster.

"I know how you feel." He put one hand out to touch my shoulder then thought better of it and pulled it back. "I was born into this life. I can't help it. If I don't consume human flesh I'll die. It might take a month or so, but a diet of only animals will slowly kill me. I didn't ask for this."

I started to feel sorry for him then stopped myself. What was I thinking?

He continued. "There is one thing I can help, though. I kill only bad people. People I find killing or hurting innocent people; mean people who torture animals, parents who abuse their children. In a way, I make the world a better place."

"But it's not up to you to decide who lives or dies. That's up to some great super consciousness, karma, God or something like that. You can't decide that."

"Well, what do you want me to do? This is my life, and I'm making the best of it." Luis sounded as though he might cry.

"I have to go. My parents..."

"Wait. Just let me say... I don't want this. I didn't ask for it, and if I could find a cure for it I'd change my life in a second. Kenley." He took both my hands even though I tried to pull away. "I do truly love you. I'd do anything for you."

I took a mental snapshot of the way the moonlight silhouetted his hair, the way his hazel eyes with their long, dark lashes practically glowed. I wouldn't be seeing his face in the moonlight again.

I pulled away and ran two blocks home, dreading the confrontation with my parents.

But luck was on my side. When I arrived at home, my parents were still asleep.

I landed in bed a mass of contradictory feelings. He loved me. But he was a monster. And could I even believe what he said about only killing bad people?

All day Sunday, I didn't hear from Luis. I didn't expect to hear from him, nor did I want him to call. No way. I chilled and hung out.

At school on Monday, Luis got me aside. How surreal, to have seen him ripping a human apart less than a day ago, and now he looked perfectly lovely in pressed white linen shirt and jeans, his hair combed back into a neat ponytail with one deliberate strand hanging in his face. "You have to let me talk to you some more."

"No, Luis. That's it for us. I'm sorry."

"I'll do anything."

I glanced around and whispered, "Find a way to break the curse."

Luis also spoke in low tones. "There is a way—kill your maker by either stabbing him in the heart or severing his spinal cord. Because I was born into this life and *our* line is patriarchal, that would be my father. I'd have to kill my father."

"I know you couldn't do that."

"I shouldn't even be telling you this but, when a person kills his maker, he reverts back to his original state."

"I don't even care." I tried to wave him away.

"Just let me talk to you some more."

"No." I turned to leave.

"Kenley, give me another chance."

"Are you out of your mind?" I said this louder than I meant to. Even though the jumble of kids changing classes whirled around us, people stared as they rushed by.

"I'm not that bad, really I'm not. I didn't pick my parents any more than you did."

"Get away from me." I rushed to my first period class.

How ironic, a week ago I would have killed to be with Luis. Now I wanted nothing more than to get away from him and never see him again.

⤖ Chapter 21 ⤛

On my way to lunch, I saw Michelle at the end of the corridor. Michelle locked eyes with me for a fraction of a second and turned in the other direction toward the parking lot.

"Wait a minute. Michelle." I ran after her, but she kept right on walking. "Don't ignore me now. I need you."

"What's the matter? Did hot-stuff break your heart? Why don't you go talk to Molly or one of those other disgusting, shallow fan girls?" She continued out the front door, and I followed her.

"Are you forgetting how much we've been through together?"

"All I know is that you're not the same Kenley who used to be my friend. You've gotten to be like one of them. You're even dressing like one of them."

I gazed down at my leather jacket, knee-high lace up boots, short tarlatan skirt with thigh-high stockings under it. I used to wear jeans and tee shirts.

Michelle opened the door of her banged-up white Toyota and got in, wincing as her skin touched the scorching seat, hot from sitting in the Florida sun, even in winter.

"I know I was wrong. Can't you be my friend?"

"In your dreams." Michelle turned away from me.

I took the hint and left.

I continued on to the lunchroom, grabbed a grilled cheese and headed over to the Claw Club table. Luis was conspicuous in his absence. Today the girls had it filled up with other, new friends. Josh and Orlando sat there, but other kids I didn't recognize sat in the spots Michelle and I always occupied. "Can I sit here?"

I expected them to say, yeah, pull up a chair. Instead, Molly looked right at me and, with exaggerated pronunciation coming from her pouty model lips, said, "No. Find somewhere else to sit."

Orlando, his hair stiffened into a full Mohawk looked at Molly with complete disgust. He curled his mouth into a sneer and glanced from one girl to the other.

"You've got to be kidding."

Sarah shushed him and shook her head.

"Okay." He put out one hand. "I'm with you people in all of the crazy things you do, but I'm not going to diss Kenley. That's bullshit." He lifted up his tray. "Come on, Ken Doll. Let's go find some civilized people to hang out with."

"I'm coming, too," Sarah said, bouncing up from her seat.

But Cristen grabbed her hand and stopped her. "You don't want to do that. Trust me."

Sarah sat slumped in her chair looking at the floor with her arms folded in front of her chest.

Molly and Cristen gave Orlando the Look of Death.

He shook his head and led me over to the other, less cool side of the room. "Where do you want to sit?"

"Orlando, thanks. I feel as though everyone is turning against me."

"Those girls suck shit. Little bitches. Who do they think they are? They piss me off." He slammed his lunch tray down onto the table.

At the same time, Brendan caught up with us. "Kenley," he said, looking at Orlando as though trying to gauge the situation. "Can I sit with you two?"

"Oh sure. You're not mad at me?" I asked Brendan.

"What? No." He shook his head, scowled and smiled at the same time.

"Kenley has just had the pleasure of being royally pissed on by the Claw Club," Orlando said as he dipped his French fry into blood-red catsup.

Brendan laughed. "You're better off."

The three of us sat at an empty table by the wall.

Orlando wiped the French fry grease on his pants and held out his hand. "Hi, I'm Orlando."

The tall sandy-haired boy beamed and shook it. "I'm Brendan."

"Oh, sorry, guys. Where are my manners? Brendan has a really interesting family. They're cryptozoologists."

"That sounds cool as shit," Orlando said. "What is it?"

"We hunt paranormal activity, like Yeti, chupacabra, vampires, sometimes ghosts."

"Interesting." Orlando gobbled down his food and chatted with Brendan for a while then picked up his tray. "Well, nice talking with you Brendan. I want to go out and get some air so I can stay awake during the bogus English lit class I have to go to next period. You're going to be okay, kid." Orlando gave me a friendly pat on the shoulder, dumped his paper plate in the trash and went outside.

"I sometimes have that effect on people," Brendan said, watching Orlando walk away.

"You think he left because of you? I don't think so. Orlando just generally does as he pleases. He seemed to like you."

Brendan looked at the ceiling and sighed, gazed at me and smiled. "I dunno. You think I'm wacked, right?"

"You're kidding. Brendan, I'm so sorry the way I acted the other day, brushing you off at the track while I was waiting for Luis. You're one of the most sane people around, especially with what I know now." I suddenly realized how I'd been ignoring this caring and wonderful guy.

"Ah, so some more has come to light about your recent... ...associations?"

"'Fraid so." I watched Orlando come in from outside and sit next to Sarah. "I don't know what to do. You're one of the few people who might be able to relate. My world has flipped upside down and my best friend has given up on me."

"Do tell."

The bell rang. I pulled a piece of paper out of my notebook and scribbled a number on it. "Call me tonight, okay?"

Brendan smiled showing even, white teeth. "Nothing will stop me. I have something important I want to show you."

We rushed off to class in different directions.

After school I busied myself in my room. I finished my chemistry homework in about five minutes. I listened to the news and searched the evening paper for something about a wild cat killing my neighbor, but found nothing. Either some other werecats had cleaned up after him or he returned later to remove the body. Very strange either way.

I tidied up a little, arranged my shelves, sat and read a book about my favorite artist, Lenore Fini. The phone rang. Luis, no doubt.

I answered it without checking caller ID. "Hello?"

"Hi! It's me, Brendan."

I sat down on the armchair next to my bed. "Oh, hi."

"Try not to sound so excited."

"I'm sorry. I'm just having a rough night."

"I certainly know how that can go. Say, how about we go out for an ice cream or something?"

I didn't really want to go but I wondered what it was he wanted to show me. Probably nothing, but my curiosity was getting the better of me. "Sure, but I don't want to stay out late."

"Understood. We can be back in an hour."

I scraped some candle wax off my dresser with my fingernail. "All right. Come on over. But just for a short time, okay?"

"Promise."

I gave him directions and hung up.

Brendan knocked at the door and Dad answered. They shook hands. "Hi, Mr. Walsh-Bohdan."

"And you are?"

"Brendan. Your last name is very unusual. Does it mean anything?"

"Proud ruler, I believe," Dad said.

"Interesting."

I peeked at him from behind the door. He stood here in his pink polo shirt and jeans. He had the kind of body that looked great in everything because of his long legs and good proportions. His sandy brown hair cut fashionably medium short and bright blue eyes made him look like was perpetually on Martha's Vineyard posing for a Ralph Lauren ad.

"I love the way you have your yard landscaped with all native plants," Brendan said.

"You like it? It looks easy to maintain, but it's not." Dad perked up.

"No, I know how much work a native garden can be," Brendan commented.

"I work on it for a couple of hours a day."

Gawd, it looked as though Dad loved Brendan.

I stepped out of my bedroom door. I hadn't made any attempt to put on anything special, just some old jeans, sneakers, tee shirt that said "Perky Goth," and a faded blue hoodie. "Hi, Brendan."

"Kenley. You look lovely."

"Liar."

Dad shook his head. "Try to be civil, Kitten. I know it's tough. Where are you kids going?"

"Just out to get some ice cream. We'll be right back," I said.

"Take your time." Dad actually stood in the doorway waving at us as we left.

"Man, you sure were a hit with my dad."

"Parents always like me. It's because I talk with them like they're human beings, not one-eyed monsters."

"Yeah, you look the part, too." I eyed him up and down.

"What part?"

"Son-in-law material."

Brendan shrugged and smiled a little bit too hard then made a move to get on his lime green Vespa.

I paused. "I don't really want to go on that. They're not safe." I realized the stupidity of my words as soon as I said them. I'd been hanging out with a murderer and I was afraid of riding on a scooter.

"You're not afraid of Sadie, are you?" He stroked it as though it were a cat.

"No, let's go." Being nothing if not considerate, Brendan had brought me a helmet which I strapped on. We chugged along, the little Vespa just barely able to carry the weight of two people. I put my arms around Brendan's waist and noticed that he had a clean scent like soap and fresh laundry.

Thank goodness it was a short ride to *Samantha's*, a cool little coffee and dessert hangout in a fashionable section of town that had shops and upscale restaurants.

Brendan got us a couple of lattés and marble swirl cheesecakes and we sat at the café-style tables located on an alleyway lined with art galleries and specialty shops. He put his backpack under the seat. The cool air felt good on my perpetually hot skin. A painting of a goddess emerging from the sea with shining water drops pouring from her pearly hair stared at us from the gallery across the way.

"What about the danger you said I was in?" I asked. "You never explained that."

"My hypothesis is that the people missing from the homeless shelter are being eaten by the growing Tampa werecat population."

"I really hope that isn't true."

"Yes, and Luis' family is at the epicenter of the whole thing."

But Luis had told me he only ate bad people. I didn't say anything, because I didn't want to admit to Brendan that I knew about Luis.

"So, having my name in that newspaper article puts me in danger?"

Brendan rested his head in one hand and swirled his coffee with the other. "I'm thinking so."

"What can I do about it?"

"I'll be your twenty-four hour body guard." He chuckled. "No seriously. Be careful. Stay inside at night. Don't go anywhere alone."

"Brendan, don't you think they're kind of like the mafia? If they want you they're going to get you?" My mouth felt dry and my skin clammy.

Brendan shrugged. "I have no way of knowing."

"What if I infiltrated them? Made them think I was one of them?"

"No, you have to stay away from Luis. He's dangerous."

"Are there other werecats at school?" I knew the answer well, but wanted to find out what he knew.

He looked at me over the tops of his eyes. "You tell me."

"What do you think I know about this?"

"I don't know. What *do* you know about it?" He leaned in closer to me.

"You're being weird now."

"Okay. Sorry. All I'm saying is be careful. Maybe if you don't raise any more suspicions, they'll leave you alone."

"I'm not planning on doing any more interviews for the *Trib*. That was a favor for a girl who lost her mother." And I hadn't even done a very good job with that. The remorse crept back into me.

"Was she a personal friend of yours?"

"Michelle and I do volunteer work at the Tampa Bay Homeless Shelter sometimes. We knew her from there."

"Gosh, I'm sorry. It's very admirable of you trying to get press coverage for them. I'd lay low now, though."

"Remember you said you were going to show me something?"

"Oh, yes." He pulled his backpack from under his seat, rifled through it for a moment then pulled out a large, hard cover book and handed it to me.

La Chat-Garou, it said across the top. *Werecat mythos in France.* I ran my hand over the mysterious-looking gold embossed cover with the Egyptian symbols on it. "What is this?"

"I swiped it from my parents. They have all kinds of esoteric books. This is the English translation of a French book written like fifty years ago. It's all about the werecat mythos. Take some time and look it over."

"Wow! Thanks." I opened it up to a random page and looked at a beautiful illustration of an Art Deco-looking cat/woman, sitting on a jewel-encrusted throne, wearing a crystal headpiece that draped down over her forehead. It held me spellbound for a full fifteen seconds. I couldn't wait to get home and read it.

"Pretty weird, huh? I think it contains some information you should know about."

"I can see that." I flipped through some more pages.

He sipped some more of his coffee and watched me.

I stood. "Well, Brendan, it's getting late. I have to go." I hadn't even finished my cheesecake.

"Are you sure you don't want to maybe go for a walk? It's such a beautiful night."

"No, I've really gotta go. I'll read this book and get it back to you."

"No, keep it; it's yours. My parents have lots of books. They won't even miss it."

We chugged home on his Vespa, and the thing was so slow it seemed like we'd never get there. Finally we arrived and I said a quick goodbye.

Once in my room I pulled out the book. As I skimmed the table of contents I saw that the book contained various werecat legends, tribes of werecats from different countries. According to the book, werecats had been around since the beginning of time. I was stunned. Or perhaps it was all the workings of a writer's overactive imagination. What was I saying? I'd been living this reality for weeks now.

The stories in the book contained secret information. The werecats would tell these allegorical stories, but they masked truths integral to the survival of the werecat race. A person just had to know how to interpret them. These stories were passed on from generation to generation as tales containing noble myths and secrets. I turned to a story that had to do with figures of Egyptian mythology—two Egyptian cat goddesses, Bastet, Goddess of Peace and Sekhmet, Goddess of War, along with Isis and Osiris, the sun god and goddess.

It is a little known fact that Isis and Osiris indulged in a secret passion, a love for the great cats. They sent emissaries all over the world to collect snow leopards, panthers, jaguars, tigers. Price was no object. Yet they kept this collection hidden from the eyes of their subjects, least Phoenician traders try to steal their lovely cats and sell them abroad. Their love of the cats grew to obsessive proportions, and they wanted to bring them to the full fruition of life.

They prayed to the great Sun God, Ra, to make their cats into humans. Ra descended from the sky in his golden chariot and mated with their precious pets. After a period of gestation, the great cat gods and goddesses were born. There were males and females, half cat and half human, all of them stunning beauties.

Thus was the Favré race born.

Two of their offspring were Bastet, Goddess of Peace and Sekhmet, Goddess of War. Both possessed cat heads sitting atop curvaceous human female bodies. Bastet had her loyal followers who gathered once a year at Bubastis in the region of the Nile delta to worship her at the Festival of Bastet.

Sekhmet also had her followers, but they were of a darker nature.

Thus the division between Favré and Rogue came into being.

The story left me in a strange mood. It had used the same words Luis had used, Favré and Rogue. Could all of the allegorical stories in the book be true? And what was all this about a division? My sense of logic revolted.

Reality intruded when I realized I was starving. I put the book aside and made a beeline the kitchen. Hungry for something other than sweets, I scrounged in the refrigerator. I found a big piece of raw steak still in the Styrofoam and plastic wrap from the grocery store. Piercing the plastic with my fingernail, I stood over the sink and gobbled the whole thing down.

It felt so satisfying in my stomach, but as I walked through the hallway I caught sight of myself in the mirror with blood dribbling down the side of my mouth and shuddered. I grabbed a tissue to wipe it then flushed it down the toilet. What kind of monster was I turning into?

On the one hand, I wished I could go back to my simple pre-werecat existence. On the other, I loved the power and sense of freedom it gave me.

My cell phone rang. Could it be Luis? I didn't want him to call, but I was pissed he was ignoring me, too. I punched the button and said in my deepest, softest voice,

"Hello."

"Kenley. It's me." Michelle sounded out of breath as though she'd been running.

"Michelle, what's wrong?"

"Horrible things."

"You're scaring me."

She breathed hard into the receiver. "Come and help me. I think they're after me."

⁂ Chapter 22 ⁂

"After you? Who's after you? Where are you?" My breath caught in my throat, and I could hardly speak.

"I'm calling you from downtown Tampa."

"For God's sake let me pick you up. Is someone after you right now?"

"I think a couple of guys are following me. I have to tell you something. Another person from the shelter went missing. But this time there's a body—maimed beyond recognition." Michelle's voice cracked. "It was mauled and half eaten like it had been torn up by wild animals."

"How do you know?"

Michelle paused. "I found it."

"Oh my God. Tell me exactly where you are."

"I'm crouched in the entranceway to Tampa Theater. I'm afraid to move to get my car, because it's parked way over at the library. 911 isn't working on my cell phone."

"I'll call 911 for you. For God's sake be careful. I'll be right there."

I called the emergency number and explained Michelle's situation then I grabbed a jacket and flew out the door.

I raced down Franklin Street, a road closed off to autos, reserved completely for pedestrian traffic. I didn't care; I had to find Michelle.

By the time I got there from North Tampa, the lights from police cars gyrated and pulsed and sirens blasted in front of Tampa Theatre. Cops in frantic activity erected barricades and strung out crime scene tape.

I could see Michelle peeking out from behind the ticket booth, but when I tried to rush up to her, a young cop with buzz cut hair politely blocked my way. "I'm sorry, you can't go that way."

"She's my friend. I have to go to her." I tried to squeeze past him but he blocked me with his arm.

"This is for your own safely, Ma'am."

Michelle saw me and said something to the woman cop who was helping her up. After that, they ushered me in.

I hugged her. "My God, are you okay?"

Michelle stood up, hobbling. "Yeah. Yeah, I think so."

"What's going on? Who was chasing you?" I asked.

"I don't know. I can't even think." Michelle held her hand over her mouth like she was going to barf. "I can't talk right now."

"Ma'am, we have to take her to the station for questioning."

"Station. I think she should go to a hospital," I said.

The woman cop looked into Michelle's face. "Michelle, do you feel as though you need to go to the hospital? Are you hurt?"

"No. I'll be okay. I just need to rest."

"She's not OK. She's in shock. Can't you see?" I felt frantically protective of her. Before I could say any more, the cops whisked her away into a cruiser.

"Can I go with her?"

"You can follow along, miss."

"Fine."

Luckily the station was just down the street. I pulled into the parking lot.

A woman with cotton candy hair pinned back into a French twist with a sweater hanging over her shoulders clipped by a pinchy chain, sat at the front desk.

"I'd like to go in to see my friend. Her name is Michelle..."

She cut me off. "I'm afraid that's impossible."

"But my friend was just brought in for questioning. She found a body on Franklin Street."

"Ma'am, I'm afraid you'll have to wait until an officer is free."

"But my friend needs me," I shouted.

She gave me a "so what" look. As she droned on in a phone conversation that didn't sound like police business, I seethed.

Finally the woman hung up.

"Can you get someone to come out now?" I asked, losing my patience.

She squeezed her eyes into a hateful look, dialed a number and talked into her headset. "Hi Herb, can someone come out here and answer this girl's questions? What's the name again?"

"Kenley Walsh-Bohdan."

She nodded her head and gave me a squinty gaze.

"Well?" I asked.

"You'll just have to wait, Miss Welsh-Bolzan."

"Walsh-Bohdan. Can I go in? My friend is very upset." I started for the door.

"Not at this moment. Sit down and wait." The woman forced a smile from her droopy face then went back to working her crossword puzzle.

I waited and looked around for something to read to calm myself, picked up the daily paper then put it down because I couldn't concentrate. Time passed, a half hour, an hour. God, what was taking so long?

Finally the cotton candy hair switchboard lady beckoned me in. "Go ahead now. Right through that door."

I rushed through the heavy metal entrance.

"Turn right at the first corridor," the receptionist said.

I started down the hallway and took a right as instructed. The station was in a state of pandemonium. People stormed around each other's desks talking on cell phones, typing into computer screens.

There, next to a beaten-up green metal desk stood Michelle.

"Are you all right?" I hugged her.

"No." Wearing jeans and a plain sweater, she looked a fright, her clothes disheveled, hair stringy, and the ghastly green color of her face and her shaking hands portrayed her inner turmoil. "They think the body is Shelly's mother."

"But she's been missing for a nearly a week."

"The body was badly decomposed." Her face twisted into a nauseous shudder.

I touched her shoulder. "How did you find her?"

"I went into one of the shelter's downtown storage units to pull out some winter clothes for the people—no one had been in there for a while—and there was a terrible stench." Michelle held her stomach and started to heave.

"Do you need to go to the bathroom?"

"No. Let's get out of here."

I helped Michelle out to the car.

"Who or what do they think did it?" I asked.

"They think one of the tigers from the Big Cat Rescue Center got loose."

The Big Cat Rescue Center was a non-profit organization that cared for displaced big cats. Circuses retired the animals when they got too old. Some people purchased them as cute little cubs only to abandon them when they grew too big and unruly. Keeping the cats in roomy, natural habitats, they did a wonderful service to the world. And they weren't that far from my house.

"And what? The cat stashed the body in a storage unit?"

Michelle shrugged. "The body was in the space between the storage units. If they knew more they weren't telling me."

"Is the rescue center missing a cat?"

"Yes. They have a new tiger that escaped somehow. I don't know the details." Michelle held her stomach as we rode home.

"I don't know how any animal could escape from the rescue center. I've been there. Those cats are so secure even the people who work there can't get to them. They're double-caged."

"The whole thing is definitely weird."

My mind raced, trying to think of an explanation, not wanting to admit the obvious one even to myself. There was only one kind of big cat that had opposable thumbs.

"Has it gotten any press?" I asked.

"No. The cops are keeping it hush-hush, because they don't want a panic. And all this time we thought it was a serial killer." Michelle touched my arm. "I'd like to call your reporter guy."

"You're way too upset. Let me call him."

"No, I want to," Michelle said.

I opened my cell phone. "I talked to Andy something, a reporter from the Trib." I wrote down Andy's number and handed it to her. "Are you sure you don't want me to call him?"

"Yeah."

I took Michelle home and settled her into bed. I was surprised when she reached for her cell phone. "Are you going to call him now?"

"I sure am." Her hands shook as she searched around for the number.

"Let me stay with you while you call."

"No, you go home. I'll be okay."

I felt like if I didn't get to bed soon I'd die so I didn't argue with her. "Just don't give him your name so he can't use it in the article. It could be dangerous."

"OK."

"Have you seen Shelly?" I asked. "I went down there last Saturday, talked to the director and called some of my activist friends to see if they could pull some strings to make sure she gets into a good home."

"They took her away." Michelle lowered her eyes to the bed sheets and shook her head.

"Can we find out where she is?"

Michelle shrugged, "I can try calling social services. Usually they can't give any information for confidentiality reasons."

Feeling tired and numb, I shook my head. "I feel so bad for her."

"Yeah, so do I. Hey, thanks for picking me up." Michelle rubbed my arm.

"Sure. I'm glad you called me." We hugged.

"Are we friends again?" I asked.

"Yeah, sure." She didn't sound that convincing.

I kissed Michelle on the cheek and drove home, my mind a morass of tumultuous thoughts. I looked at the clock. Three a.m. The next day was a school day. I'd be beat.

I made it home somehow, lay down in bed and closed my eyes. As I turned over on my left side and hugged my pillow I heard a clawing sound against the window. I rose with a start.

Then I told myself it was a branch scraping and settled back down. But it grew more insistent, followed by a pounding.

What could I do? There was definitely something out there. And with Michelle just having outrun two werecats, I knew I could be in grave danger. My heart nearly blew out of my chest. If I escaped out the front door, it could get me, but nothing could break through these hurricane-resistant windows.

For a second everything quieted down, and I peeked out through the Venetian blind. There sat a full-sized jaguar.

Luis.

My heart fluttered, and before my brain could catch up with my emotions, I opened the window and let him in.

The jaguar bounded in through the window and sat there growling at me.

I backed away. I'd made a mistake.

This one wasn't Luis.

⁓❦ Chapter 23 ❦⁓

It had different markings. I'd let in a completely strange animal. How could I have been so stupid?

I tried to back up toward the door, but the hissing cat positioned itself to my right and swiped at me, backing me into a corner. My parents wouldn't hear, because their bedroom was on the other side of the living room and gallery room.

As the thing growled and snapped at me, it started to change. It sprouted shoulder-length black hair, long red fingernails and small, pointy breasts.

"Molly. What are you doing here?"

"Bitch. You stay away from him," she hissed.

"Stay away from who?"

"As if you didn't know. Luis, you dumb slut." Molly pushed me down onto my bed and leaned over me, her hot breath in my face.

"For one thing, it's none of your business what I do. For another thing, I'm completely finished with him." I tried to push her off me, but Molly slammed me back down.

"Yeah, right. Nice try. Do you know how long I've been playing the part of his best friend, secretly wanting him so much I could die?"

"You're pretty pathetic, Molly."

"Shut up." Molly slapped me hard. "You're the one who's pathetic. You're not one of us, so stay away. I have him where I want him, and you are not going to ruin it."

I put my hands up in the air. "Listen, I wouldn't think of it. He's all yours. Be my guest. Knock yourself out."

Molly narrowed her eyes. Apparently unselfconscious about her nakedness, she placed her knee in my chest and grabbed me by the hair. "If you change your mind, I'm going to hurt you. Not kill you, just maim you so you're ugly. You and I both know that's worse than death."

Molly pulled me up, slammed me onto the floor, gave me that obnoxious model pout and dove out the window.

I sat back feeling as though I'd been hit by a cyclone. Hurricane Molly. I had no idea the girl was so psycho. She could have Luis. Fine.

I went back to bed, tossed and turned—a restlessness night for my bewildered self.

The next day, Tuesday, I noticed that Molly had cornered Luis against one of the lockers. What was she trying to do, catch him so he couldn't escape? The bitch. But he had his head turned away from her then finally slid under her arm that was blocking him and left.

As I carried on with my day, Luis seemed to be everywhere. Once in a while I'd catch him giving me a wistful look, but I'd turn away before I made any real eye contact. I noticed that he looked disheveled and drawn, not his usual hot self. Not good at all. I wondered what was wrong with him. He looked so vulnerable and thin, sad even.

I had to stick to my guns and not get back with him. I'd seen him devouring a human. I had to remember that.

Michelle had stayed home after her horrible night, so I couldn't talk to her.

Brendan was waiting by my car after school. "Have you seen the headlines?" He held out a copy of the *Trib*. "Woman eaten by escaped tiger."

I scanned the article. "That's great. They're going to be out looking for a poor, innocent tiger instead of for the real monsters who did this."

"My sentiments exactly."

I told him about Michelle's episode with the killer. I did not tell him about the Molly confrontation, however. I don't know why, I just didn't.

"This is kind of bad," Brendan said.

"Yeah."

"What I mean is that they're getting sloppy, leaving bodies around. It's as though they're so confident they don't have to be careful any more. I suspect that their numbers have grown to huge proportions and more people are going to start dying."

"Hmmm. What do you make of them thinking it's a tiger that escaped from the Big Cat Rescue Center?" I threw my book bag into the back seat of my car.

"I'm wondering if one of the werecats was hiding out there or something. It would be convenient. I mean, he'd blend in."

"But how would he get out?" I asked. "The enclosures are all double-caged and double-locked."

"Obviously, he could turn back into a person and pick the lock. The cages are cat-proof, not people proof. They could have entered as a cat and exited as a human." Brendan was so logical.

"Bizarre. I have to go home. I'm beat." I climbed into my car.

"Just remember, be careful." Brendan gave me a sweet little kiss on the cheek. One that made me feel truly special.

"Thanks, I will." Maybe I could get to like him after all.

I stopped by The Starlight Coffee House to get a soy latté to take home. Who should be there but Luis, sitting in a corner facing outward. Looking pale and tired, he broke his zombie-like stare to gaze up at me.

Had he followed me there? No, how could he have known I was going to stop here on my way home. Was he stalking me? Using his werecat intuition to figure out where I'd go? I tried not to look at him.

While I was standing off to the side waiting for my latté, he came up to me. At first I pretended not to see him, but then I turned to face him. His eyes were ringed with dark shadows. "Kenley, I have to talk to you for a second."

"There's nothing to talk about." I didn't like to be like that, but I had to draw the line and hold my ground.

"I'm going to give up eating..." He didn't say the words, but I knew exactly what he meant. He was going to give up eating people.

"You can't, Luis. It'll kill you." What was he thinking?

"But it's the thing that makes me repulsive to you, and I can't live without you." The surface of his eyes grew shiny like he was on the verge of tears.

Something about his sadness started to get to me, and I put my hand over his. "You're not repulsive to me."

"Then why won't you..." Luis hesitated, swept his glance around the room, then lowered his voice. "Why won't you be with me?"

I practically whispered to him. "I can't live with the vampire cat thing. It's just that it's not for me." The girl called my name and I grabbed my soy latté off the shelf and put the heat sleeve around it. "Maybe we can figure this out. like an antidote or something."

"I can't kill my father," he whispered. "Can't we go somewhere else to talk?"

I wasn't going to leave with him, no matter how much I still loved him. "Maybe there's something else. Doesn't anyone in your family know a cure?" I asked.

"Oh, like I can ask *them*? They're batting for the other team." He gave a pained smile at his own lame joke. "Can I call you tonight?"

What was I doing? I couldn't get sucked in by him again. I shook my head and started to leave. "I don't know, Luis. I need some distance."

"Please. I'm going to find a way to change. I promise."

How was he going to give up eating people if he needed it to survive. I sighed. "Okay." Lots willpower I had, right?

I headed for the exit, wondering what I'd gotten myself into by saying I'd talk to him again.

That night I waited, but Luis didn't call. Then I got worried and called him, but he didn't answer. How long of a period could they go without making a kill before they'd die? I paced the floor worrying about him. Kenley, stop being a sap. Don't let him reel you in again. After working myself up into having a raw stomach, I had to do something, so I grabbed my keys and headed to my car and headed to his house. I couldn't help myself. Driving past all the palatial estates, I had to wonder what in the hell I was doing. Why didn't I leave well enough alone and let both of us go our separate ways? I wondered what drove me to go on this crazy cruise to damnation.

It was the bond between us that compelled me to try to help him. I'd never felt so strongly about anyone in my life. I thought I never *would* feel that way about anyone ever in my life. Granted I realized I had my whole life ahead of me, but I suddenly wondered, if I lost out on this intense love, would I ever find another one?

I didn't want to run into Enrique, so I snuck around the side of the house. Seeing Luis' bedroom light on, I crept up and knocked on the window. After two tries, I heard some movement in the room. Luis stuck his head out of the window and said, "Who's out there?"

"Luis?" I looked up at him from my place in the bushes feeling stupid and stalker-like. "I was worried about you."

"Kenley! I'm sorry. I fell asleep." He sounded really weak.

"You didn't answer your phone."

"I didn't hear it because I was out like a light. Hang on. I'll be right out."

We sat on a stone bench in the huge, manicured garden in back of his house. The garden had brick paths, neat rows of roses, crepe myrtles, mums and zinnias with statues tucked here and there. In the moonlight it was utterly magical, but that night it just felt sad.

He looked so beautiful, his hair disheveled, his eyes dark and brooding. His usually bronze face looked like milk. Even in shorts and a tee shirt, barefooted, he was a creature of incredible majesty and splendor.

How different the mood was this time compared to last time. "Luis, are you dying?"

"Not right away. It's just that...I don't want to live without you, and I'm an abomination to you the way I am. Then I heard about the body they found in downtown Tampa." He cringed.

"You didn't have anything to do with that, did you?"

"God, no. My family may have, but not me. I keep my distance from all of that."

"Listen, Luis." I started to put my hand on his thigh then thought better of it.

"You have nothing to do with all of that. That's your father's generation. Just get along as best you can. You need to eat, so if you just kill bad people, I don't think there's anything wrong with that. There are enough of those to keep all of you fed for life." I wasn't so sure I really thought that, but I wanted to tell him anything that would make him eat again and keep him from dying. I couldn't stand the thought of a world without Luis.

"Could *you* do it? Could you kill bad people for food?"

I hesitated and considered lying but decided against it. "I don't think so."

"That's what I thought."

As I looked at him sitting there in the moonlight, all thin and fragile, I thought about the male energy that still exuded from him. Even in his weakened state, I felt the magnetic pull toward him.

Sometimes something happens to you to make you feel a little bit differently about something, but you're not sure why. That's what happened to me at that moment. Damnit, of all the stuff people did in this world, maybe killing some baddies for nourishment wasn't all that terrible. My brain turned some kind of corner.

"Wait, maybe I could...kill bad people."

"I don't think so, and I wouldn't want you to. I have to tell you something else." He briefly touched my forearm.

This didn't sound good.

"I've been giving it a lot of thought, and I know in my heart that you're right. You and I shouldn't be together. You should continue on your high-minded path of helping people with your volunteer work, associating with nice people." As he looked down at his hands, his unruly hair fell into his face, and he pushed it back. "I'm damned. I'm cursed. You shouldn't have anything to do with me."

"What?" I tried to stroke his hair, but he pulled his head away slightly, making me put my hand back in my lap. Somehow he looked even more delicious in his dilapidated state.

"Don't put another minute of energy into liking me. It's no good. I need to be with my own putrid kind. Kenley, you're too good for me. Too pure."

"I'm not that freaking pure." Shoot. Why hadn't I ravaged him in the swimming pool when I had the chance?

"Yes you are. You'd have to be with a Rogue and you're too good to make that change. I don't want to be with anyone but you, Kenley, so I'll spend my life alone."

Was this one of the "It's not you, it's me" relationship talks? Was he trying to diss me?

At that moment, I wanted so badly to be with him my insides physically ached. I couldn't lie to myself anymore, couldn't make myself want the nice Brendan. "I want to be with you anyway."

"I don't think so. It's not going to work." Luis kissed me on the cheek and walked back into his house.

I drove back home and tore off into the forest running. I hid my clothes in the neighbor's bushes and fled into the woods. Changing into cat easily now as I ran down the suburban street, I found I could go into some kind of overdrive mode and sprint so fast I'd hardly be visible to the human eye, so great was my speed and strength.

I felt invincible. I didn't need him. Right?

This time I spotted an owl on a branch. Carefully gauging the distance, instinctively knowing the force I'd need to exert, I leapt, graceful as a swan, and nailed the owl with one big paw. The thing never knew what hit him. I munched contentedly on the ground. After napping in the woods for a bit, I walked home. In no hurry, I padded along, enjoying the feel of my powerful, elastic muscles and the scent of orange blossoms. Some of the plants had a unique green pepper smell. The sounds of night birds singing, bats flapping their wings, house cats crawling in the underbrush, stalking mice—all this delighted me and made me feel better about the Luis situation.

Then I grew relaxed, a little too relaxed and off-guard.

I didn't spot the woman until I walked directly in front of her house.

❦ Chapter 24 ❦

We looked each other in the eyes, the woman so still she could have been a statue. But she wasn't. I could smell her.

The woman didn't scream, didn't move a finger.

Shit. I rushed down the street, changing back to human as I ran, found my clothes, put them on and rushed home. Once I had changed back to human and was fully dressed my curiosity got the better of me, so I walked back to house of the woman who had spotted me. I remained at a safe distance.

Damn, a police car pulled up. No, two. The cops got out and talked to the woman who gesticulated wildly.

"It was a cat, a huge black killer cat. Probably the same one that killed the homeless woman."

"Now hold on a second, ma'am." One of the cops pulled out his pad to take notes, the other one tried to comfort the woman.

Cop cars invaded the area like wasps, stinging the air with their piercing lights. They looked as though they intended to comb the neighborhood. I went home to bed thinking that I'd just ruined it for myself. The local police would be watching. Now I'd have to be so freaking careful.

The alarm clock blared way too early. It seemed that since I started changing, I required even more sleep than I had before, but now I was getting even less. Didn't cats sleep about eighty percent of their lives? I needed the excitement in my life to calm down for a while so I could catch up and recharge my batteries.

I finished my double latté while walking through the parking lot to school and threw my empty cup into the trash barrel in front of the building.

At least Michelle would be in school today.

I took the back way to homeroom in order to avoid Luis's locker. But there he was right outside of my homeroom class looking paler and weaker than ever.

Pulling him aside, I said, "Luis, you have to eat."

"I don't want to. What's the use?"

The bell rang and I had to go into class.

I plopped into my seat next to Michelle. I'd try to think of my friend for a change instead of being so selfish. I leaned over and took Michelle's hand. "How are you doing? I've missed you at school."

"I'm slowly regaining my sanity. The Claw Club ditched you, huh?" She looked at me sideways and pursed her lips. "They suck anyway. Are you going to be all right?" she asked.

"It's a little more complicated than that. It's like I ditched them, actually. And, yeah, Luis and I broke up." I looked down at the floor.

"Ken, he's a shallow, egotistical shithead. You don't need him."

"I know. Doesn't make it any easier, though."

"What about that new guy I've seen you hanging around with?" She raised her eyebrows.

"Brendan?" I asked.

"He's a babe. If you don't jump on that one, I'm going to." She looked at me sideways, as though gauging my reaction.

"Yeah." I sighed. "Brendan likes me, wouldn't you know. You can have him. You're welcome to him." Everything felt so hopeless. If I couldn't be with Luis, I simply wanted to die.

"I have to show you something." Michelle whipped out a newspaper.

It was *Creative Loafing*, a local alternative rag that you could pick up for free in various locations in the area. The front page read, "Local Police Involved in Cover Up of Serial Killer." I skimmed the article.

Tampa police are saying that an escaped tiger is responsible for recent series of gristly murders, but are they hiding a much darker killer? Some say that a creature formerly known only in horror novels is responsible.

The bell rang.

"Kenley." Michelle touched my arm. "Thanks for calling 911 for me that night. My buttons must have jammed or something, but I had you on speed dial."

"I'm so happy I was there to call...that I could help."

"You saved my life, you know."

My eyes misted over. So did Michelle's.

We hugged and headed to our classes.

It seemed as though I saw Luis everywhere.

I got an apple for lunch and sat down on the other side of the room from the Claw Club and their growing number of groupies.

Brendan walked over to me, giving me a shy smile. I had the feeling he could read my mind or something. I always felt as though he knew more than he was letting on. His look and his tentative approach made me, in some weird way, think he knew what I was going through with Luis. Not so weird, actually. He could tell we weren't talking, but Luis and I never did talk all that much in school.

"Hi," Brendan practically whispered. "Can I sit down?"

"Oh sure. You don't have to ask."

He sat across from me, sighed and handed me a newspaper. "Have you seen the front page of the *Trib*?"

"Oh, shit. Big Cat Seen in Tampa Neighborhood."

"That's one street over from your house, Ken." Brendan had taken to calling me Ken.

"We've got to talk. Not here, though." I really did need to talk to someone who'd understand the whole werecat situation.

"How about going for a run with me after school?" he asked. "I need to blow off some steam."

"Sounds good."

We ate lunch and made light conversation. All the while I was distracted by stupid stuff I knew I shouldn't even be thinking about. Why were the Claw Club girls ignoring me? Not that I wanted to be with them, but I hadn't done anything to them. The bigger question was why did I even care? Had the momentary taste of popularity corrupted me?

Finally the bell rang. Brendan and I hurried back to our classes.

All day, the specter of Luis, sallow and weak, tormented me.

Between fourth and fifth period, Sarah and Orlando came up to me in the hall. "Hey," Sarah said, twirling a piece of her blue-highlighted hair between her fingers.

"Hey," I said back.

Orlando threaded his arm through mine. "How are you doing, Ken Doll? I see you've broken up with Luis. Don't let it get to you, you don't need him."

I decided to risk asking them the Big Question. "You guys, let me ask you... Are you both Rogues?"

Orlando opened his eyes really wide while Sarah turned and away and hid her "o-face" with her hand.

"Listen I know the whole story. Do you kill and eat people? I'm asking, because...I'm just curious."

"Ah..." Sarah nudged Orlando and put her fingers over her mouth.

Orlando cleared his throat. "We're not supposed to say. You know how that goes."

That was just as good as a yes. "Sure, I understand."

"Things are heating up around here." Orlando pulled his fingers up through his Mohawk, his full-sleeve tattoos showing from under his tee shirt. "I can't say any more."

"That's okay. Thanks, you guys for being my friends, kind of."

Sarah perked up. "Anyway there are a lot of other cool guys around town. We'll take you out to a rave sometime."

"Sure. That sounds like fun." Not.

"Gotta go, kid." As Orlando hugged me, the hall traffic went around us like river water around a rock.

That made me feel better. Sort of. At least I knew someone in that group thought about someone other than themselves.

I half expected to run into Luis at the track. Not that he'd be running, but he seemed to be everywhere. But no. The outdoor running area in back of the school was Luis-free. Brendan was already dressed in white shorts and tee, stretching by putting one of his long legs on top of a fence and bending over it.

"Nice legs, Brendan." I looked them up and down, grinning.

"You noticed. Yeah, I try to stay in shape."

"Let's start running. I'm ready to spill."

"Lead the way and spill away." Brendan jogged along with me at an easy pace.

A cool breeze blew through the palm trees, actually resembling a fall day. The track gave off a vague rubbery scent.

I told him the whole deal about discovering my werecatism. About Luis being a Rogue, about Molly threatening me.

He gave me a meaningful look, eyes slightly narrowed. "I know all that Kenley."

"Then why did you let me go on thinking you didn't?" I came to a complete stop.

"You had to come about telling me in your own way." Brendan was so wise and so understanding.

"But how did you know?" I started running again.

"Ken, my parents are in a network of people who are obsessed with this kind of stuff. They track any—what they call paranormal—activity going on everywhere in the world. Tampa, Florida, right now, is world renowned in cryptozoologist circles as a hotbed of werecat activity."

"Then why doesn't CNN cover it or something?"

"Because it's under the radar. But the way things are continuing, it's not going to stay that way for long."

"There's something going on, isn't there?" I easily kept up with Brendan and his long legs.

"Yes, but we're not exactly sure what. The Rogues are planning something; that's my guess." Brendan waved to a couple of kids who ran passed us in the opposite direction.

I sped up and Brendan kept right up with me.

"You okay, kid?" he asked.

"I'll live."

"I know what you're going through with Luis."

"You do?" I slowed down again.

"Yeah," he said softly, nodding.

"How?"

"I'm sensitive to your feelings, that's all." He gazed over at me kind of sheepish, looked down at the ground then at me again.

"Thanks, Brendan." I smiled and touched his arm. I wondered to myself how he knew so much about werecats? Could he possibly be one himself? No, I banished the idea from my head.

"I know that having everyone in the world say, 'He's dangerous, stay away from him, bla bla bla,' isn't going to make you feel any differently. It's human nature to have to learn by your own experiences, not by what people tell you."

Brendan rocked. Why couldn't I be in love with him? I banged my head with the heel of my hand. Stupid.

He gently took the wrist of the hand I'd used to bang my head. "Hey, don't be so hard on yourself. You're going through typical teenage angst to the power of ten. Exponentially increased by your werecat-ism."

"Brendan, what would I ever do without you? I'd go nuts."

"You'd do just fine."

I started running again, loving the feeling of the bouncy track against my shoes. "I have one question: Once a person has been turned into a Rogue, is there any way to undo it?" I knew what Luis had told me, but I wanted to get Brendan's take on it.

"I should say, 'No, once you become a Rogue it's permanent,' but I know that's not true, and I can't lie to you. I know that there is an antidote. What that is I'm not exactly sure."

I glanced away, thinking.

"Kenley." He stopped me and pulled me around to face him. "Don't even think about letting him turn you."

"What? I never said anything about that."

He shook his head and put his hand up like a stop sign. "I'm just sayin'... We don't know what the antidote is. We don't know if there's a time limit on it. You can't take that risk."

I said nothing.

"I'm going to keep investigating the situation until I find out the exact nature of the Rogues' plans," Brendan said.

We started on our second lap. "You've got to be careful with them. They're lethal, you know," I said.

"Me? What about you? I *am* careful, believe me. I don't want to be WC dinner." Brendan paused. "Would you do me one favor? Besides not seeing Luis—would you do me another favor?" he asked.

"Sure." We slowed down.

"Can I watch you change?" Brendan glanced at me sheepishly as though he were asking to see me undress. "Into a werecat, I mean."

I grinned as I realized I'd run over a mile and wasn't at all out of breath. Actually, I'd hardly exerted myself. "Yeah, I think I could arrange that. Come on over later tonight."

I went home and tried to do homework, but I had the attention span of a month-old kitten. I played on the Internet, took out some colored pencils and doodled, rearranged my shelves.

Remembering the werecat book, I pulled it down from the shelf and read some more.

> *Bastet fell in love with a beautiful human male named Tristan. One day while they were lounging next to a flower-filled pond she asked him, "Do you mind that I am a woman from the neck down but the rest of me is cat?"*
>
> *"No, my love." He caressed her abundant breasts and kissed her cute cat mouth. "This is*

what I love about you." As he ran his hands over the rest of her body, a figure emerged from the pond, standing on a large lily pad. It was a woman, perfectly formed with long, flowing blonde hair and an amply curved body. She beckoned the man to her.

The man rose as though in a trance and followed the water-woman. He stood on the lily pad with her, cupping her face with his hands, kissing her human nose and lacy eyelashes. Locked in a lover's embrace, they slowly sank into the water. Just before the woman's head sank into the water, she revealed her true form, that of a cat with a woman's body.

"Sekhmet!" Bastet screamed at her. "He's mine, you cannot have him."

"I'll have what I want, you sap."

At that moment, Isis (Bastet's best friend) rose from the water. "From this moment on, Sekhmet I curse you to be a vampire cat. You will be feared and ostracized by humans and werecats alike.

Incisors grew from Sekhmet's mouth. She turned and promptly bit the man, turning him into a vampire. "Now your lover will also be feared and ostracized." She spat the words at Bastet.

"You will now both be part of a race of damned beings known as Rogues," Isis said with venom coming out of her countenance.

"Great Isis, I will always stand by you," Bastet said as she bowed down low before the great goddess. "But my Tristan has done nothing to deserve this."

"Ah yes, you are right," Isis said to Bastet in a most kindly way. She pulled a magical pouch from her pocket and sprinkled a handful of star dust upon him. "Tristan is now returned to human."

Tristan emerged from the water and returned to his beloved Bastet."
That is how Sekhmet came to be forever ostracized from the peace loving werecats.

A cure, there was a cure! But this was only legend; could it be real?

I tried to take a catnap but the marching men of my thoughts invaded my brain. I curled up into a fetal position, grasped two handfuls of my hair and pulled as hard as I could. Was I losing my mind thinking that killing bad guys was romantic somehow?

I turned on the TV and watched the news. A dark haired thirty-something man dressed in a business suit stood knee deep in reedy wetland. Scores of protestors joined him. "Tampa attorney, Santiago Malik has assembled a coalition to protest the building of a nuclear power plant on the wildlife preserve, Weedon Island," the news anchor said.

Then Malik spoke. "This sensitive coastal land that has previously been protected has now been re-zoned to allow this atrocity of a nuclear power plant. Scores of animals will be killed by the change in water temperature resulting from the production of power in this area. Plus, we all know the dangers of a nuclear power plant melt down, which is something that has happened in the past. We are not going to let this take place. Please join us by reading the information on savethewetlands.com and giving us your support."

The man spoke with strength and passion, gesticulating at each sentence.

Oh my God! That was Luis's father. But at thirty-something, he looked too young. Then I remembered about the immortality thing. They must freeze in the prime of life, early thirties or so.

After that thirty-second news flash, the weather came on. I barely had a chance to look at him. So I flipped around channels trying to see if someone else was carrying the story, but no luck.

That got me thinking about all the good I could do for this world if I had immortality like Luis's father.

I knew I'd hate myself for it, but I called Luis.

Unbelievably he answered. "Hullo," he said in his sultry voice.

I swallowed hard.

"Luis, I have to talk to you."

"Say when and where."

"The woods near my house. The usual spot in, say, half an hour."

"Sure."

"You're not too weak to go, are you?" I thought of him lying in his bed starving to death.

"No. You have my word, I'll be there."

I washed my face and put on some makeup then slid out my window again, circumventing my parents, and sprinted down the street into the park's secret entrance.

Luis sat on a park bench waiting for me. Because it was so dark, I could barely see his face. I sat down next to him, and he seemed distant and stiff. When I thought about how affectionate he used to be with me, it made me ache. What I wouldn't give for him to put his arm around me and pull me toward him, kiss me with his warm mouth.

He remained silent, waiting for me to speak.

I took a deep breath, inhaling the pine scent of the forest. "Luis, this is killing me. I have to be with you. Every time I see you, I feel a pang in my heart."

"I'm sorry. This whole thing is so crazy." He paused and turned his head toward me. "Kenley, you're a goddess. You can get anybody you want, any time you want, so what's the big deal?"

"The big deal is that I want you." Now was the time to lay it on the line. I'd held too much back for too long.

"You know that's impossible." He visibly stiffened, sitting more upright.

Now I felt like a real loser. "I know. But how could you feel that way about me one minute and not the next? I don't understand."

"I'll never stop loving you, Kenley. It's just that I don't want this life for you."

"So if I were a Rogue, things would be different?"

"No. I don't know." He shrugged. "If you became a Rogue, you'd have to make a human kill within five days or die yourself."

"Don't you think I'm good enough to become a Rogue?"

"Like I said before, I think you're too good. I won't do it." He glanced at me.

The clouds must have parted allowing the moonlight to shine into his hazel eyes. His beauty made me ache.

He sat silent again. "The problem is, Kenley, that I love you."

"What?"

"I love you too much to expose you to this life." He took both of my hands in his and pressed them together. "If I didn't love you quite so much, I'd turn you to Rogue in a second. Then we could be together forever."

Together forever with Luis. "And I love you too much to not be part of your life, whatever that may be." I searched his face, trying to gauge his reaction.

"You're not just saying that?"

"I've never been more serious in my life."

"No, Kenley." He got up and walked away. Just like that.

I ran after him. "Luis wait."

"No." He left again and this time I didn't follow him.

In response, I tore off running into the woods, ditched my clothes in one of my usual hiding places and made the change. As always when I morphed into cat form, I felt as though I owned the planet. I was the most regal creature in the universe and had the right to obtain anything I wanted in life. And damnit, I wanted Luis.

I laid low over the weekend, sure that Luis would call me. To occupy myself, I helped Michelle out at the homeless center. We were actually able to find out where Shelly, the girl whose mom disappeared, was living and visit her. To my amazement, my parents' friends were in the process of adopting her. She lived in the Cheval section of Tampa in a gorgeous house with two nice people for parents. When we spoke with her, she seemed sad, but the novelty of living in a mansion with all kinds of clothes and great stuff around her was quelling the pain. That was good. It also eased my guilt at not having been able to do more for her. I went through all of this in a kind of daze.

I'd been so sure Luis would call, but he didn't. Saturday night I went out for a drive by myself, and ended up going past his house. Okay, I told myself not to, but I couldn't help it. I don't know what I thought I'd see. His bedroom was around the side, and I could see that lights were on, but I didn't see any activity.

Knowing that I shouldn't, I parked my car way down the street and walked. I told myself I'd walk past and that would be it, but I found myself creeping up to his bedroom window. He had the Venetian blinds pulled down, but he also had the light on and I could see through a crack in the side. Knowing that I shouldn't have been spying on him, I peeked through the side. My heart hammered like crazy. I didn't know what I thought I'd see, but I saw Luis sitting on his bed, alone, staring off into space. It made me feel good that he wasn't with anyone else. I decided to abandon my stalking.

As I took one last look at him, I felt a hand clamp onto my shoulder. "What are you doing here?" a gruff male voice demanded.

Chapter 25

I turned to see a handsome Latino man in his thirties dressed in some loose shorts and an aqua polo shirt with a Ralph Lauren emblem on the front. His thick black hair had touches of gray at the temples. It was Luis's father, the same one I saw on TV making the pitch to save the wetlands from the nuclear power plant.

"Mr. Malik." I stood and held out my hand as though we were meeting at a Sunday afternoon tea party. "I'm Kenley. I'm a friend of Luis's."

His face immediately lit up into a smile. "Kenley. Why didn't you come through the front door?"

I shrugged. "I don't know, I just..."

"I know you kids. It's more fun to sneak around. I used to be that way myself, climbing in and out of windows." He made a throw away gesture with his hand and laughed.

The leader of the evil order of werecats was a nice guy. How odd. "Yeah..."

"Let me get Luis for you." He started to walk toward the front of the house.

"Wait a minute," I said sheepishly. "We kind of broke up, and I'm really not supposed to be here. I'm just, you know, having a tough time with it."

"Oh, you teenagers. He's crazy about you, but I'll let you work it out for yourselves." He stood and looked at me as though he hoped I'd change my mind. I'd scarcely gotten such a nice reception from a parent when I was invited to their house, let alone when I was caught stalking.

"Maybe some other time. But thank you so much for your invitation." I don't know why, but I hugged him.

Just as I was doing that, I saw Luis peek around the side of the front door. Shit.

"Kenley? Did I hear your voice out here?"

I didn't know what to say, but his dad spoke up for me. He turned toward Luis. "You know, when I was your age I wouldn't have let a beautiful girl wait around outside in the night air."

Luis pursed his lips. "Well, if I'd known she was out here..."

"Sorry," I said.

"You have nothing to be sorry for. It's my son who should be apologizing."

Luis stood there with his hands clasped together in front of his body. "You're right, Dad. I'm sorry Kenley. I shouldn't have let things get like this between us. Come on inside."

Mr. Malik walked toward the garage. "I'm going to be out for a while. Maybe all night." He winked. "You kids have fun."

"Wow, what a nice guy," I said as I watched Luis's dad pull out in his gold Jaguar convertible.

"He has his moments," Luis said. "He's certainly mellowed out over the years. But he's right. What was I thinking to risk losing you?" He took my hand. "Come on into the house. Enrique's out of town, so we'll have it all to ourselves."

We sat in a cozy corner of his room that had a cushiony love seat, and he rubbed my hand softly. "How did we let things get like this between us?"

"I don't know. At first I couldn't handle the Rogue thing. Then I could, but you were having no part in turning me."

"And I'm still not."

"But you know, I mean, meeting your father just now. He's a decent guy. He's not the devil I pictured him to be. I wouldn't mind being part of this family. You're normal, just like any other family, except you..."

"Yeah, except we..." Luis ran his hand through his long hair, thinking. "Where do we go from here?"

"Turn me. I want to be with you always." I took both his hands and squeezed them.

He pulled away, which gave me a pang of rejection. "No. I won't do it," he said.

"But I want to be part of your life, a permanent part."

He closed his eyes and turned from me then shook his head almost imperceptibly. "No."

"I've thought it over very carefully, Luis." I reached out and touched his arm. "I know it'll change my life forever, and I'm prepared for that."

He stared into my eyes as though trying to read my mind, closed his eyes again, exhaled deeply, started to say something then stopped.

"Go on. Say what you're thinking." If I had to coax him, so be it.

After another pause, he finally said, "You'd have to fully understand what you're getting into."

He was starting to relent. My heart sped up. "I do understand."

"You know you'd have to kill humans."

"What are a few less murders and rapists in the world? We might just get a few ponzi scheme organizers while we're at it."

"You're making light of this, but it's very serious. It's a lifelong commitment. There's no turning back. And when I say lifetime, we're immortal, so that is forever."

His dark eyes bore into mine like soft lasers.

I thought about being with Luis forever. "I want that. More than anything. To be with you for eternity, I mean."

"You're willing to embrace the Rogue lifestyle? To let me turn you?" He searched my face as though trying to get to the truth of my emotions.

"Yes."

"Maybe." He looked away, considering.

"Please."

He gave a heavy sigh. "I love you so much, Kenley. I want what's best for you, and this can be a difficult life."

My heart gave a little jolt. He told me he loved me. Now I was more sure than ever.

"I love you, too. So much. That's why I want this."

"That reason isn't good enough. I have to be sure. This is a serious matter, Kenley. Serious and permanent. Are you ready to give your life over to being a Rogue?"

"I'm so ready, Luis."

He scowled then something must have changed within him, because I could see the doubt and tension disappear from his face. "Okay." He nodded to himself. "Do you want to do it now?"

❦ Chapter 26 ❦

The possibilities pounded in my brain. Even though I often had trouble deciding what to wear to school, often took a half hour deciding what color nail polish to buy, I said, "Yes," to this life-altering decision without having to think at all.

Luis hugged me, held me at arm's length, looked into my eyes and kissed me, little nibbles on my lips at first then deeper contact. His satiny lips on mine made me feel as though nothing else in the world existed.

"Wait," I said. "After we do this, will you be truly mine?"

"Totally. No one else can hold a small flicker of light to your beauty and intelligence. The two of us are truly meant to be together. Nothing in heaven or hell will be able to tear us apart."

"What about all of the other girls in the Claw Club?"

"They're only friends. You and I represent the true royalty of our lines. Together we can do anything. We can bring peace to our shattered families. And we'll be together throughout all of eternity."

I wanted to believe him. I did believe him.

"Let's go to my garden." He stood and pulled on my hand.

"What about your father?"

"He's got a new girlfriend. He'll be out all night, and my brother is out of town."

"OK, let's go." I let him pull me.

We walked through the sumptuous house with its marble floors and crystal chandeliers through a Florida room that held Moroccan patterned brown wicker furniture and enough plants to furnish a medium-sized arboretum.

We passed the freeform swimming pool and waterfall with its bluer than blue water on our way to the formal garden and stood at a circular center with round multi-tiered fountain. Four stone benches surrounded the fountain, and garden spokes radiated from the center. White flowers I couldn't recognize glowed in the moonlight. It reminded me of a Renaissance estate.

"What's this going to involve?" I asked this not exactly caring, I was so lost in the euphoric blindness of desperate love.

"It's a blood exchange."

"Will it hurt?"

"Hardly. I'll do everything I can to make you feel comfortable. You have to take off your blouse."

I unbuttoned my white shirt, slowly with my heart pounding and finally dropped it to the ground still wearing my bra. Even though I was more than ready for this moment of intimate contact with him, I looked at him feeling suddenly shy.

Luis stared into my eyes. "Are you having second thoughts? We don't have to do this."

"No. I'm fine. Undress me."

When he reached both arms around me, my pulse quadrupled. He slowly and carefully unhooked my bra and slid it off. Standing back a little, he traced one finger from my lips down to my waist. "You are so beautiful," he said.

After that everything moved in slow motion.

Luis removed his shirt and spread it over one of the stone benches. "Please. Lie down."

I did, and he kneeled beside me. When I touched his naked flesh, electricity flowed through my fingers and ran into my body, igniting me. A small breeze kicked up, making me keenly aware of the feeling of the night air on my naked chest. It tingled and exhilarated me. I felt vulnerable yet ecstatic. I looked up in the air and exhaled, then saw the bright, pink moon, partially covered by fast-moving clouds. I looked around me and noticed the cool breeze swaying oak branches and palm trees.

But my main focus was on Luis. The scent of his clean, spicy cologne mingled with night-blooming jasmine was so sweet and erotic it made my body quiver.

He put his head to my breast, just over my heart and made a little nip in the skin. I jumped, but soon the feeling of him sucking the fluid from me made me float in a cloud of silvery moonlight, warm and cool at the same time with a mild, undulating breeze. I watched the top of his head as his long black hair spilled over my white flesh and moved like flowing water as he drew from the spot on my chest.

He raised his head and kissed me with my own salty blood still on his lips. I could only describe the feeling as opium flowing through my veins. I cared about nothing but him.

But the sound of a siren off in the distance broke the mood. A moment of panic overtook me. "Luis, I'm not sure about this. It's so permanent. Let's stop it now."

His eyes softened into a hurt expression. "Whatever you want, I want the same thing. If we stop now, I should take you to the hospital for a transfusion, since you are fatally low on blood."

"Hospital? Luis."

He hugged me. "Whatever happens, however you want to go with this, I'll take care of you. If you're Favré or Rogue, I don't care. I've never loved anyone so much in my life."

I raised my head to see him better and felt a wave of nausea overtake me.

"Be careful, my love." He cradled my head.

"Keep going Luis. I'm ready."

"You're sure?"

"Yes."

He slit a spot over his own heart, gently lifted my head and placed it on the wound. "Drink it down," he said.

I sucked at the gash as though by instinct. As the life-giving fluid poured down my throat, I started to feel a pressure build deeply inside my core.

"Luis."

"I know. It's normal to feel aroused during the transition. Try to enjoy it."

I continued drinking as he held my head to his chest. I wrapped my arms around him and enjoyed the smooth, warm feeling of his flesh.

A sensation like tickling took over my brain and traveled through my body. My breasts felt super-erotic and sensitive. I momentarily rubbed them against him and moaned. As I continued drinking from him, the feeling moved down to my genitals. They felt swollen and moist; they pulsated. All this driven by Luis. As the tickling, throbbing sensation increased, I let go of sucking on his flesh. A mind-shattering orgasm rocked my body. Luis held me as waves of pleasure filled my body like surf crashing against the shore. It lasted for what seemed like minutes, then it began to quiet, and I lay back spent. Luis held me with my head on his chest.

I fell into a light sleep for a few moments then opened my eyes. "Oh my God."

"Everything in our life together will be that intense." He tapped my chest. "So get used to it."

"Wow. I don't think I can even stand up."

"Want to stay here with me tonight?"

There'd be all hell to pay in the morning with my parents but what the heck. "Yes."

In those first few hours after the change into Rogue, I didn't feel that great. My blood bubbled and zipped through my veins. My body chemistry must have changed completely, because I tasted an acid residue in my mouth. All of my molecules felt like they were doubling inside of me, making my body more dense.

All through this Luis comforted me. Brought me ice to chew on when I grew feverish and hot tea when I felt chilled. He stroked my forehead with his smooth hand as I felt like I had the worst flu of my life.

After a while I felt better and Luis and I lay in his smooth, white sheets. I kept my eyes open, watching him. He was even more beautiful asleep, and I wanted to remember the way he looked forever.

In the morning, he rose and kissed me, but I felt like Juliet waking up that fateful morning with her Romeo. I hoped this story ended better.

"Kenley, I love you so much." He tried to hold me in his embrace, but I had to go.

"I love you, too, my sweet Luis." I said my goodbyes and hurried home.

As predicted, in the morning demons overtook my parents, my mother especially, and I *did* have all hell to pay.

❦ Chapter 27 ❦

Mimi Walsh-Bohdan stood in the doorway in her white silk bathrobe, her arms crossed tightly over her chest.

She flung the front door open and yanked me into the house. "Don't you know what you put us through staying out all night? With all these murders in the area? Don't you have any consideration at all? We've been up all night waiting for you." I could practically see the steam coming out of her pores.

Dad stood in the background. "Kenley, we're very disappointed in you." That one phrase from him had always made me feel so remorseful I'd do anything to make amends.

"I'm sorry. You have to realize, I'm coming into my own as a werecat. That takes some nighttime activities. Just because you and Dad are in denial about it, doesn't mean I am."

"Oh sure. Try and make us feel guilty." Mom's face grew red as a bloody steak. "I don't know what I'm going to do with you."

"You have to give me some space. It's senior year and I've just found out I'm a werecat. Gimme a break." I headed off toward my bedroom. "I'm going to be late for school."

"And that nice boy, Brendan, showed up to pick you up, and I had to tell him you weren't here."

"Oh, Brendan." I'd completely forgotten.

"You're not even considerate of your friends."

I closed my eyes and shook my head. That was bad. Standing up Brendan, the one person who truly stood up for me and tried to protect me, made me feel horrible. But, I snapped myself out of my feelings of guilt and realized I needed to get ready for school.

163

In record time, I showered and dressed. When I stepped out of my house, every blade of grass, every leaf on our big oak tree jumped out at me in 3D.

I hopped into my Jeep but didn't even need to stop at the Starlight Coffee House for my morning jolt. Last night had been enough of a jolt. On the way to school, it hit me. What had I done? I'd been turned into a Rogue. What happened now?

The trip to school was like a ride at Disney World, or maybe it was like an acid trip. I wouldn't know. Colors brighter than I'd ever seen before danced in my vision. I could hear people talking in the cars all around me. In fact, the noise nearly deafened me until I figured out a way to make an internal adjustment and turn it down.

The heat I felt radiating from my skin was complemented by a God-awful hunger that made me pull into McDonald's and get pancakes, sausages and hash browns to go. Usually I'd worry about my figure, but I knew I was burning the calories like crazy.

I really had to concentrate on driving my car and not getting lost. It was so tempting to turn off and go to the beach or go to Phillippe Park, sit on the Indian mound and look out across Tampa Bay.

But alas, I held my concentration and motored on to school.

When I passed Brendan in the hall, he looked away from me.

"Brendan, I'm sorry..."

He passed by me like I was a ghost. I deserved it.

I sat down next to Michelle in homeroom.

"What happened to you?"

"What do you mean?" I wondered if it was that obvious.

"You look weird. I can't quite place it. Kind of wild and your face is flushed."

"Last night with Luis."

Michelle shook her head. "Ken, you're playing with fire."

"I know that. I don't care."

"It was that good, huh? Well, if you're happy, I'm happy. So how was he?"

"All I can say is oh-my-God."

Michelle looked serious. "Be careful with him. But...I want all the details later."

"You don't disapprove?"

"Hell no. He's a babe. He may be a little fickle with girls, but so what? You had fun, right?"

"Yeah, uh, fickle with girls? What does that mean?"

Michelle shrugged. "Oh, nothing, just, you know, he was seeing Kristen, then you then Molly, then you. I didn't mean anything by it."

"Okay." I nodded, feeling less sure of everything than before.

"I didn't mean to upset you."

"It's fine." I didn't know he'd ever been involved with Kristen.

"See you later." She wriggled her fingers at me.

Luis waited for me after homeroom and gave me a quick kiss on the cheek. "How are you feeling?"

"Great!"

"Any after-effects?" He caught me around the waist with one arm.

"Not that I can tell. Mom and Dad gave me fits this morning, but I expected that. I think I might be grounded for a while." Just the sight of him, even in the mundane morning school hallway, intoxicated me.

"I can teach you how to get out of being grounded. It's called time-shifting, like matter transfer."

"Wow."

"Your parents didn't teach you that?"

"Duh, no."

Molly passed us in the hall, not saying anything, but giving me the Look of Death.

"What's with Molly?"

"She wanted us to be together, but she's like a sister to me. I need to have a talk with her. She'll get over it."

"I'm scared of her. I didn't tell you that she threatened me."

"She threatened you?" he said with grave concern on his face.

"Yeah, she said if I didn't leave you alone, she'd disfigure me."

"She can't disfigure you, because whatever anyone does to you will heal in a couple of hours. Outside of severing the spinal column. That does cause death."

I sighed. "I hate conflict."

"Welcome to my world."

"Um, Luis. Did you ever go out with Kristen?"

His glance darted away for a moment, and then he looked back at me with a pained expression. "Just for a short time. It didn't work out. I hope that doesn't bother you."

Fickle with girls. "Not at all, I was just curious."

"There's nothing between us—Kristen and me. You know that, right?"

"Yeah."

As we parted for class, he mouthed the words "I love you."

A feeling of warmth traveled up from my toes to the top of my head. I was impossibly gone.

"He told me he loved me." Michelle and I waited in the lunch line.

She gave me a skeptical look. "Right in school?"

"Yeah."

Once we got our food, Michelle headed for the tables across the room from the Claw Club until Cristen came over and took my arm. "No, no, no, you're sitting with us today."

"You guys are so schitzo. Yesterday you hated me."

"That was yesterday. Today is today, and you are sitting with us, because we have to plan the Winter Solstice Fete. It's going to be huge. It's a fund-raiser for the Big Cat Rescue Center."

Michelle shrugged. "I'm all for that," she said.

"Great. Let's be all one big, happy family then." Kristen virtually bubbled over with enthusiasm.

I didn't see Luis again for the rest of the day.

At home my parents were waiting for me. They hadn't forgotten about my all-nighter.

"We're grounding you for a month," Mom said.

"I can live with that." I knew they'd forget about it in a couple of days.

"What? You're not going to put up an argument?" Mom scowled at me.

"No, not at all. I broke your rules, and I'm willing to pay the consequences."

Mom and Dad looked at each other in disbelief. "That was easy then." Dad smiled.

"While we're all home, I want to talk about some things." I tossed my book bag onto the counter.

"Sure."

We all sat in the living room. "You've told me something about our side of the family, but I'm hearing about another side called Rogues."

Mom answered quickly wrinkling her nose a little. "They're the antisocial side of the family."

"They're flesh eaters, meaning they eat people. It's not a good thing," Dad pursed his lips and shook his head.

"Yes, there are only a handful of them in the world, and they keep to themselves. I don't think there even are any of them in the States, right, Bruce?" Mom's gaze rested on Dad.

Dad nodded his head. "That's what I heard. They live in Bulgaria or something with all the old-world vampires."

"They're nothing for us to be worried about." Mom shot Dad a concerned look. "Why do you ask?"

My parents were really *really* out of touch.

"No reason. I hear tales, that's all."

"We're the civilized side of the family. That's all that counts," Dad said.

While I had their attention, I was going to get all of the information out of them I could. "Are people born Rogues?"

"No." Mom jumped in quickly. "All werecats are born Favrés, the pure strain, and are then turned into Rogues."

"Once someone is turned into a Rogue, is there any way to reverse it?" Granted, this question would have set off red flags for most parents, but mine were such a tightly wrapped bundle of their own concerns, they didn't even read between the lines.

Dad jumped right in. "There is one old legend. In ancient times a woman agreed to be turned into a Rogue in order to save her village from invading foreigners. She allowed herself to be turned and then found out that the invaders had already ransacked the village. The man who turned her came back to hold her captive. She escaped from him, and asked the village shaman what to do. The shaman gave her the Dagger of Bastet to kill him. She didn't expect it to do anything but kill him, but the aftereffect was that it reversed the Rogue curse. She became mortal once again."

"That's very interesting."

Dad walked over to the curio cabinet and unlocked it with a key from his key chain. He pulled out a dagger with a purple amethyst handle that had been sculpted into a cat's head. It was the same one that Luis had admired. "This is it," Dad said. "It's the real deal."

"It's just a copy, isn't it? It can't be the original."

"There are five originals in the world. We possess one of them." He handed it to me.

As I held it in my hand, I felt it pulse with energy.

"Tell you what, though," Mom said. "The whole legend is a just a bunch of crap. Any old dagger will do when it comes to killing the maker to release the spell."

The muscles in Dad's face sagged into a frown at Mom's correction of him.

"I don't understand," I said.

"Like so many myths and legends, you find that there is some basis in reality, but it's watered down. Granted, stabbing the Rogue who turned you—in the heart—with the Dagger of Bastet will release you from the curse, but any other knife will also. The dagger has a few other magical properties though, like the blunt end can be used to freeze people into position. And the Dagger of Bastet will leave Favrés unharmed." Mom looked pleased with herself for proving Dad's story to be incorrect. He sat there and took it as usual.

"You mean there's no other way to reverse the Rogue curse?" At this point, I was still euphoric from my night with Luis, so I wasn't asking for myself, but it didn't hurt for me to have the information as long as they were in the mood to give it. Who knew if I might need it some time in the future?

"There might be, but I don't know what it is."

As usual, they were too wrapped up in their own little world to realize what was going on with their daughter. They weren't bad people, they just tended to be oblivious.

"Thanks. I'm just going to go to my room to do some homework." I picked up my book bag.

"Didn't you want to talk about anything else?" Mom asked.

"Maybe later. I want to get some work done before I get sleepy. I'm planning on having an early night tonight."

"Kenley," Mom said. "Did you apologize to Brendan?"

"Yeah, I did."

"You know, if he wants to come over and work on homework with you while you're grounded, your father and I don't mind."

"All right. Thanks."

Brendan would probably never speak to me again.

At around eleven, a tapping sound on my window startled me out of my pleasant doze. My chemistry book clattered to the floor as I jolted out of bed.

⁓❦ Chapter 28 ❦⁓

"Oh, Christ. Is that Molly?" I wasn't scared anymore; I was over it.

Then I heard the tapping again. I turned out the light and peeked through the blinds. All I could make out was a dark shape under the window. When the shape moved, I saw an upturned face with long, black hair.

"Luis." I fell all over myself lifting the blinds and opening the window. "Come on in."

He hoisted himself through the window like an Olympic gymnast, barely exerting any effort. He stood close to me in the half-light wearing a loose black shirt and black pants with an ivory choker around his neck. His hair flowed freely about his shoulders.

The sweet scent of citrus blossoms drifted through the window and mingled with Luis's spicy cologne.

He didn't say anything. He just stood there staring into my eyes. I wondered if I should do something. As Luis edged imperceptibly closer, I felt the heat creep up my neck. I stepped closer, too. Luis pressed his face in near mine, still not touching me.

I moved forward until our faces just barely met. With one stroke, Luis brushed my hair back from my face and pulled me in to kiss him.

Nothing had ever felt so incredibly right to me before.

"Luis, stay with me tonight," I whispered.

"I'd love to. I'm going to teach you something amazing tonight."

"You're amazing."

He still held me close. "Remember I told you about time and space shifting?"

I halfway wanted to just keep him in my room and ravish him. The time shifting thing sounded like work. "But I just want to be with you."

"How about being with me in, oh say, a Moroccan palace?"

"Huh, what?" I grinned.

"My father has a palace in Morocco. We could go there, but I need to teach you to shift first."

"Oh, wow! I'm in. Let's go."

"Let me explain. First you must turn into cat mode. Then there's a mental process that takes place. You must turn your attention inward and place it upon your desired destination."

"But I've never seen your dad's palace. How can I visualize it?"

"That's the good part. Until you can do it on your own, you can ride along on my vibrations." He leaned in to me, all excited.

"This is like matter transfer?"

"Exactly."

"Now I'm scared."

"Nothing to be scared of. I promise." He touched my nose with his index finger.

"Not be scared that my molecules are going to be rearranged while traveling through space?"

"This is hard to explain, but it's a natural process for us," he said.

"Is it a Rogue thing?"

"Rogue and Favré both; we all do it."

"My folks were holding out on me."

"Yeah, they completely neglected your werecat lessons, so I'll have to pick up the slack."

"I'm so glad." I beamed.

"Ready?"

"Sure."

"We have to take off our clothes." He held me close to him and pressed his body into mine then quickly released me.

"Is taking your clothes off always part of the deal with shape shifting?" I grinned.

"Yeah, 'fraid so. You might end up getting a zipper caught in your flesh, and you wouldn't like that very much."

We both peeled off our shirts and dropped them to the floor. Luis undid his ivory choker. "Don't forget rings and things."

Next we removed pants and underclothes. The naked Luis standing before me was almost more than I could bear. His coffee with cream skin, the smooth muscles silhouetted by the moonlight that streamed in through the window mesmerized me. Not to mention that he had the most beautiful genitals I'd ever seen, though I hadn't seen many. Then it struck me as odd that I'd never actually touched them. We'd never had sex, even though I felt as though we had.

"Ready to shift? Can you do it by yourself?"

"I think I've gotten fairly good at it now, but I always seem to have to be out running."

He gripped my arms at my elbows. "Close your eyes and concentrate. See yourself shifting."

I pressed my eyes shut and tried to feel it—the fur sprouting from my pores, ears pushing out from the top of my head, claws popping. I stood and imagined, and as I did I felt Luis's hands become furry, and I heard him drop to the floor with a thud and the tapping of his claws. The pressure was on now. I willed it, and began to feel the subtle shifting of my molecules.

"Come on, Kenley, you can do it," Luis thought to me.

I felt the familiar tightening of my skin. It happened faster than I was used to. I lowered myself to the floor and experienced the shift. There was an odd pleasure in it now. I nuzzled up to Luis's sleek fur.

You are magnificent, my love. Jaguar-Luis licked my neck.

And so are you. Now what do we do?

Get on my back and close your eyes. He lowered himself to the ground.

I looked at him and cocked my head.

Go ahead. This is how we teach our little ones.

I'm confused. I said.

Somehow the proximity of our bodies makes us move together.

I'll trust you. I climbed on top of him and situated myself. It felt kind of nice.

Ready? Hang on.

I clamped my arms around his neck, closed my eyes and pressed my face into his back, so warm and good.

Something happened, and I felt a weightlessness that made me lose all sense of my body. As I clung to him, everything went into overdrive. Objects whizzed past me; the air rushed through me giving me a feeling of loose, disjointed molecules. I was no longer able to hold on, because I didn't have any arms. *Luis, I'm scared.*

Almost there, Love.

I had the sensation of the winding down of a gyroscope, and even heard that kind of a sound. Things grew still. It seemed we had touched down.

Cautiously, I opened my eyes and saw Luis's golden, furry pelt. Lifting my head up, I viewed a bedroom straight out of the Arabian Nights. A huge bed covered with silky bedding held a canopy draped with gossamer material. Outside a golden sunset filled a desert canyon.

Luis, where are we? I climbed down off his back.

We're in Morocco, just as I promised. We can change back now.

I easily made the shift to human.

Luis changed so fast I almost missed it. He reached behind a door and tossed me a shimmering robe.

We settled down on the huge bed. Luis held me and stroked my hair. "The great thing is that we can make time stop. Literally no time is passing back home."

"You're kidding." I couldn't stop smiling. How could things be any better? I had to pinch myself.

"Not kidding at all."

I buried my face in his chest and inhaled the unique scent I loved. If God existed at all, it would never allow us to be separated.

He pulled me so close to him I could feel him breathe. "And now, Miss Walsh-Bohdan, you are completely mine."

"You know, I've never done this before."

"We don't have to do anything you don't want to." He stroked my side and nuzzled my neck. "I'd be happy just to lie here and kiss you."

I'd never felt anything so incredibly right before in my life. "All I know is that I want you so badly."

He leaned me back and planted kisses all over me then put his mouth on mine and kissed me deeply until I started to see fireworks under my eyelids. Wow!

I can only say, I spent the night delirious and drunk on love. He was part of me and I was part of him and I didn't for a moment regret what I'd done.

That wouldn't come until later.

◦◦◈ Chapter 29 ◈◦◦

We spent the entire night together in Morocco and still arrived back home in time for me to get a full night's sleep and be completely refreshed for school. Amazing.

As I drove to school on Friday, I had an entirely new perspective. For one thing, I'd had the most incredible night of my life with Luis. Yes, it had been uncomfortable at first, even a little painful, but he *so* made up for it with his tender touches and incredible technique. God, he was good.

For another, I had immortality, the most highly sought-after but elusive commodity in the entire world. What would people pay for immortality? Billions? Some would even sell their souls for it. I had it now.

I felt so hot, despite the frost on my windshield that was uncharacteristic of Florida. I wore a tank top and jeans and was just comfortable.

An overwhelming hunger, even worse than what I'd experienced before, gripped my stomach. I stopped at a different fast food restaurant, bought two breakfasts and shoveled them down while I drove. Still, it didn't quell the emptiness inside me.

In gym class, I volunteered to jump the hurdles first. It crossed my mind to try to be not quite so good so I wouldn't arouse suspicion, but I decided not to. The fun of being super-girl outweighed the possibility that people would talk. I hadn't bothered to join the track team, but that had only been a means of getting to know Luis anyhow.

As I sat on the bleachers, Michelle looked at me as though I'd grown a beak. "What in the world is going on with you? I think you just set an Olympic record."

"I've been working out, getting enough sleep, eating right, you know."

"No, I don't know. That was frigging weird." She looked away from me and crossed her arms in front of her chest.

"Hi, Kenley." Kristen put her hand on my shoulder and bent over me until I could smell her baby powder plus coconut scent. "You were amazing out there. I wish I could be as good."

Michelle gave me a weird look and left to go run her hurdles.

"It's just since the change, you know," I said.

Kristen looked around and put a finger to her own pink, silvery lips. "Careful talking about that stuff."

"Oh, sure."

"I know at first you want to tell everyone," she said.

"No, I definitely want to keep it to myself."

"Are you and Michelle having lunch with us today?" she asked.

"I am. I don't know about Michelle."

I watched as Michelle did a good job of jumping the hurdles. Perfectly fine, nothing spectacular.

"No matter, as long as you'll be there. Molly might be disappointed if Michelle isn't there, though. She likes Michelle. Well..." Kristen tapped me on the shoulder. "I have to get out of here before the gym teacher calls on me. I could do it, but I'm just not into it. *Ciao.*"

"*Ciao.*" Her comment about Molly liking Michelle seemed odd, but I didn't think anymore of it after that.

After doing an adequate job in running her hurdles, Michelle returned to her seat. "You *are* going to explain all of this to me later."

Along with my senses, my cognitive powers intensified a thousand fold. I breezed through my classes, no sweat. Mr. Wizofsky called on me for answers to questions about the periodic tables. I rattled them off no problem. The teacher stared at me slack jawed. "Well, Miss Walsh-Bohdan, you have been studying, haven't you?"

"Yes. Yes, I have." I smirked, satisfied with myself. Any trepidation I might have had about my change fled my mind.

I was able to rattle off formulas and periodic tables like nobody's business.

At lunchtime, the Claw Club girls had saved me the prime seat at the head of the table. Molly had picked up some new boy-toy and sat at a nearby table working her powers on him. Not that she needed to do much.

We talked about plans for the Winter Solstice Party. "It's going to be huge," Kristen said. "It isn't too early to start thinking about it."

"Oooooh, I can't wait." Sarah clapped her hands together and jumped up and down in her seat. Orlando watched her boobs visibly jiggle.

"I'm up for whatever you need," I said. I hoped I wasn't getting in over my head, like doing fund-raising stuff or something. I hated that. But I thought about how I could wear some of the new clothes Luis had brought me for the ball.

After school, Luis waited for me by my car. Facing me, he cupped his hands around the back of my head and kissed me. "How was your day?"

"Wonderful." I couldn't wipe the smile off my face.

"Can I come over again tonight?"

"You don't even have to ask."

"Good. I wouldn't want you to get bored while you're grounded." He wrapped his arms around me and kissed me again.

"Ha! Hardly. Not with you around."

"I'm glad to hear you say that." He squeezed my hand. "We have something really important to do tonight."

"More important than last night?"

"Mmmm..." He grinned. "I don't know about that."

"More cat lessons?"

"Yes, of course." He held me. "And some more of just being with you. I can't get enough of you."

"Me, too. I feel the same way."

"See you tonight then?" He pulled away and waved to me as he left.

"Sure."

I was glad my parents were always busy with their art collecting and their various parties. That meant they usually weren't home until later on at night.

My cell phone rang. Looking at caller ID, I saw that it was Michelle. I didn't answer it because I didn't want to have to explain my life to her. Not yet. Besides, I'd been sworn to secrecy.

The one thing that troubled me was Michelle. I didn't want to lose the longest-lasting friendship of my life. Michelle seemed okay with everything for now, but she wasn't going to be satisfied with superficial answers to her questions. I'd do something about that tomorrow—ask her if she wanted to go do volunteer work at the shelter together or go out to a movie then start breaking things to her gradually.

I did my homework easily. All I could think about was Luis. What was I going to wear? I tore through my closet searching for something that would make me look as amazing as he does.

I wondered where it would all lead. Then my old doubts crept back in. Would he get tired of me? He could get any girl he wanted. Molly and Kristen were so much hotter than I was. Molly, with her full model lips. And Kristen with her Euro trash wardrobe looked more put together than a model from *W*.

Stop it. You're beautiful yourself. And interesting. I looked in the mirror at my long, hair, my complexion flushed from excitement. "Yer okay kid," I said to my own reflection.

The night dragged on. I bathed and lotioned and buffed, applied some new *parfum*, dressed myself to look as though I didn't care what I was wearing, as though I'd thrown something together at the last minute. We all knew it took hours to achieve a look like that.

Luis arrived at eleven sharp, through the window as he had the previous night. "We have something really important to do tonight."

I stood on tiptoe to kiss him. "Are we going to another exotic location through matter transfer?"

"No, actually, we're going in my car."

"Oh, where?" That surprised me.

He grasped my arms at the elbows and stared into my eyes. "We have something very important to do tonight, and you have to trust me, okay?"

Luis crawled out the window and turned around to lift me outside into the chilly night. We could have gone out through the front door since my parents weren't home, but I let him be chivalrous.

We walked down the street in silence, holding hands. He opened the door of his Jaguar for me.

"Are you going to tell me where we're going?"

As he pulled out, he took my hand and rubbed it. "This is an important night for you, Kenley."

"Hmmm? Why?" I said, enrapt in the mere presence of him.

He took a deep breath and shifted his gaze away from me. An odd expression like pain or regret flashed through his countenance. "You have to make a kill."

Chapter 30

"A kill?" I felt my throat tighten. "But I've already made one."

"This will be a human kill. You knew you'd have to, right?"

"Yeah. I guess. I mean..." I felt the nighttime sky closing in on me. Though I knew this moment would eventually arrive, I'd thought of it as more of an abstract concept.

"Kenley," Luis pulled over to the side of the road and turned to face me. "You have to make a human kill within five days; if you don't, you'll die."

"You never told me that."

"Yes, I did."

"I don't remember that." All the blood drained from my head.

"I tried to discourage you, remember?"

I felt as though he'd put a knife in my heart and twisted it. "Yeah," I said softly.

He touched my face gently. "You knew that as a Rogue you'd have to make a human kill."

"I knew, but it didn't really hit me until this moment. All I really thought about was being with you."

"Kenley." He hugged me and rubbed the back of my head. "I should have listened to my instincts. You're too good. I've led you into a life you can't handle."

"I can handle it. I just have to get used to the idea."

Luis leaned back and sighed. "I've made a mistake with you."

"No you haven't. You'll see." I had to wrap my mind around this thought. "I need a pep talk."

"A pep talk. Let's see." He paused. "You have to learn to connect with your Rogue nature. You're feeling some hunger inside, a hunger you can't quite satiate, right?"

"Yes. I'm eating tons, and it never seems to fill me up."

"That's because your body craves a different kind of nourishment—living flesh. I'm surprised you can even stop yourself. As the days go by you'll start to feel feverish, desperate, weak, and then you won't be able to control the hunger at all. You'll go after the first person you see alone on a dark road at night. And that won't necessarily be the right person to kill. If we do it now while your hunger is still controllable, we can find a bad guy and kill him. Think of yourself as a superhero, an avenging angel. That's the only way I've been able to live with it."

It was wrong to kill people. My throat clenched up; I knew I couldn't do it.

Luis put his hand over mine and rubbed it. "I remember my first time. Like your family of Favrés, Rogues don't turn until after puberty."

"Tell me about your first time."

"I didn't like the thought of killing at all. I wanted no part of it, in fact. My father made me do it. He's different from me. He thinks all humans are fair game. We drove out to the countryside, in a small town in Connecticut, found some guy walking down a road and pulled up as though we were asking for directions."

Luis looked straight ahead as he talked. "Father got out of the car and changed into cat mode faster than I had ever seen anyone change. He went for the man's jugular and took him down in one swoop. We shared the meat. The next time he made me do it by myself. He wanted me to go out and find a young girl, because he thought she'd be easier for me to handle, but I couldn't do it. So instead he commanded me to kill a teenage boy who was working in the field picking apples. I did it, but very badly. He wasn't quite dead and still thrashing around. Father had to finish it off for me. I hated myself for killing that innocent boy. Ever since then I've sworn not to kill innocent people."

"You mean like the way they're killing the homeless people?"

"Exactly. Those people never hurt anyone. That's why I use my powers of perception. It's kind of like ESP but a little different. I can teach you to have it too. Anyway, I can sniff out bad guys."

"Like a superhero, huh?" I tried to look on the positive side.

"I like to think of myself that way. I'm determined that once my father has turned over his position to me, that's the way we'll all operate. No innocent person will ever die. Feel better about it now?"

"Yes. It's just that it's not our place to decide who's bad and who isn't."

"When I find someone beating up an old person or woman or a child, that person is as likely a candidate to be my dinner as any."

"I have to do this or I'll die. I have to think about it that way." The terrible wrongness of my decision to become a Rogue pressed on me like a ten-ton anvil.

"Let's do it then." Luis started the Jaguar and took off.

We ended up in St. Pete in a bad section of town. Crumbling brick buildings and small, wooden houses with peeling paint and torn-off shutters lined the street. Kids hung out, boys in the uniform of white tee shirts and straight-leg jeans, woman in midriff tops, hip hugger jeans or mini-skirts and platform shoes.

"Do you always go to the poor sections of town?" As I said that I remembered that he'd made a kill in my own neighborhood.

"No. There are plenty of high-income bad people. They're harder to get to because they're usually behind closed doors. It's not impossible, though. I know. It doesn't seem fair, does it?"

"No. What if they have some kind of disease?"

"That means nothing to us. Our bodies purify the flesh and blood as we digest it. We can't experience disease. So you don't have to worry about that, okay?"

I nodded.

"Look." Luis pointed down a side street. "We've found our food."

"I don't see anything." I strained to see what Luis saw.

"There's a man attacking a woman in an alleyway."

"How come I don't see anything?"

"You'll develop the sixth sense. It takes time." He pulled over onto a side street. "Take your clothes off and change, quick."

I broke a nail trying to pull off my jeans in the tight car. "Damn." I sucked at the spot that had broken below the quick.

"Make sure to open the door before you make the change. You can't open a door with paws, you know. Hurry."

"I'm hurrying." I finally got my turtle neck sweater and bra off, and put all my concentration into making the change to panther. I looked over at Luis and saw the sleek jaguar sitting up awkwardly in the driver's seat. He turned and slid out the door, graceful as a ballet dancer.

My change, on the other hand, wasn't going so well. After a minute I still couldn't feel the transformation. I couldn't do it under duress.

Luis poked the door open with his nose and waited patiently.

Finally, I felt the change overtake me and looked down to see the intricate rosette pattern in my fur that looked like black from a distance.

I followed Luis down the street and into an alley. The stench of garbage turned my stomach. A compact, muscular man with short black hair threw a young girl down to the ground and pushed his knee into her stomach. She had blood coming out of one corner of her mouth. The man tore her blouse off and held her down with his left hand as he tugged at her skirt with his right.

The girl screamed, her platinum blonde hair dragging on the filth of the alley, her young skin torn in spots from the rocky dirt of the ground.

Luis launched himself at the man. He seemed to grow into a larger, fiercer version of himself as he tore into the back of the man's neck and flipped him around.

The girl's eyes widened and she scrambled backward, crablike. She looked on in terror as Luis held the man down with his powerful paws. He thought to me. *Come on over here and rip out this bastard's jugular.*

Chapter 31

At once horrified, numb and queasy, I couldn't move. *I can't. You do it.*

Do it now. This is a perfect opportunity.

No, next time. I sat, frozen.

Arrgh... Follow me, then.

What do you mean?

The man yelled and struggled as Luis had him pinned. Make sure you're touching me somewhere. Here, hold my ankle.

I put both paws around his ankle and found myself making the space leap through alien planes of existence and scrambled matter and landed in broad daylight in a field that smelled like hay and wild flowers.

I looked over at Luis. He had dragged his prey with him through time and space. He clamped the man's throat in his teeth as the man struggled and made whimpering sounds. No doubt his vocal cords were being squashed.

I bent over and vomited. *I can't.*

Pull yourself together. Do you want to die of hunger?

No, but I can't. You do it.

OK. Luis ripped into the left side of the human's neck, and when the blood gushed out, he lapped at it with his big tongue. *At least come over here and have a drink.*

I was curled up in a ball with my paws wrapped around my stomach. *No way. You go ahead.*

I looked up to see him tearing into the man's flesh, eating it in big, greedy gulps. I tried to think of it as a National Geographic special, but I couldn't. This wasn't a gazelle he'd taken down, it was a human.

You don't want any? Luis called.

No. God, no. This was why they never left any bodies. They dragged their prey off to another dimension. Very clever. The werecat who killed Shelly's mother must have gotten sloppy. Either that or someone wanted to get the werecats busted.

I lay curled up until Luis finished and nudged me with his nose. *Ready to go home?*

Yeah.

We rode back in silence.

"I'm a failure, huh?" I couldn't stop crying. What had I gotten myself into? I knew what Luis was thinking, that he shouldn't have turned me. He was probably disgusted with me. I couldn't believe he still cared.

"It's okay, Kenley." He rubbed my knee. "You can't be expected to be able to do this right away. You still have time."

"What if I can't ever do it?"

He shrugged. "We won't think about that."

We climbed back in through my bedroom window. Luis hugged me.

"I think I need to be alone, Luis. I need some time to think."

"Sure. Don't feel bad, okay? Remember how much I love you and that I'd do anything in the world for you." He kissed me on the cheek and left through the window.

On Saturday morning when I thought I'd be able to sleep, Brendan woke me up bright and early.

My dad said, "Kenley, wake up. Brendan's here." Dad continued his love affair with Brendan.

I woke, washed quickly and pulled on jeans and a hoodie.

Brendan and I went for a walk down the street. "I can't believe you're still talking to me. I'm so sorry about the other night."

I noticed that Brendan was clenching and unclenching his fists. "What in the world are you thinking, Kenley?" It was the first time I'd seen him actually angry.

I walked next to him mutely.

"I know what you've been doing." The sandy-haired boy pressed in toward me, his eyes blazing.

"What *have* I been doing?"

"Hunting." If words could stab, that one word would have killed me.

"Shhh. What makes you think that?"

"Stop playing games with me. I told you what a wide network of cryptozoologists we have. They're watching this area and everything that happens here." He stormed off in front of me, not able to contain himself.

"Are you watching my bedroom?" I hurried after him.

"No. But we do watch the streets."

"Let's get further away from my house before we talk," I said.

We walked to a small park about a block away. One magnificent royal palm stood sentinel over a rose garden and several benches. Even though the morning had started out cool, the sun put a warm glow over everything.

"Admit it. You let Luis turn you into a Rogue." He spit out the words as though I disgusted him.

I hesitated, wondering if I should tell him. Then I thought, why not? He knows anyway. "Okay, I admit it. Yes." I sat down on one of the benches and crossed my arms in front of my chest while Brendan stood over me.

"Have you made a human kill?"

"No. Not yet. And I know it sounds ugly, but..."

"You know that once you make a human kill your soul is the property of the Dark Lord," he said.

"The devil?"

"Who else?"

"The devil doesn't exist. That's religious dogma. And would you please sit down next to me?" I wouldn't have him taking that superior position with me, and I didn't feel like standing.

"Tell the Devil he doesn't exist. Whatever you call it, your soul will be eternally damned."

I didn't buy the eternally damned part. I wasn't even sure I believed in hell. "You think you know everything. So tell me, what's the cure?" I knew what I'd been told, but I wanted to see if Brendan knew any other options.

He looked at me intently. "Stab your maker in the heart."

That was the same thing my parents and Luis had told me. "Kill Luis?"

Brendan took my hand and squeezed it. "Yeah."

"Isn't there any other way to do it?"

"Not that I know of."

I sighed.

"Your parents have the Dagger of Bastet. I saw it in their curio cabinet when I was at your house. Using that special knife will make it easier."

"How will the knife make it easier?"

"It's made for killing Rogues. It slides very easily into their hearts."

I felt nauseous at the thought of stabbing Luis. No way I could do it.

"But the knife won't even injure someone who's not a Rogue."

"That's convenient."

"There's also a way to use it to freeze people for a period of time. Not sure how that works exactly."

That was a new one, something that could come in handy. I'd have to get the details on that.

"There's more. The plan Luis's father is organizing is to kill ninety-nine out of every one hundred humans in order to save the werecat habitats. People are ruining the planet. That's a given. The Rogues want to take matters into their own hands—keep enough humans for food, but not enough to make a dent in the environment."

"That sounds like an exaggeration. How could they possibly do that?"

"We don't quite know that yet. Remember, werecats are magical creatures. They have means beyond the ones we know."

"True, but Brendan, that seems so fantastic, like something out of a sci fi novel."

"You didn't believe me when I told you to watch out for Luis, either. Was I right?"

"Can you find out one thing for me? Is there any way other than killing your maker to end the Rogue curse?"

"I'll try to find that out, but I'm not promising anything." Brendan's anger had faded into mild aggravation.

"I've got to go get some lunch. I'm starving."

As I rose to go back to my house, Brendan put his hand on my shoulder. "You're craving human flesh, you know. Nothing from your fridge is going to satisfy that."

"Yeah. I'm all too aware of that unpleasant fact of life. So how come you're not afraid of me?"

A hint of a smile played on his lips. "Because I know you wouldn't hurt me."

"You're right, I wouldn't." We'd made the short walk to my house. "Brendan, I have to go."

"Call me if you need anything." He said as I walked into the house.

As an afterthought, I turned and hugged him, inhaling his fresh laundry scent. I knew Brendan was right, but at that point I had to deal with what my life had become.

As I ate a rare roast beef sandwich, I pondered what Brendan had said about Luis's father wanting to kill off most of the human race. Frankly, I didn't see how it was possible, and why would they want to cut off their source of food?

I knew one thing. I wanted out of the Rogue business. It had been a mistake—the biggest mistake of my life.

I felt the way people must feel when they find out they have a terminal disease—a crushing, oppressive fear with no hope in sight. If I had cancer I could go to a support group, do some creative visualization, get sympathy from my family and friends. But this I had done on my own against the advice of Brendan who had turned out to be my one true friend. And where was Luis when I needed him? Looking back at the string of events, I felt manipulated. Had he made me feel sorry for him so I'd weaken and beg him to be turned into a flesh-eating monster. How could I have been so dumb?

I walked into the living room in tears. My parents were nowhere around. I wanted to call Michelle, but then I couldn't exactly say anything to Michelle, because she didn't know the situation. I couldn't very well tell her.

How could I have gotten myself into a mess in which I couldn't even talk to my best friend?

Still hungry, I looked in the refrigerator, found some raw meat and gulped it down. I didn't feel any remorse this time, because, after all, it wasn't human. After washing it down with a ton of water, I did some homework. Even in my agitated state, my increased cognitive powers let me breeze through the calculus that had been the bane of my existence.

After that, I roamed around the house like a caged animal. I wanted to go out and run, but I didn't want to encourage my Rogue tendencies. What if I stumbled upon a human in the woods?

The eating of human flesh had nauseated me, but what would happen if my hunger overcame me so much I couldn't control myself?

Tonight I'd stay put.

Thoughts of killing Luis to overcome my suffering crossed my mind. Then, of course, I couldn't believe I'd even considered it.

Luis wasn't calling, the bastard. Even though he knew what I was going through, he let me stew in my own tortured thoughts.

I found the key for the curio cabinet, snagged the Dagger of Bastet and tucked it away in my room. Just in case.

At around midnight, I decided I'd call Brendan and thank him for everything, admit to him that I'd been a lunatic and tell him I cared about him deeply. I searched my phone for his number. There it was.

I dialed, and, to my surprise, a woman answered.

"Hi, Mrs. Fournier? This is Kenley. I hope I'm not calling too late, but can I talk with Brendan?" I felt sheepish for calling so late and getting his mom.

"He's not with you?" The woman's voice sounded high-pitched and shrill.

"No."

"He's not here. Do you know where he is?"

"No. We talked for a little while this afternoon, and that's the last I saw of him."

"When Brendan didn't come home tonight, I started to worry, because he's always so considerate about calling if he's going to be late. Now that it's midnight, I'm really concerned. It's just not like him."

No. Dear, sweet Brendan wouldn't make anyone worry needlessly about him. "I don't know, Mrs. Fournier. Can I do anything?"

"Just call us if he turns up at your house or if you hear anything, okay?"

"Definitely. Have you called the police?"

"We're just thinking about it now." Brendan's mom's voice trembled a little.

"Let me know if he turns up."

"We will, dear. Bye now."

I should have gone to bed and forgotten about it. Brendan was probably out sulking somewhere. But that wasn't something he'd do. I knew something was wrong. Maybe he'd been nosing around about Rogue business a little too much. Or maybe it was nothing. Maybe he'd gotten lucky. There was a thought. He was a handsome guy. Michelle said she was interested in him, didn't she? I felt a twinge of jealousy.

I lay down and tried to sleep. My pillow felt too thick and the sheet made an uncomfortable ridge under my arm. I turned over trying to get settled. A jumble of thoughts and impressions filled my head. How could I abandon the one friend who'd stood by me through all of this mess? I got up and dressed.

I was going to find Brendan.

But as I walked out the door, my cell phone rang.

Glancing at the caller ID, I saw it was Luis. My heart tumbled over in my body to the point that I had to hold my chest. Damn, I hated myself for loving him. Don't answer it.

No, I had to.

"Hello."

"Kenley?" His voice sounded whispery.

"What's wrong with your voice?"

"I have a sore throat. Come over to my house. I have to see you."

"Do you know what's happened to Brendan?" I asked.

"That's what I want to talk to you about."

"Fine then. I'll be over."

I parked on the next block, well away from Luis's house, in case his brother or father was around, left my stuff in the car and walked towards his house. At first I pounded on Luis's front door, but no one answered, so I crept around the side of the sprawling house and knocked on one of the windows. No response. I thought I remembered which room was Luis's, but maybe I was mistaken. I moved over one and knocked again. I couldn't tell if his car was there, because it could have been inside the massive garage.

Was he playing games with me? Damn him. I hated him, but I was doing this for Brendan.

I knocked one more time, hard.

In mid-knock, someone grabbed my wrist from behind. I turned around and gasped.

"What do you think you're doing?" A man grabbed me so hard it felt like he was breaking my arm as he spun me around.

Chapter 32

My heart hammered up into my throat, then when I saw it was Luis's brother, I got really mad. "Enrique. I want to talk to Luis. It's none of your business what I'm doing here anyway."

"Everything that goes on at my house is my business." He practically hissed the words.

"Let go of me." I jerked away but couldn't get out of his grip. "What do you think you're doing. I came here to talk to Luis."

Tan muscles bulged from under his black tee shirt as I struggled to get away from him. He caught my other wrist in a car-crusher grip. He had short, black hair and the same striking features as Luis, but a sneer twisted his lips and a permanent scowl creased his brow. I could tell he'd been the kind of kid who liked torturing small animals.

"Luis is out with some honey, I do believe."

A wave of jealousy flooded into me like the wake of a tsunami. "You're lying."

"And you're obviously a very naïve young lady." His lips curled into a smirk.

"I don't have anything to say to you. Let go of me." My anger compelled me to give another good jerk. My werecat-ism made me uber-strong, but he was stronger.

"Hello, Kenley," he whispered. "I want to see you so bad."

"That was *you* on the phone?"

"No shit, Sherlock."

"Let go of me." I kicked at his shins, but he managed to hold me away.

"You seem like a sensible girl, so I'll tell you this right up front. If you struggle, you're going to get hurt. If you come with me easy, you won't."

"All right, I'll go along." I wasn't going to let that bastard take me anywhere. "Just let go of my wrists and explain something to me. What do you want with me?"

When he turned away briefly to collect his thoughts, I jabbed my palm up under his nose as hard as I could, hoping to drive the bone right up into his brain. When he doubled over cupping his hands around his nose, I slammed my knee into his groin. That'd teach him to mess with me.

I hauled ass down the street toward my car, frantically digging the car keys out of my pocket. Damn! They weren't where I'd usually put them. Then I realized I'd left them in the car.

Before I was able to get anywhere near my car, Enrique tackled me from behind and knocked me to the pavement smashing my face into the hard stone.

Stabbing pain shot though my face and shoulders as he grabbed my arms from behind and wrenched them back.

In one swift movement, he hoisted me over his shoulder. When my stomach hit his hard muscles, it knocked the wind out of me. I pounded, kicked and bit him, but I was no match for him. I'd never seen such superhuman power and agility. Very aware that he could crack my spine, I stopped struggling. But this time, he didn't loosen his grip. He opened the triple wide garage door using a remote and popped open the back of his van.

I closed my eyes and tried to change into a werecat so I could fight him off, but it wasn't working. I couldn't concentrate.

"You're not going to put me in there," I yelled, kicking and struggling.

He said nothing, just tossed me into the back of the van as though I were a crash dummy and slammed it shut.

Visions of torture chambers flashed through my brain. I felt so senseless with panic. I didn't know what to do.

The first thing I did was try to open the back doors. Of course they were locked. The pitch black of the inside of the van made me feel like I was in a tomb. As Enrique backed the van out of the garage, I felt the inside of my surroundings to find a window or something but only grasped metal all the way around. I remembered hearing that if you were locked in a trunk, you should try to kick out the taillights and wave your arm out the hole so a cop would see it and stop the car. But I felt around the back, and everything was solid. I found a panel on one side but couldn't find a release. It must have needed a screwdriver to open it. I pounded at it with my heel trying to break the compartment. Everything else in the world was plastic, why was this van still made of metal?

I sat against the side of the van and held my head.

Was he going to kill me? He could have killed me right at the house. Did he have some kind of weird torture in mind? I felt my stomach starting to heave.

I had no sense of time. I wasn't wearing a watch, and my cell phone was back in my car. My car... It was back at Luis's house. Surely someone would see it there and put two and two together when they found me missing. That was some hope.

It seemed we'd been driving for an awfully long time. He must have been taking me way out to Timbuktu.

The van stopped. After waiting a torturous amount of time, Enrique opened the door.

"Get out," he said gruffly.

I looked around and saw miles of Florida scrub pines and palmettos. We could have been anywhere.

"Are you going to tell me what's going on?"

"Sure. Since you asked, our father is anxious to see you take the final step in becoming Rogue."

"Well, he's too late. I already am a Rogue, Bozo."

He slapped me hard across the face. "Don't smart-mouth me, slut. You haven't made a human kill, have you?"

I remained silent.

"Father wants you and Luis to get married and form a nice little Rogue dynasty—the first marriage between Favrés and Rogues."

"You mean your father put him up to going out with me?" I felt I'd been slammed in the gut.

"You got it, doll." Enrique smirked. "And that first night when he rescued you—don't think that was an accident either. Our father orchestrated the whole thing."

"I don't believe you." The thought that Luis had been put up to going out with me crushed me inside and made me lose any ability to fight back. But maybe Enriqué was counting on that, making me believe that to break my spirit.

"It doesn't matter if you believe it or not."

I should have known I wasn't hot enough to get a guy like Luis without him having some ulterior motive. No, stop that! Luis was scum for taking part in it. "Why are you telling me this?"

"So you'll realize your potential part in werecat history."

He started walking me toward a medium-sized warehouse, this time firmly grasping my wrist.

"You idiot. I'm never going to cooperate now."

He slapped me hard again. "I'd like a little more respect, Miss Walsh-Bohdan. Can I call you miss hyphen? Miss hyphen, I like that. Not only are we going to seal your fate as a Rogue, we're going to kill your parents." He snickered.

I held my stinging face. "Why? They don't bother anybody." Surely he was just saying that as a threat. If my parents were gone, I'd be completely alone in the world. Who would care about me then? I swallowed hard trying to keep it together.

"Then you'll be the only remaining purebred Favré royalty."

"Bastard."

Enrique laughed. "Doesn't matter what you think of me. We're going to stick you into a cage with a human. Day-by-day, you'll get hungrier and hungrier until you won't be able to resist eating."

"And what if I don't?"

"Hmmm, let's see." He rubbed his chin with his free hand. "You're on day three of being turned. It's simple. If you don't eat within two days, you'll be dead."

As I closed my eyes and shook my head, my world spun around on itself.

Enrique opened the warehouse door with a remote control unit on his key ring. I noticed the sparkling steel on the side of the building. It was new.

We came to an internal corridor and another locked door, which he opened with a card like you'd get in a hotel. Jeez, this place was tighter than Fort Knox.

Enrique opened the door fast, pushed me inside, and pulled the door shut.

I looked around. How bizarre. It could have been the inside of a room at the Marriott. King sized bed, TV inside of a hutch, comfortable couch, a table with two chairs. Some cage this was.

I heard the toilet flush. Someone was in the bathroom. Had Enrique taken some poor homeless person captive? Maybe he'd given me a tough guy so I'd have to kill him to survive. My skin prickled with fear. As I heard him rustle around I started imagining what he might be like. Some biker skinhead, tattooed and mean? Maybe a crazed crack addict who'd want to tear me apart with his bare hands or worse?

A sandy head poked through the bathroom door.

"Kenley?"

Chapter 33

"Brendan? What are you doing here?"

"I could ask you the same thing." He hugged me and brushed the side of my face tenderly. I flinched at the sting as he touched the place where my face had hit the road.

"Who did this to you?"

"Luis's brother, Enriqué, the scum. He tackled me, and my face landed against the pavement. Who brought you here?"

Brendan looked bewildered. "A bunch of guys I don't even know. I was coming out of a bookstore on Dale Mabry and they jumped me, took me down just like nothing. I thought they were going to kill me for nosing around in the Rogue stuff too much. But now this is a pleasant surprise having you here." He smiled like we were on a date at an ice cream parlor.

"You know why they put me in here with you, don't you?" I asked.

"They wanted to make me deliriously happy?"

"No. They want me to eat you."

He grinned. "Well, that's torture I could take."

"No, guy. I'm on my third day of being a Rogue and I'm constantly hungry. My body is craving human flesh, but my mind can't accept it. They're betting my Rogue instincts will overcome my humanity and I'll have you for lunch."

"Oh." He shrank away from me and sat down on the couch. "I know you wouldn't do that...would you?"

"Of course not." As I said that, the smell of his blood, more delicious than any roast beef sandwich, made me salivate. "But I don't know. I could lose my mind or something." I licked my lips.

"Don't get any ideas now, okay?" He looked genuinely nervous, kind of twitchy and tense.

"Brendan, you're supposed to be mad at me. I've treated you horribly." I held his forearms and looked into his eyes.

"I know. The trouble is, I can't stay mad at you no matter how hard I try."

"Oh, Brendan." He was gone over me the way I had been over Luis. "Do you have any idea what time it is?"

"No, there aren't any clocks in here."

I walked over to the television and pushed the power button.

"It doesn't work. I don't even know why it's in there."

"I feel like I'm in the episode of *The Twilight Zone* where they had people in a human zoo."

"Really I wonder if they're watching us."

"Without a doubt." I sat down next to him on the couch, but his human scent made my stomach grind. Why was it I hadn't been able to bring myself to eat the rapist the other night, but I was craving Brendan? I got up.

"Was it something I said?" He tried to be jokey but looked relieved that I'd moved away from him.

"No, Brendan. In fact, over these past few days I've realized that you're my only true friend. You're the only person who would stand by me through anything."

His sandy brown hair fell over one eye "Oh right, the loyal friend, the..." he made quote marks with his fingers, "nice guy. Nice guys never get the girl, though, do they?"

I turned to face him. "Yeah, they do." I paused, wanting to be sure about what I was going to say to him. I sat on the couch and took his hand. "Brendan, I care so deeply about you."

"I...I'm stunned. I don't under—." He stopped himself abruptly and shook his head. "Oh, you mean like a friend, right?"

"No, I mean, whatever it is in my screwed up childhood that made me go for bad boys, I'm over it. I want you, Brendan, you're a hunk; you could be a GQ model. And you're sensitive and caring and deep. I should have my freaking head examined for having wanted Luis. I'm so over him."

"Really?"

"Yeah. Look, I'm in trouble, and where is Luis now, huh?" I raised my palms and looked around. "Nowhere. Out with some chick."

"Kenley, I'm flattered, but are these true feelings or are you rebounding from Luis?"

"I'm not rebounding. In fact, I keep thinking about what you said about killing your maker releasing you from the curse." Luis had never loved me. It was all an act because his father wanted us together. The more I thought about it, the more sure I became that I could stab Luis. Right in the heart the way he'd stabbed me. Right now I had to concentrate on keeping myself away from Brendan.

"Could you do that? Kill Luis?"

"At this moment, yes. In fact, I took the knife out of my parents' cabinet and put it in my room." Unable to resist the urge, I moved in a little closer to him.

"I'm encouraged," he said.

"And you know what they told me? Any old knife works. Just stick it through the victim's heart." I sat back down next to Brendan on the couch and put my head on his chest. The beating of his heart nearly drove me crazy. I loved him. Loved him and wanted to eat him at the same time.

I licked his neck.

"Mmmmm." He let out a sound of abject pleasure, then sort of caught himself and I felt his body tense and start to pull away.

Then I bit his neck, just lightly, felt the tender pulsing of his jugular. Just as he really struggled to get away from me, my senses overcame me. I crawled on top of him and pinned him down. He tried to resist, wriggling and curling beneath me, but was no match for my strength. When that didn't work, he tried to strangle me, but I pulled his hands away from my neck, as though they were child's hands. For a moment I paused, amazed at my own strength.

Full of awe at my own power, I pressed myself against him, flattening him down on the couch. As Brendan struggled beneath me, I felt the quickening of my pulse, the ears sprouting on top of my head, claws springing from my fingers.

"Kenley, what' happening?"

Still pinning Brendan to the couch, I felt my sinews tightening, my muzzle pushing out. Fur sprouted everywhere.

Then I stopped myself. What kind of a monster had I become? I knew that if I let the change overtake me, my resistance would completely evaporate, and I'd kill the only boy who had ever genuinely cared for me.

"Brendan," I said while I could still talk in a human voice. "Get away from me, now." I pushed myself away from him with hands that had claws where fingernails should be.

"How?" He pushed himself away from me on the couch, his face a mask of abject terror.

"Lock yourself in the bathroom." I hurriedly got out of my clothes while I still had opposable thumbs.

"There's no lock on the bathroom door." His voice rose in panic.

"Jam a chair under the knob. Put the dresser up against it. Do something. Fast." I could feel my snout pushing out—always the last thing to change.

Brendan scrambled up from the couch, pushed one of the heavy chairs into the bathroom and slammed the door.

I was total panther, and my stomach ground on itself as though I'd swallowed Drano. My insane hunger overtook me like a crack addict's need to freebase.

Knowing there was a human in the other room who could alleviate the pain didn't help. It also didn't help to know that I could have mown down the bathroom door as though it were a stage prop.

A hunger that drove me to the point of insanity took over my body as though I were a remote-controlled robot. Self-restraint wasn't even possible at this point. I backed up, wiggled my hindquarters and lunged for the door.

At virtually the same time I broke through the bathroom door, the outer door flung itself open.

"Let her go. Now!" a voice shouted with a frenzied urgency.

It was Luis.

Enriqué stood behind him wielding a huge dagger. "This is what father wants."

"Bullshit. If she's going to answer her Rogue destiny, it has to be of her own free will."

I was so shocked I instantly changed back into human and scrambled to put on my blouse and jeans.

"I don't give a flying rat's ass what he thinks. We are *not* forcing Kenley into doing something she's going to regret." Luis looked beat. Stringy hair hung over oily skin and dark circles ringed his eyes. "It's bad enough Father sent me on a wild goose chase to get me out of the way. Let her go."

His father had sent him away. He hadn't been with a girl after all.

Enriqué made a move to gash Luis with the knife. Luis jumped to the side. "What do you think you're doing?"

"Carrying out Father's orders."

"Since when are you so damned obedient?" Luis was able to grab the handle of the knife and the two brothers struggled with it.

Brendan whispered to me. "Let's get the knife and you can kill Luis. You'll be free."

"First we have to get the knife away from Enriqué." I looked for anything in the room that could be used as a weapon. Enriqué had Luis pinned to the floor.

I lifted up a monster lamp and crashed it over Enriqué's head.

Enriqué stopped momentarily as though a mosquito had bitten him, but it was enough for Luis to be able to smash him in the face, sending Enriqué flying in one direction and the knife in the other.

Brendan lunged for the knife and grabbed it, and Enriqué went after him. So fast I could hardly see it, Brendan stabbed Enriqué directly in the heart, then pulled the it out again and held it in a death grip as he backed away. Brendan gasped and held his chest with his other hand.

Enriqué stared down at his chest then back up at Brendan with an abject look of disbelief. As he pressed on his wound, a gusher of blood soaked through his shirt and splattered down to his pants. Enriqué fell backwards onto the floor.

Brendan had hit him in a werecat's one vulnerable place, his heart.

Luis leaned over his brother and pulled him up into his grasp, but that only caused the blood to gush out more.

"Enriqué! No!" Luis held him. "You can't die." He gazed up at Brendan and me in disbelief. "Why did you do this? Nothing can be done for him now."

Brendan and I looked at each other, so shocked we didn't know how to react. "He would have done the same to us." Brendan's voice shook so badly it sounded as though he were underwater.

Luis hugged his brother, crying, as the blackish fluid collected into a pool on the floor. I couldn't get over the thought that it was so dark, not like the bright red you see in the movies. I had such mixed feelings of relief for us, but sadness for Luis.

Brendan handed the dagger to me. "Kill Luis. Go ahead. This is your chance to break the curse."

I took the dagger in my hand and stared at Luis on the floor holding his dying brother to his chest.

Brendan gave me a nudge.

I held the knife up in the air poised directly over Luis.

☙ Chapter 34 ☙

Then I let the knife clatter to the floor.

Brendan took my hand and pulled me toward the door. "I knew you wouldn't be able to do it."

"We can't just leave him." I couldn't take my eyes off of Luis, now a crumpled heap on the floor holding Enriqué, whose eyes had frozen into a dead-stare.

"Let's go." He practically dragged me, and I went with Brendan, but my heart remained behind with Luis.

Brendan and I wandered out into the scrub forest that carried the sweet smell of dense foliage along with some underlying scent I couldn't quite identify. The dark moonless night would have been impossible for most people to navigate, but my heightened senses allowed me to see in the dark. Even though I wanted to go and collapse somewhere, I could feel the hunger grind in my stomach.

I explained to Brendan that I had to eat, so I quickly made the change to werecat, hunted, took down a deer and ate almost the whole thing in order to momentarily quell my appetite. I did all of this out of his sight, and when I was finished, I returned to find him sitting on an overturned tree.

"We'd better stay here until sunrise. Then we can probably find our way to a main road and hitch back home," Brendan said.

"I can't believe all of this has just happened." I held my hand against my pounding heart and sat down next to him.

"I can't believe you wouldn't kill Luis. We had the perfect opportunity."

I knew I was going to hear this over and over again from Brendan. "He came back to save us. How could I kill him? It's not that easy to kill someone, you know? Not for me anyway."

He had a hurt look in his eyes. "You still love him, don't you?"

I remained silent for a long time, really wanting to be honest with Brendan. I said, "No, I don't. He's a jerk and a bastard."

"We're out in the middle of nowhere and it's getting cold," Brendan said. Cold in autumn in Florida was about fifty degrees. Still, neither of us was dressed for it.

"Enriqué told me the Rogues are going to kill my parents. We have to get to them now and warn them." I stood, took Brendan's hand and tried to pull him.

"We can't do anything until morning. I have no idea where we are. We have no cell phones. We'll be wandering around aimlessly."

"I need to go now. They're going to kill my parents. Come on, please?" I pulled on his hand.

"Kenley, with no light to guide us, we could be stumbling around in the forest all night."

All I could think about was that we killed Santiago Malik's son, and the next time I saw him, he wouldn't be the nice, friendly guy I'd met while I was peeking into Luis's bedroom window. "Come on. We have to go." I started walking until Brendan was nearly out of view.

He called after me. "Come on back. You're just going to get lost."

I sighed. "I'm such a mess, I don't know what to do."

Brendan came over and hugged me, and the warmth of his body felt wonderful. I must have expended a lot of my body heat, because I felt uncharacteristically chilly.

"I think we should settle down and try to go to sleep. When the sun comes up, we'll know better what direction to go in."

"No. We have to get going now. Wait. Did you hear that?" I tipped my head toward the noise to listen better.

"I don't hear anything."

The unmistakable sound of cars drifted through my head. "It's the highway. Come on." I grabbed Brendan's arm and pulled him in the direction of the sound. It wasn't close, but it was walkable.

"Are you sure?" Brendan followed behind me.

I wasn't paying that much attention to him as I attempted to lead us in the right direction. I took a deep whiff. "Do you smell something like animal droppings?"

Brendan sniffed the air. "No. I know your senses are a lot sharper than mine are, but I can't smell anything except pine trees. I think we should stay the night in the woods."

I was not going to lay down in fire ants and palmetto bugs. Besides, I had to get to my folks. "No. Trust me on this one. We're going to come out near a farm or something."

We walked a few miles in silence. Brendan continually lagged behind, I guess as a statement of his belief that we'd get ourselves miserably lost in the dark. Then, yes! We came out on Highway 589, a fairly busy road.

"I knew it. We're on the outskirts of the Big Cat Rescue Center. I've done volunteer work there. We're only a couple of miles from my house. Enriqué must have driven me around for hours to confuse me," I said.

"It worked. His buddies did the same thing with me, and I had no idea where I was," Brendan said as he arched his back to stretch it.

"Is the Big Cat Rescue Center some kind of Rogue hiding place?" I asked.

"I'm not sure, but it would appear so."

"We have to get to my parents' house." I couldn't think of anything else. I didn't want my stupidity to be the cause of their deaths.

We tried to hitch a ride and were unsuccessful until I told Brendan to hide in the bushes, and I stood out there alone. A big red truck came to a screeching halt, and the young trucker guy was none too happy when Brendan came into view, but he was nice enough about it. I made Brendan get in first, and I climbed in after him.

"Where you headed?" the trucker asked.

"Could you drop us off at the front gate of Somerset, off North Dale?" I asked. That was where Luis's father lived.

"Are you crazy?" Brendan looked at me as though I'd lost my mind.

"No, I'm not crazy. I have to get my car before anyone finds out about Enriqué."

Brendan slammed his hands down on his lap. "Luis is probably at the house already. Is your car worth more to you than your life, and mine?"

"I parked the car about a block away, so it's not actually at the house. And Luis will be in his own little world tonight. He's not going to be thinking about my car."

"Will you two make up your minds." The trucker sighed, aggravated.

"Yeah. Somerset please," I said quickly.

"You got it, babe. I'm going right by there." He shifted and the truck started to roll.

Brendan shook his head.

"I need my car, Brendan. How else am I going to get away?"

Brendan sat, silent with his lips pursed.

Since it wasn't that far, we arrived fairly quickly. I thanked the trucker then jumped out of the truck with Brendan reluctantly following behind. We stood directly at the gate. Tiers of beautifully-kept flowers supported a marble sign that said, "Somerset—Live the Life." A line of royal palms illuminated by spotlights created a fitting backdrop.

"Come on. It's not far, and we don't have to actually pass Luis's house. You can stay out here and wait for me if you want."

Brendan thought about that for a moment then said, "No, I want to be there for you if anything happens."

"Thanks, Brendan. I appreciate that."

We hurried down the street like cat burglars, past massive houses with endless rolling lawns, perfectly manicured gardens, and carpets of petunias, zinnias and impatiens.

"Let's hurry up. I don't like being in here any more than you do," I whispered.

A car crept by us. "Oh, no," I said.

Before I could react in any way, Brendan grasped me into a clinch that could have steamed up the cover of a romance novel and gave me a passionate kiss. After I caught my breath, I said, "Are you trying to make us look innocent?"

"Yeah, a couple in love out for an early morning stroll."

"Guess it worked." I was still worried about the car that passed us, though.

We ramped up to a slight jog, and soon my trusty green jeep came into view. I was never so happy to see it. I opened the door and started to climb in, but Brendan put out a hand to hold me back. "What if it's rigged up to an explosive?"

His comment gave me pause. Now I didn't want to get in. "What should we do?"

"I'll get in."

"No, I will. These werecats don't work like that. They eat people, they don't blow them up." I got into the car, held my breath and turned the key.

The engine started like a charm and no, we did not blow up, even after Brendan got in and we rolled down the street.

"Brendan, can you look in the back? Is my purse still there?"

He rummaged around and pulled out a purple messenger bag. "You mean this?"

"Yes. Okay, that's one good thing on this sucky night. Now we have to go to my house and warn my parents."

At the first pink rays of dawn, we pulled up to my parents' house and parked in front. As we headed up my driveway, I said, "I'm going to get my ass kicked for staying out all night. You might not want to come with me." Then I stopped dead. "Plus, I have to convince them about the Rogues."

Brendan looked intently into my eyes. "I don't care about being yelled at. We're in this together now. Let's go inside."

When we were halfway up the walkway, the door exploded outward, followed by my mom, fuming like a steam engine. "Young lady, you were supposed to be grounded. Do you know your father and I have been up all night worrying our guts out? You are the most selfish...If you don't straighten out, we're going to have to send you to school in...England. See how you can fraternize with your trouble-maker friends then."

Dad came over and hugged me. "Oh kitten, we were so worried about you. Thank God you're home."

"You'd better have a really good explanation." Mom looked at Brendan confused that the boy who was perfect son-in-law material had led me astray. "You mean you were with Brendan?"

"I'm sorry Dad, Mom."

"Sorry, Mr. and Mrs. Walsh-Bohdan." Brendan smiled a little then sighed and cast his eyes downward. The perfect son-in-law had disappointed his future in-laws.

"You'd better have a good explanation." Mom tapped her finger against her folded arms, a little less angry once she realized Brendan was in the picture.

"I do. Mom, Dad, Rogue cats captured us. They were trying to...turn me."

"They didn't, did they?" Mom scrutinized me.

"Um, no. We have something really important to tell you, though."

Mom raised her eyebrows. "You're not pregnant, are you?"

With everything that was going on with my life, my mom picked this one thing to obsess over. "Oh, I wish that was all we had to worry about. No. You've got to get out of here. The Rogue cats are going to come and kill you." I pulled on Mom's arm trying to get her to move. "Hurry. Pack a bag and let's go."

"Wait a minute." She remained planted in her spot. "I'm not going anywhere."

"Mrs. Walsh-Bohdan," Brendan said.

"Call me Mimi."

"Mimi. There has been an influx of Rogue cats into the Tampa Bay area. They're using it as a home base for this huge massacre of a good deal of the human race," Brendan said.

"We've always thought that there were just a handful of these vampire cats. We didn't even think any of them were in the States," Dad said.

"They've been gaining in number for the past few years, turning out new Rogues like an assembly line." Brendan put his arm around me.

"I need a moment to absorb all of this," Dad said.

"And you and your husband being in the royal Favré line, they're going to go after you and kill you because they'd like to get rid of all the Favré royals."

Mom held her hand to her chest. "Well, uh, we're not anything like that. We're just normal people."

"It's okay, Mom. You're officially out of the closet. Brendan knows everything about us."

"Mimi," Dad looked directly at her, really serious. "I think we should leave. Pack a couple of bags and head off for the weekend. It couldn't hurt."

"Nonsense," Mom said. "With our security system, our house in like Fort Knox. No one could ever possibly penetrate it."

"These people are monsters. They'll break your doors down." I couldn't believe my mom's stubbornness. "Mom, Brendan just killed the Rogue leader's oldest son in order to...save me." It just hit me that Brendan had rescued me, not Luis.

Dad took both of my hands in his. "You and Brendan killed the leader's son? Mimi, I think we should listen to Kenley and leave."

"Absolutely not." Mom made a downward motion with her hands.

I could have killed her myself for her unbending stubbornness. "Mom, you are so pig-headed. Just for once, could you please listen to me?"

"Kenley, don't talk to your mother that way. Mimi, if you don't want to leave, I'm with you," Dad said. "I know that the house is extremely secure, hurricane-resistant, and made of the best high-tech materials available."

"So on the off-hand chance that we're going to be attacked by Rogues, though goodness-knows, I don't know why they'd bother to kill a couple of middle-aged ex-royals. We'll be safe." Mom looked satisfied with her conclusion.

Hot tears streamed down my cheeks. "I'm pleading with you now because I love you both. Granted, we've had our differences, but come on. Give me the benefit of the doubt and let's go."

"No." Mom planted herself in the doorway, her legs rooted to the spot like tree trunks.

"What are you going to lose by getting out of here?" I pleaded with her, trying not to break down into a sniveling mess.

"I just don't see that it's necessary, Kenley. Even if you're not exaggerating, our house is extremely secure."

"Fine. Go ahead and think I'm exaggerating. I've tried my best." I stormed past them to my room, grabbed some of my favorite things, along with some toiletries, cash I had on hand and a credit card and threw them into a backpack and duffle bag and hurried down the stairs. Then I went back to get the Dagger of Bastet, wrapped it in a towel and threw it in my bag along with the werecat book Brendan had given me. As an afterthought, I dashed into my parents' bedroom and snagged my mom's big address book. I was going to need if I was ever going to find my roots.

"Where do you think you're going?" Mom tried to stop me by grasping my arm.

I pulled away. "I'm going to save my own life, and if you don't want to come with me, I'll miss you, but I can't make you leave. Bye, Mom. Bye, Dad." I hugged and kissed both of them, feeling as though I was leaving part of myself behind. "Come on, Brendan, let's go."

We took off toward the forest in my Jeep. "Brendan, you've got to excuse me, but I have to eat. Feeding on animals seems to quell my hunger to some extent."

"Go right ahead. Better them than me."

All the while I was driving I kept looking in my rearview mirror expecting the Rogues to be pursuing us. But then they wouldn't be so obvious; they'd be sneaky and catch us when we weren't looking.

I parked by the side of the road and dashed into the woods. I'd gotten so good at hunting that it took me only minutes to stalk a deer and bring it down. With my stomach pleasantly full, I returned to Brendan. I wiped my mouth with a tissue to make sure I didn't have blood on my lips.

"Feel better?" he asked.

"Oh, yeah. At least I feel kind of human now."

"Human is good."

We headed north until we came to a sign that said, *Welcome to the Orange Blossom Motor Home Park—Where the livin' is easy.* "Turn right here," Brendan said.

"You live in here?"

"Yeah. My parents have been dragging me around the country chasing various phenomena ever since I can remember. It's a pretty nice RV park as they go."

"That must have been rough on you, moving so much."

He shrugged. "Yeah, I suppose."

We passed by a recreation center, tennis courts and a pool. This place obviously housed snowbirds who liked to travel in comfort. "Turn left after the pool."

We pulled up to Brendan's family home—a super deluxe RV.

"This is huge." I'd never seen anything so big in my life. Silver with royal blue swooshes across the outside. It even appeared to have an upstairs. The sides pushed out to make the inside bigger.

"Not so huge when you have to live in it with your parents. That's why I spend a lot of time outdoors."

Mrs. Fournier rushed up to us on the front walkway dressed in jeans, tennis shoes and a purple hoodie. Tall and thin with chin length brown hair, she hugged Brendan then me. "Thank God you're all right. What happened? I know you would have called if you could have."

How different these parents were who trusted their son instead of always assuming the worst like my mom and dad. Mom and Dad. I swallowed hard at the thought that I might never see them again.

Brendan's little sister played by herself with a couple of My Little Ponies in the front yard. She looked like about five.

"This is Aubrey," Brendan said. "Aubrey, this is Kenley."

A little cherub with curly blonde hair and big blue eyes, she gawked up at me with interest. "Hi." She raised a chubby little hand and waved.

I waved back. "Hi, Aubrey. Whatcha got there?" I crouched down next to her.

She held up a purple pony. "This is Dancer." She spun the pony, making it do a little pirouette in the sand. "And this is Belle. She likes to dance, too." Belle joined Dancer in a gallopy trot.

"They're beautiful, Aubrey." I petted one of the little ponies then straightened up as Mr. Fournier hurried down the steps to the RV, pulling a stylishly faded sweater over his well-toned body, and clasped his arms around his son.

"Oh Brendan, we were so worried. Thank God." He was tall with salt and pepper hair, an older version of Brendan. "Where have you been? Why didn't you call us?"

"I couldn't, Dad." Brendan sighed and squeezed his eyes shut, his arms still firmly wrapped around his dad.

Mr. Fournier patted his son on the shoulder. "I just put on a pot of coffee. Come on inside."

His family was not at all what I expected. I guess I thought being cryptozoologists they'd be strange—hippie or biker types. These people looked completely normal.

We walked up the steps of the massive, elaborate motor home. It had two bedrooms, with a short loft for Aubrey, sides that pushed out electronically to make more room and a wide screen, high definition television. The Pre Raphaelite paintings on the wall caught my attention. Waterhouse and Rossetti. Strange for a motor home. We sat in high-backed chairs at an oak table in the spacious kitchen facing the living room engulfed in the aroma of freshly baked muffins, waffles and sausages. Brendan's dad poured steaming coffee. The smell of waffles already in the waffle iron made my stomach growl since hunger constantly consumed me.

We told them the whole story, leaving nothing out, and remarkably enough, his parents believed us. Every word.

Mr. Fournier dished out sausages and waffles with maple syrup talking about werecats as matter-of-factly as if he had been discussing baseball scores. "We've been watching these werecats for years. They've been growing in numbers, and we think they're planning something big, a coup of some sort."

I couldn't get over how Brendan's family looked as though they stepped out of an LL Bean catalog, like they should have been at the summerhouse in Maine, not in a glorified trailer in Florida hunting werecats. Plus they all looked so calm, even knowing that the Rogues were most certainly after us.

"Yeah," Mrs. Fournier dished some strawberries over her waffles. "We've been nervous as heck about Brendan nosing around the WC's. They're a vicious lot. And you can see they'll do anything." She touched the back of my hand. "I'm not saying your parents are like that, dear. They're a different sort. We know that they're peace loving."

As I ate waffles and sausages that didn't even come close to satisfying my hunger, I wondered how these people could calmly eat their breakfast when their son had just killed the son of the Rogue leader, and the world as they knew it was shattering all around them.

"We've got to get out of here." Mr. Fournier said as he wiped his face with a linen napkin.

Mrs. Fournier's face clouded over. "We need to talk." She pulled her husband by the arm into the bedroom.

"Your parents are kind of calm about this," I said.

"It's been their world for so long these strange phenomena don't phase them. They get off on it in a way."

Though I didn't want to eavesdrop, my super senses let me hear the parents bickering in the other room.

"We can't just pick up everything and leave, Cliff."

"You know those people. They'll hunt Brendan down, and they won't stop until they kill him."

"But the girl has been turned. She might rip us apart in our sleep," Brendan's mom said.

"That's kind of dramatic."

"Dramatic, I'm being realistic. You've let this spook-hunting destroy any kind of normal life we might have had."

"That's just the thing, Marcia. I don't want a normal life."

"Well I do. We're not going."

"We are. We can't let those monsters get our son."

"If you hadn't insisted upon coming to Tampa to find them, they wouldn't even know about our son. If you hadn't been adamant he make friends with Kenley, he wouldn't be in this danger."

"Brendan. You mean your parents put you up to being friendly to me?" I felt like I'd been stabbed in the heart. Again.

"What?"

"I'm a werecat. I can hear your parents talking in the other room. He put you up to making friends with me."

"Yeah, well, my father did, but he didn't tell me to fall in love with you, which I have." His glum expression led me to believe he regretted his feelings for me. I didn't wonder why.

"You fell in love with me?"

"Yeah." His eyes rested lightly on me then darted away.

I put my hand over his. "Thanks, Brendan."

"For what?"

"For making me feel wanted. I have feelings for you, too." I wasn't sure what they were yet, but I definitely had them.

A spark lit in Brendan's eyes and he gave me a slight smile.

"How did your parents even know about me?"

"They're all hooked in to the cryptozoologists network. They knew you were the last of the royal Favré line."

"How did they know when *I* didn't know."

Brendan shrugged. "Like I said, they have a network."

It was all too weird. I pictured myself being in a feature article in the *Cryptozoologist Gazette*. Luis's father had wanted him to marry me, and Brendan's parents had wanted him to make friends with me. Didn't anyone like me for myself? "I can't help all of this." I felt like I was going to lose it again.

"Come on." He put a finger under my chin to lift my face up toward him. "Don't give me that look. Everything's going to work out."

"Now your dad likes me and your mom hates me."

"No, Mom's just a worrier. She'll come around." Brendan leaned over and kissed me on the cheek. "We'll take care of you. Don't worry."

As he did that, I felt as though I really did care for him. I could make a life with this person who was so infinitely understanding and loveable.

The parents' conversation continued.

"Look, Marcia, she's a real werecat. We'll never get the opportunity to study one this closely. It might never happen again."

"I don't know about this."

"Besides, we have to think about the girl. We have to rescue her so she's not pressured into a barbaric life with the Rogues. Maybe we can help her out, you know, find a cure."

"And how are we going to do that?"

"We have the resources."

Mr. and Mrs. Fournier emerged from the bedroom. His mom looked as though she'd been crying. His dad had his arm around her. "We've decided we're all going to get out of town. It's getting a little too dangerous around here. Kenley, I'll go hook up your car to the back of the rig. Let me have your car keys."

"Wow! Thanks." I handed over my key ring relieved that we'd be leaving.

"What about my Vespa? Brendan looked pained. I can't leave Sadie."

"You can load her into the back. There's plenty of room."

"Okay. That's good."

Brendan's dad went outside and walked around to the back of the RV. I heard him start my car.

Mrs. Fournier slid into the back bedroom leaving the two of us alone for a moment.

"See? I told you they'd help us."

"They're pretty cool."

"I'd better go outside and help." Brendan pressed my hand, gave me a nod and went outside.

As Brendan and his dad hurried to get the outside of the motor home ready for the trip, I sat alone at the kitchen table. Brendan's mom peeked out of the bedroom, no doubt hoping I'd be gone. Seeing I wasn't, she probably felt she had to make some conversation. "Want me to give you the tour?" She smiled with her mouth but not with her eyes.

"Yes, please. This is a beautiful RV."

"Thanks. We like it. It had to be roomy and comfortable to fit the four of us. This is the bathroom. You'll see that there's a full shower and stackable washer dryer."

"Wow. This is full sized."

"Then the bedroom. Notice the queen sized bed." She led me into a room with plush comforter and matching curtains. "Watch this." She flipped a switch and a flat screen TV emerged from a cabinet in front of the window. "And this is the amazing part." She opened a door in the back center.

"Another room?"

"Yes. This RV is called a toy-hauler, because it's made to haul people's motorcycles, and such, but we've made it into a bedroom for Brendan." Bookcases abutted a small light colored wooden desk. The single bed against the back wall folded up into a couch. I saw Brendan and Mr. Fournier through the back picture window as they connected my car to the trailer hitch.

"This is the most amazing thing I've ever seen." The room told a lot about Brendan, the neatness, his love of learning.

"Yes, we knew that he needed his own space."

We walked through the lavish motor home back out to the front. "You'll notice that there's a little loft in front for Aubrey." A narrow staircase led to a loft with a twin bed and pink dresser surrounded by safety railings.

The loft was cute, but I could just imagine what it did to a little girl to be constantly uprooted.

"How often have you moved in the past?

"Too often."

I could tell by the tension in her face that was a sore subject. She started doing the dishes.

"I just want to say, thank you so much, Mrs. Fournier. I mean for upsetting your lives for me."

"Don't thank me. I didn't want to go. Brendan and Aubrey have just gotten settled in their schools and I've made a few friends. I hate being constantly uprooted. It's worse than being in the military." Brendan's mom busied herself quietly making something that looked like brownies. "And we're not leaving just to protect you, it's for Brendan, too." Her mouth formed a hard line as she talked.

"I'm sorry." I wanted to shrink down into nothingness and fall into the crack of the ivory leather sofa.

Something inside of her seemed to thaw. She stopped fussing with her food prep and looked over at me with a sad expression. "Ah, it's not your fault you're in this situation." She shook her head. "I know that."

"Maybe it *is* my fault."

"Look on the bright side. This is going to be an educational experience for all of us." She dried her hands on the dishtowel and sat down next to me on the couch.

"How so?"

"We can help you get in touch with your werecat nature in a way your parents never could...or never wanted to."

"Really? How?

"We've been studying these creatures..." Mr. Fournier glanced down at the floor. "Uh...the werecats for a long time, and we know virtually everything about them."

Well, thank you Mrs. Fournier." I still didn't get a warm and fuzzy feeling from her, even though she was making an attempt to be friendly. And this was the woman who was going to be my new mom? The madness of the situation hit me. "I'd better go out and help the guys."

Brendan and his dad had everything wrapped up and ready to go in an hour, and we were on our way.

"Where are we going now?" Aubrey asked, irritated about having been pulled away from playing with her ponies in the sand. She climbed up to her little loft and lay on her stomach in her bed facing us with her hands on the safety bars like a prisoner. The sight of her broke my heart.

Brendan and I sat in his back bedroom on the fold down couch watching Tampa, Florida, disappear as we headed north. Brendan had his arm around me, giving me the only feeling of protection I had in the whole world.

I hated myself for the fact that I couldn't think about anything except Luis. How he risked his life to set me free. The vision of him in tears, bent over his dead brother, played over and over in my mind. This mixed in with our first night together was fast sending me into a spiral of despair. Tears rolled down my eyes; I couldn't help it.

"What's the matter?"

"I'm a Rogue now. If I don't feed in two days, I'll die. Your mom doesn't like the fact that I'm a Rogue."

"She'll adapt. She's had to put up with my dad all these years." He gave a little chuckle then, seeing that I didn't respond, took on a pensive expression.

"She's worried I'll go berserk and kill everyone."

"I know you wouldn't do that. My parents trust you. Mom was just getting carried away today." I felt sadder and sadder as we drove further away from Tampa.

"If they trust me, they don't know anything about Rogues because sometimes we can't help ourselves. That's the honest truth. I would have taken you down if Luis hadn't burst through the door."

"In the end, I don't think you would have."

"Maybe you're right. I don't know." Maybe he was.

He hugged me as though he never wanted to let me go.

My cell phone rang. "I wonder who that could be."

"Please don't answer that," Brendan said with a pleading look in his eyes.

It had to be Luis. When I looked at the number and didn't recognize it, my misery factor multiplied. "I have to answer it." I pressed the button. "Hello?"

"Kenley. Thank God you're okay. Where are you?"

"Who's this?"

"It's Orlando." Orlando, the one member of the Claw Club who had some shred of humanity.

"Hi!"

"Listen, I have to tell you something, and I'm probably going to get freaking crucified for it, and you'll hear it in the news eventually, but here goes. Kenley…" He hesitated.

"Tell me."

"All right." His voice caught and cracked. "The Rogues broke into your house and killed your parents. Not just killed them but tore them apart and demolished the whole house." He was silent for a few moments then said, "The house is practically like matchsticks. I was worried you were in there, too."

I couldn't speak. Even though I'd known it was coming, nothing could prepare me for it. I had the outside hope that maybe they'd come to their senses and left.

"Are you sure Mom and Dad were in there?" There had to have been some mistake. They couldn't have gone that way.

"Yes, they found the bodies and identified them. I hate telling you this, but I don't know who else would." His voice sounded small and quiet. "You okay, kid?"

Worried that if I tried to actually talk I'd fall apart, I squeaked out a "Yeah."

"You're not alone, are you?" Orlando asked.

"No, I'm with a good friend."

"That's a relief. You know you've got to leave town, right?"

"I'm already out of the area."

"Smart move, kid. Is there anything I can do to help?"

"No, thanks, I'll be okay."

"Who is it?" Brendan pressed his head up against the outside of the phone to try to listen.

"Orlando, hang on a sec, okay?" I shook my head, too numb even to cry and said to Brendan, "Mom and Dad were killed." After I said that, sadness flooded into me. I had to purse my lips to keep myself together, to keep from falling apart. "Mom's so stubborn. I should have tried harder." I pressed my fingers against my eyes to keep from crying, but it didn't work. Tears started trickling down my cheeks.

Brendan grasped me by the shoulders and looked directly into my eyes. "You did everything you possibly could. I don't want you blaming yourself. It was completely out of your control."

"Yeah." I took some deep breaths and put the phone back up to my ear.

"Okay, I'm back," I said to Orlando.

"There's something else." Orlando cleared his throat. "They have Michelle."

"No! God, no! Are they going to kill her?"

"No. Those Claw Club bitches have gotten their hooks into her. They're going to turn her."

"Thanks, O. You're the only one of the Claw Club who ever cared at all."

"Don't mention it, kid. Listen, you keep in touch. Let me know where you are and what you're doing." Orlando hung up.

I sat there in silence and shock for the longest time, unable to speak or think, as Brendan held me. Then the reality of the whole thing hit me and I collapsed into myself, crying silently so hard I couldn't take a breath. The only way I could get any air was to take short gasps. Finally I had to let it out and sob until I felt like my guts would explode.

"I know. I know." Brendan pressed me against his chest and rubbed circles on my back.

"They're all I have."

He kissed the top of my head. "We're your family now, Kenley."

I sat there settled into his arms for a good long time as we watched the highway pass behind us. I shook my head to clear my senses and sat up. "Brendan, we have to go back."

"You're kidding."

"I'm not. They have Michelle. She's like a sister to me. We grew up together."

He stiffened and sat upright. "But we just left. And Luis father is going to be after the both of us."

"I can't abandon Michelle."

"What about abandoning me? You'll be leading the werecat mafia right to me." He looked at me with a hurt, ruddy expression, like he was trying to keep his emotions in check but couldn't quite do it.

"They want me, not you. My marrying Luis is key to their plans, but that is not going to happen. I could never trust any of them again."

"No. You can't put me and my family through this and then change your mind. Besides, you wouldn't be safe back in Tampa.

"Ask your parents, please?" I'm begging you, Brendan. I need to go back. I can't leave Michelle to those monsters." I clutched at the front of his shirt.

He paused, thinking. "All right. We'll go back under one condition."

"What's that?"

"You have to promise that in order to break the Rogue curse and live a normal life, you'll kill Luis."

"Kill Luis? The Rogues would put out a contract on me if I did that."

"Are you kidding? Since you've already screwed up their plans they're probably going to kill you anyway. No doubt they have someone trying to find you right now."

My muddled mind couldn't make sense of anything at that point. "I'll think about it."

"Don't think."

"OK." I hesitated. I thought about the ways Luis had betrayed me, the fact that he didn't love me at all and had just been doing his father's bidding when he went out with me. "I promise. I'll kill Luis."

⚜ Chapter 35 ⚜

"Let's break the news that we have to go back to your parents," I said, trying to get him out of his seat.

Brendan shook his head. "No, I can't tell them; you tell them.

"I hate doing this, but okay. I can't leave Michelle to the wolves." I made my way up to the front, careful to hold onto the wall as the RV bounced over some uneven highway. Aubrey sat in her loft playing with some glam hip-hop Barbie dolls, making a blonde and brunette doll talk to each other, trying to make up for her lack of playmates, obviously. Maybe this life would make her more creative.

Mrs. Fournier, who sat reading, looked up at me and I could tell she wanted to like me, but she felt really awkward with me. What I was about to say wasn't going to help things a bit.

I staggered out to the front room, my face a tear-stained mess, and sat down next to her. "Mrs. Fournier, you've all been so great to me..." I broke up crying, unable to speak and sank down onto the couch.

"What is it?" She pulled off her reading glasses and looked at me. Her eyebrows pushed upward causing her forehead to wrinkle.

"The Rogues killed my parents."

"What?" Mr. Fournier craned his neck looking back at me and nearly ran into a gas tanker.

"Careful, Cliff."

"What did you say?" He looked straight ahead at the road as he talked.

"The Rogues. They killed my parents." My chest heaved and I cried again, and Mrs. Fournier got up to comfort me.

She sat me down on the couch and held me. "I have to go back home."

"We have to stop and talk about this." Mr. Fournier pulled off at the first exit and parked in the nearest gas station.

Brendan wandered in from the other room. He sat in one of the living room chairs, stared down at the carpet, crossed his legs and nervously tapped his foot. He looked sad, angry and loveable all at the same time.

"They have my best friend, Michelle, and they're going to turn her into a Rogue. I can't let that happen. She wouldn't even have been involved in any of this if it hadn't been for me."

"Cliff, I think we should take Kenley home," Brendan's mom said.

Mr. Fournier sat down in a chair across from the couch. "Kenley, it's not safe for you to go back there. You have to think about the consequences of your actions." He sat leaning toward me.

"I can't think about that. I have to help Michelle. I know I've been selfish throughout this whole thing, and now I have to think of someone besides myself."

"But we planned to help you find other relatives, find out about your roots. We offered you all that, and you're giving us up for someone who didn't care enough to find out the truth about what was going on with your life?" Mr. Fournier said.

"Mr. Fournier, she's like a sister to me. If those monsters turn her I'll never forgive myself."

"And most importantly, we have to find the antidote for you," he said.

He didn't have to say that. My mortality was ticking off in my head like a time bomb. I had a day and a half left. "If I don't drink human blood, which I am not going to do, I have a day and a half left to live."

"Cliff, I think we should let Kenley help her friend," Mrs. Fournier said.

"We need to discuss this some more." He pursed his lips and rubbed his finger against the side of his nose.

"There's no discussing it." Brendan, who had been silent, stood up. "Kenley's promised to stab Luis in the heart. That's the real reason we're going back. I think we should let her."

"That's right." I nodded my head and looked away, knowing well that wasn't my entire reason.

"For God's sake, Brendan. Be a little more sensitive to Kenley. She just lost her parents, don't pressure her into killing Luis," his dad said.

Brendan looked remorseful then said, "I didn't pressure her. It's what she wants."

"I'm your father and we have to think about your safety, too. You were the one who actually put the knife into Enriqué."

"I could get in my Jeep and drive back alone. That would let you take your son to safety."

Brendan stared at me. "You'd leave us just like that?"

"I can't help it."

Brendan stormed into the other room and slammed the door.

"Oh, Brendan." Mrs. Fournier started to go after him then stopped herself. I could almost read her mind, saying, *See what this girl has done to our family?*

"Let me go back to Tampa by myself. I don't want to put Brendan in danger."

"No, I can't let you go back by yourself. If we go back, we're all going back together."

"Like I said before, I can't leave Michelle at their mercy. I'd never be able to look myself in the mirror again."

Mr. Fournier gazed at me intently. "I know you can't, nor should you desert your friend. Hang on. I'm turning this baby around." Mr. Fournier started up the RV and u-turned onto the highway heading south.

The ride back was strained. I sat in a chair in the living room, because I didn't especially want to be alone with Brendan, because I felt guilty. Guilty that he loved me in a way I wasn't sure I could return and guilty that I said I'd kill Luis when I knew I probably couldn't.

As Mrs. Fournier drove, his wife sat in the passenger seat and it seemed they were making some sort of plan for Brendan's safety, like maybe sending him away. I was too nervous to listen.

I felt terrible. I also wondered about my real motive. Was I going back to rescue Michelle or be with Luis? No, after I found out that Luis's father had put him up to pretending to be in love with me, I could never go back to him.

We finally crossed the city line into Tampa, pulled into the RV park and settled into the same spot we were in before all of this took place.

Mr. Fournier quietly unhooked my Jeep. Brendan was acting a little chilly toward me. He was so sensitive and intuitive he could probably tell that I still had feelings for Luis.

"Do you want to stay with us?" Mr. Fournier removed the trailer hookup from the rear bumper.

"No. Thank you, though." I nodded my head.

"Where will you go?"

"I'm going to go find Michelle. She's the reason I came back after all." As an afterthought I said, "I don't even think the werecats will be after Brendan. It's me they want."

"Good luck to you, Kenley. Remember, if you ever need help, we're here." Mr. Fournier held out his hand and I shook it, then he hugged me and patted my back.

"Thanks, Mr. Fournier I truly appreciate all you've done for me."

I left, not wanting to put them in more danger than I already had.

I was kind of glad Brendan was distancing himself from me because I wouldn't have to keep my promise to kill Luis. I was sure I couldn't do it anyway.

What a wild goose chase. What a stupid thing to put Brendan and his family through all this, then in the end to reject their unbelievable kindness. Maybe I'd been wrong to go back for Michelle. Was I doomed to always second-guess myself?

I drove the long way around so I wouldn't have to go by my house. For one thing, I wasn't emotionally prepared. For another, there could be Rogues waiting to kill me. Brendan was right. If they thought I wasn't going to cooperate, they would come after me to make sure I didn't start up the Favré royal line again.

Actually, if they were waiting for me, going to my best friend's house didn't seem like the smartest option either. But what else could I do?

Barely holding myself together, I pulled over to the side of the road a few blocks away from Michelle's house and lay my head down on top of the steering wheel. I had only one and a half more days before I'd die if I didn't eat human flesh or figure out a cure. Could I have been more screwed?

At dusk I decided to risk it and drive past Michelle's house. Just my luck, Michelle's beat up white Toyota was gone. Her Mom was out, too. Luckily, I still had her key on my key chain.

I parked my car down the street from Michelle's house.

My cell phone rang. When I looked at the caller ID, my heart nearly stopped.

Chapter 36

"Luis?"

"Where are you?"

Damn, I'd have to be absolutely crazy to trust him. Every fiber of my being knew I shouldn't even talk to him. I hesitated. "Why do you ask?"

"Because I'm worried sick about you, for God's sake."

"Stop being so fake. Enriqué told me how your father put you up to turning me."

"No. Yeah, initially that was true, but I fell in love with you. That's why I seriously tried to discourage you from taking up The Life."

"You're so deceitful; you put me off in a way you knew would make me beg you to be turned. And it worked, didn't it?"

"I didn't want it to work. I swear. You have to believe me."

I rubbed my temple. "What about Michelle? I heard some Rogues were trying to turn her."

"Oh, that's the Claw Club girls. It's just because they like her and want her for themselves. I don't think they've done it yet."

"If they were going to, when would they do it?"

"Probably tonight in the special clearing in the woods."

The Rogues might have wanted to lure me there to kill me. "I don't trust you. I don't trust anybody. The Rogues want me dead, don't they?"

"No one ever wanted you dead."

"I don't believe it. What about my parents? They weren't bothering anyone. They didn't want anything to do with the family."

"Oh, Kenley, I'm so sorry about that. You have to believe I had nothing to do with it."

"I don't know what I believe."

"The Rogues wanted to kill everyone in the royal line except for you, because you were going to..."

"What."

"You were going to marry me and unify the two houses."

I felt like he'd stabbed squarely in the gut and then twisted the knife.

"Can I see you now?" he asked.

"No. Are you crazy? After your henchmen killed my parents?"

"Kenley *they* aren't *me*. I want nothing to do with them. I despise them."

"I have to think. A lot has happened, and I don't even know what my feelings are." Besides, I had to wait for Michelle, but I wasn't going to tell him that.

"You sure? I'm so worried about you. I don't even know where you are."

I took a deep breath. "Yeah. And it's going to stay that way." Then I had an afterthought. "Luis, promise me one thing."

"Anything. Name it."

"Don't let them kill Brendan or his parents. He was just trying to protect me when he killed Enriqué."

He hesitated. "Yes, because it's what you want, I'll make sure of it."

"Thank you for that." I hung up.

I waited some more, but no one came home, so I left my car parked down the street, grabbed my overnight bag and headed for Michelle's house. I inserted my key into the door, hoping they hadn't changed the locks. It didn't open. *Damn.* I twisted it some more and the lock clicked over.

Once inside, I realized just how beat I was. I looked around Michelle's room. It was such a girl's room compared to my old room that didn't exist anymore. Flowered Laura Ashley sheets had curtains to match. No posters of grunge and Goth bands like my bedroom. Instead, she had framed prints: a goldfish in a cylindrical container by Matisse, a girl with red hair sitting on a park bench in Paris by Manet. There was an eerie lack of clutter.

No matter. A (probably false) sense of security kicked in and I keeled over onto Michelle's foo-foo bed and crashed.

It must have been hours later when I heard the front door open. "Michelle?"

"Who's there?" A trim, petite fourty-ish woman wearing a bright green sweater, jeans and matching green sandals burst into the room. She took one look at me and screamed an ear-shattering, "Aaeeeiiiiiii!"

"Mrs. Paglia." I jumped up and shook the sleepiness out of my head. "I'm sorry I just came in to see Michelle. I didn't know where else to go."

"Kenley! Oh my God!" She held her chest as though she was having a heart attack. "We thought you were dead." First she pressed her hand flat against her throat and stared at me, then she sat down and hugged me. "Honey, I'm so sorry—horrified—about what happened to your mom and dad. We heard the sirens from blocks away, there was such a commotion. Everyone's been worried that the people who killed your parents kidnapped you. I can't believe you're okay. Thank God!"

Her burst of emotion brought on another crying jag. I tried to calm down. "The truth is that I left because I knew what was going to happen. I tried to get Mom and Dad to leave, but you know how stubborn Mom can be." At that moment it hit me. I'd never see my parents again—never be embarrassed at their crass materialism or exasperated at Mom's pig-headedness. How I wished I could have them back. A constricted feeling in my throat turned into a rush of pressure in the backs of my eyes. I started crying so hard I thought I'd choke.

Michelle's mom held me. I sank my head into her fragrant sweater. "I know it's horrible, but it's going to be all right," she said.

"I'm sorry." I gagged, hardly able to talk.

After several minutes I still couldn't stop.

Finally, I pulled it together enough to talk. "Where's Michelle?"

Mrs. Paglia rose and sat in the frilly chair next to the bed. "I don't know. I'm worried about her. She's been acting so strange lately. She hasn't been doing her volunteer work. She's been hanging around with these girls: Molly, Kristen and Sarah."

"The Claw Club."

"The what?" Mrs. Paglia's eyes widened and her mouth hung open.

"It's just a bunch of girls and their posse at school."

"I'm worried that they're a bad influence on her. Michelle's always been so sensible." Michelle's mom fussed with the doilies on the arm of the chair.

"Really. I used to be sensible, too."

"Sounds like you had your head in the right place to get out of town and save yourself. Speaking of that, you need to go to the police and tell them you're safe." She made a move to get her cell phone.

I shook my head. "I'm afraid the killers will come after me."

"How do you know who the killers are?" she asked.

"They kidnapped Brendan and me, but we got away."

"You're kidding. Who are they?" She put up her hand like a stop sign. "Wait, I don't want to know."

"They're bad news, that's all I can say."

"Did they follow you here?" She looked left and right.

"No, absolutely not."

"Maybe you can get in the witness protection program."

"There's no witness protection from these people."

Mrs. Paglia knit her brow and leaned forward whispering. "Is it mafia?"

That struck me funny in a weird inappropriate way. "I wish. They're worse than that. Much worse."

She gave a quick gasp. "Does this have anything to do with the change in Michelle?"

To tell her or not to tell her. "I don't think so. She'll be okay." Yes, I should have told Michelle's mom to get her away from these people, but I couldn't. I had to leave that decision to my friend. I knew damned well her mom couldn't have stopped her anyway.

The front door opened and Michelle rushed into the room. "Kenley! You're alive. I was worrying my guts out." Since I was still sitting on the bed, Michelle leaned over and hugged me.

"I'm alive all right, beat to hell, though. It's so great to see you. You have no idea." I shook my head, grasped Michelle's hand and felt the tears start to well up again, but I swallowed my feelings and stopped myself.

"I'm sorry about your parents," she said, nearly sobbing. She held my hand. "More than sorry, but I don't know what else to say."

"Thanks, Michelle. You're the best."

"Are you girls hungry?"

We both said "Yeah" at the same time. I was sad, upset, crazed and grief-stricken, but I could have eaten a bear. My hunger for humans only flared up when something provoked me, like being alone with Brendan in the hotel room. I had to think about why that was. Probably because I got physically excited and the hunger went along with it.

Mrs. Paglia cooked us hamburgers, which we sat in Michelle's room and ate.

I practically inhaled two burgers without taking a breath. Michelle looked at me a little weirdly for eating so much, so fast, since I used to pick at my food and take my time.

"Michelle." I took a sip of my iced tea. "We could beat around the bush here, but I don't have much time. I know they've been trying to turn you. Orlando told me."

"Yeah, so what of it? You're a werecat, aren't you?" Michelle said this so casually I couldn't believe it.

"You know?"

"Uh, yeah," she said as she wrapped her mouth around her burger.

"I am, but that's because I was stupid. I let my insane crush on Luis sway me into being turned. Also, I was one already by nature. But you know what's really involved, right?" I put my food aside and said this right into her face.

"You have to eat people. So?" She pulled away and took a sip of her drink, all nonchalant.

"So? You know that the Rogues are killing the homeless people don't you?"

"Yeah, I know, and I had a hard time with it at first, but now I'm thinking I don't have to be like that. I can just kill bad people."

I was shocked. "How can you be so indifferent? You've dedicated your life to helping these people, and you're going to join the Rogues who are trying to wipe them out?"

"Yeah, I know." She wrapped her arms around her stomach as though it hurt.

"At the rate they're creating Rogues, there aren't going to be enough bad people to go around. I think half the school's been turned," I said.

"You're exaggerating. Anyway, what's 'bad?' It's a subjective thing. Becoming a Rogue means immortality, you know that, don't you?" Michelle said that last part as though she didn't want to admit that was a big part of her motive.

"I know, but listen. You could be a Favré and live for a thousand years. Why would you want more than that? You know the difference, right?"

"Yeah, I do. My mind's made up."

"Do me a favor. Just give it some more thought. You can always do it later. Luis took me out and tried to get me to make a kill, and I couldn't do it. It was horrible. And you know what? If I don't kill someone in another day, I'm going to die, which is most probably what's going to happen."

"Kenley, no. You can kill someone. Go out and find a murderer. Or a corporate CEO." She smirked then quickly frowned.

"It's not up to me to take those people's karma into my own hands."

"You've been brainwashed by all those hippie environmentalists you hang out with at your Environmental meetings. Karma. Sheesh." She looked up in the air.

"Listen, nobody escapes karma, and I'm not going to be the one to take the law into my own hands."

"We'll see. I'm going out." Michelle gathered up our dishes and took them out to the kitchen then returned for her jacket.

"Michelle, think about it, please. You're going out to be with the Claw Club, aren't you?"

"No. I have a date." Michelle scooted before I could stop her.

I knew where Michelle was going—out to the clearing in the woods, the place where Luis had first helped me turn into a werecat. I'd wait a few minutes then go out there myself.

But what if it was a trap?

Chapter 37

I crouched in an area about a thousand feet from the clearing. The jungle drums played their hypnotic beat, and the bonfire glowed and popped, its evil purple and orange tongues reaching out into the night.

The Claw Club girls, in their ornate, gilded cat masks, escorted the new inductee into the circle. It was Michelle, of course. She wore the usual white gauzy robe, and a cat mask that looked like a wildcat.

They did their crazy orgiastic dance during which everyone stripped their clothes off and went wild, hopping and spinning like whirling dervishes.

Everything stopped. I stood shocked as the girls removed the white robe from Michelle. They'd let me keep mine on. She stood naked, the white skin between her tan lines glowing in the moonlight. I almost wanted to look away; I didn't really want to see my best friend naked, but my fascination overtook my sense of propriety.

What could I do to save my friend? I wracked my brain. Burst in and break the whole thing up? I didn't think that would work. Use my cell phone to call the cops? If Luis were here, maybe I could talk some sense into him, but he didn't seem to be. This appeared to be an all-girl affair.

A male walked into the circle—the person who would turn her. He wore a jaguar mask, and for a moment I hoped it was some other person who would turn Michelle, but there was no mistaking the long lean muscles and shoulder-length hair. Luis.

I remembered the night he'd turned me, the intimacy of his sucking on the spot near my breast, and the shattering orgasm I had when I felt his blood rush into me. It had been one of the most intimate and intensely erotic moments of my life and now my boyfriend—ex-boyfriend—was sharing that with my best friend.

I crept away then fled into the woods. There was nothing I could do.

At 1:00 a.m., I knocked on the back window of Brendan's family's motor home. The window opened and a familiar face appeared. The one person who had stuck by me through everything, Brendan. "Kenley? Forget it. I'm not talking to you. Go away."

"Please listen to me."

"No." He started to close the window.

"They've turned Michelle. It happened tonight."

"Oh." He cursed softly under his breath. "Hang on a sec. I'm coming out."

We sat in my jeep, running the heat every few minutes to take the chill out of the air.

"I'm over you. I'm a trusting person, and you've done nothing but use me. I thought you were serious about wanting to get out of town, but you used the Michelle thing as an excuse to get back to see Luis." He folded his arms across the front of his flannel-shirted chest.

"I'm sorry. My life has been a mess. I'm doing the best I can." I tried to rub the back of his hand, but he pulled it away. "I don't know where else to turn."

He sighed. "Okay. Tell me what happened."

"They turned Michelle tonight. She's a Rogue now. I feel so horrible. I don't know what to do."

"There's nothing you can do, and it's not your fault, so don't beat yourself up over it." He put his arm around me and it felt better to me than anything else had in a long time.

God, he never stayed mad. He was a saint. "You're forgiving me for my abominable behavior?"

"You know..." He pulled his arm away from me, pushed his hands into his pockets and looked down at his feet. "I get mad at you, but I can't stay that way. I wish I could. I'm such a sap."

"You are not a sap, you're a wonderful person."

"Yeah, yeah."

"I had Luis promise not to let their guys hurt you."

"You talked with Luis? After what happened?"

"He called me and I picked up the phone."

Brendan shook his head then raked both hands through his hair and looked at me exasperated. "Well, at least thank you for not letting them turn me into cat food."

"I'm so frigging confused, I don't know which end is up."

"You're not confused, you just have conflicted allegiances. First it's Luis then me, then Luis then me."

Damn, he could see right through me. "I'm bad. Shoot me."

He hugged me. "You may be bad, but I can't seem to get enough of you. Why is that?"

"You're a masochist?"

"I must be."

We sat in silence. I felt more ashamed of myself than I ever had in my life. "I've botched everything up. I'm even responsible for my parents' death."

"You are not. I was with you when you tried to get them to leave, remember? You did everything you could."

"No, I mean getting involved with Luis and everything."

"Honey, he had you pegged. You practically had nothing to do with it. You were set up for this whole thing."

"You think?"

"I do." He turned to look at me. His blue eyes and sandy-haired good looks had never been so appealing to me. "So, are you going to kill Luis?"

"Oh that again?" I grabbed my hair with both hands. "I don't have it in me to kill anybody. That's why I'm a miserable failure as a Rogue. I have the magical Dagger of Bastet with me."

"Can I see it?" Brendan asked.

"Sure." I opened my backpack and unrolled it from its towel. The knife was a purple sliver of stone with a cat's head sitting on top. I turned it over in my hands reverently. "This is Bastet, isn't it? Egyptian cat goddess."

"That's right. It's thousands of years old," he said.

I looked away. "I don't think I can kill Luis."

Brendan grasped me by both shoulders. "You don't seem to understand the gravity of the situation. If you don't make a kill by tomorrow, you'll be dead. If you do make a kill, you've in essence sold your soul to the devil. If you kill Luis, on the other hand, your nightmare will be over and you'll be able to go back to your regular life."

"You make it sound so simple."

"You can't do it because you still love him." He let go of me.

I didn't say anything.

"Admit it," he said.

"I don't know. I do know that I really care for you."

He hugged me again. "You drive me nuts. What am I going to do with you?"

"Right now, I'm going to go back to Michelle's house and sleep, and in the morning I'll decide what to do."

"Stay with me." His eyes pleaded.

"What about your parents?"

"They love you, too," he said.

"Even after my little escapade of taking them on a wild goose chase and turning them around to come home?"

"Doesn't matter. They know what a tough time you're having," Brendan said.

"They think I'm going to eat them."

"No, they don't."

I kissed him on the cheek. "I'm going to Michelle's. Bye."

Truth be told, I didn't know what I was going to do exactly, but an idea was swiftly forming in my mind. Sunrise would be day five of my Turning. If I didn't make a kill by midnight, I'd die.

I heard Michelle come in at around 4:00 a.m. and get into the other side of the queen bed.

Michelle shook me. "Wake up. I've got to talk. I've had the most amazing night."

"I really don't need this," I said, so sleepy I felt as though I was waking up from a coma.

"Kenley, I'm in love, but I have to talk about it."

"What? You think I want to hear you gushing over Luis? You and every other female in this town?"

"That's just the thing, Kenley. I'm not in love with Luis. I'm in love with Molly."

Chapter 38

I sat up. "Jeez. You mean to tell me that after all this time we've been friends, you've decided you're a lesbian?"

"Molly's just so sexy. She makes me feel things I never thought were possible." She ran her hands down over the curve of her hips.

"But Luis turned you tonight."

"How do you know? Were you watching?"

"No, I mean..."

"Admit it." She poked me in the sternum, then kind of missed and poked one of my boobs, which made me wonder if she'd ever been excited by me.

"I was worried about you," I said.

"Luis didn't turn me, Molly turned me," Michelle said.

"But I saw Luis."

"He was there, but Molly did the ceremony. And Kenley," Michelle clutched my shoulder. "I had the most unbelievable orgasm of my whole life."

I started giggling in a kind of hysterical, uncontrolled madness. But it turned into tears and I doubled over sobbing and clutching my head.

Michelle held me. "I know, it's all too much, isn't it?"

"That's an understatement."

"Let's go to sleep. Things will be less insane in the morning."

"Why don't I believe that?" Despite everything, despite all the craziness, it seemed I could always sleep.

The next morning when I heard Michelle getting ready for school, I sat up in bed and said, "Michelle, no matter what happens, remember that I'm your friend, and I love you."

Michelle sat down on the bed next to me and searched my face. "That sounds kind of final."

"Nothing's final. Just remember that, okay?"

"I will. I love you, too." As she hugged me I thought about all our years together, all the stuff we'd been through. I never wanted to let go of her softness, her unconditional love for me. These things meant a lot when you were about to lose everything.

I took a shower, got my stuff together and headed downtown to the bank.

I withdrew all of the money in my savings account, which would hold me for a while. When I turned eighteen in a couple of months, I'd be able to draw out all of my parents' considerable assets with no problem since they had so trustingly put my name on all of their accounts. Then I'd be set for life. That was if I lived past this day.

As I headed north on I-275, I felt like a diver plunging into deep water, each telephone pole and nameless palm like a depth marker in my journey into unknown waters.

My friends, my home—not that there was much left of that—grew farther and farther away from me. Ever since my parents' death I felt as though their souls were moving farther and farther away, until there'd be nothing left of them, a little pouf of smoke in the nameless dimensions beyond this earth.

Tears trickled down my face. My parents were dead. There was a name for that—orphan. I was an orphan. I started crying so hard I couldn't catch my breath or see the road.

I turned off at the next exit—some hick town like the millions of others that lined I-275. I pulled off into an orange grove, leaned my head on the steering wheel and heaved out the torrent of tears.

I'd never see my parents again. Never see Luis or Brendan. And this was day five of having been turned into a Rogue.

Realizing I had to find strength within myself now more than ever, I sat and concentrated on directing my werecat telepathy. I sent it out in a radiating circle ten miles around myself, then twenty, then one hundred. I knew that I was searching for a needle in a haystack, but I had hope.

The sun was sinking into the horizon like an anchor tossed over the side of a ship. I pulled myself together and got back onto the highway.

Every mile put between myself and the Tampa Rogues would mean that much more safety. Luis said they didn't mean me any harm, but Brendan seemed to think they would be after me, and I was certain that since I was responsible for Enriqué's death, Luis's father would want me dead.

When I saw the familiar Florida visitor's station with the signs that said, "Free Orange Juice," I knew I was nearly at the Florida/Georgia border. It reminded me of road trips with my parents when I was a kid. They always stopped at the visitor's welcome station. But now at 11:00 p.m., the station stood closed-up and dark like a summer pavilion in the dead of winter.

I knew I had to step up my search. If I was going to pass out of this human existence, I was going to go out with a bang and maybe help someone along the way, too.

A strong feeling made me pull off the highway and down the main road of a tiny town that had a post office, gas station and 7 Eleven. With even the convenience store closed up and dark, the place looked more like a ghost town than a living community.

Driving further down the street, I came to a motel right out of an Edward Hopper painting. It had about twelve units with the requisite pool and plastic lawn furniture up front, and a bright coffee shop sat to the side. One lone trucker rested his chin on his hands at the counter as the waitress filled his cup with steaming brew.

I pulled into one of many vacant parking spaces and walked into the office feeling like a zombie. The small room with two chairs and a tiny front desk smelled like twelve-day-old coffee. The man behind the counter with alligator-tanned skin and a big shirt, gave me a momentarily suspicious look. He probably thought I was awfully young to be traveling alone. He was right. But when I pulled a roll of money out of my backpack, he smiled, said, "Thank you, miss," put the cash into his old-fashioned register, and handed me the key. Room number three.

Predictably the room reeked of mildew. I looked around at the stained carpet, the corroded air conditioner, towels thin as slices of ginger and wondered. Was this the place where I was going to die? A cheap motel room?

Not if I could help it.

I pulled back the bed covers and collapsed onto the sheets. The clock radio said 11:50. In ten minutes I'd be dead.

Chapter 39

When my super sharp hearing picked up a faint noise, I raised myself up onto one arm and cocked my head. No mistaking it, I heard a child screaming. No regular person could have detected it.

I hurried to the front door and listened, then stepped outside. The noise didn't seem to be coming from the hotel at all, rather it radiated from the woods behind the building.

There it was again—it sounded like a little girl crying and begging, punctuated by intermittent shrieks.

That was my chance. I tore off into the woods, fearless. Did it occur to me that it might be a trick to lure me out to an isolated spot and kill me? Yes it did, but I was beyond caring about mostly everything now.

The woods behind the hotel contained the typical Florida mixture of junky palmetto palms that stuck up from the ground like hands with claws, scraggly oak trees and razor-sharp briars. I easily flattened any offending brush or leapt right over it.

The feeling of body heat and the sound of the little girl's screams, combined with the overwhelming sense of evil I detected, made it easy for me to zero in on them.

I came face to face with a man who looked like any government office worker you would see anywhere—white shirt, gray tie and black pants, salt and pepper hair.

He held a little girl by the throat and was trying to remove her pink playsuit.

The startled look on the man's face changed to smug gloating when he realized the person who had discovered them was merely a teenage girl.

Without even thinking, I kicked the man in the face and sent him spiraling backward, grabbed the little girl and practically flew, carrying her back to the hotel room. I sat her down on the bed, told her everything was going to be okay, not to answer the door for anyone and locked the door behind me as I walked out.

Soon I was bounding across the underbrush toward that horrible monster of a man. Still woozy from his thrashing, the guy bent over with his head hanging and struggled to get to his feet.

I grabbed him by his collar and brought his face right up to mine.

The surprise on his face that such a delicate-looking girl could be so strong was priceless. I laughed in his face. "Like to mess with kids, huh? Well, I'm going to mess with you."

I felt the shift coming on—a prickly sensation under my scalp that traveled down my spine then out my arms and legs. The tops of my hands and feet felt bubby then claws sprouted. I tore off my clothes leaving them in a pile.

I'll spare you the description of what I did to the man. Suffice it to say I sat contentedly gnawing on his sorry carcass for a good half hour. The taste of human flesh quelled my hunger the way nothing else ever could have. And the fact that I had killed a monster and saved a little girl made it all the sweeter.

The little girl. I chewed up the last few morsels of his flesh I could stuff into myself, then I changed back and dressed in record time.

Sirens, flashing lights and cops surrounded the motel. When I unlocked the door to my room, the little girl was waiting there as instructed. Poor kid, she shrank back as I entered, looking petrified. I put out my hand. "It's okay."

The girl couldn't even talk.

"We're going to bring you outside and find your parents."

When I walked her outside, the cops were all over me. "Wait a minute. I heard her screaming and found her out in the woods."

The cop knelt down and talked to the girl. "Is she telling the truth?"

I wiped my chin, hoping I didn't have blood on myself anywhere.

When she didn't say anything, I thought, oh brother, I'm probably in trouble. But then she spoke up. "The man took me into the woods. And she kicked the man and saved me." She hugged me around the thigh, her tiny hand clutching at my shirt.

"You were able to overpower a grown man?" the cop asked me.

"Yes. Martial arts." I shrugged.

A car skidded up to the curb and a young couple hurried out. "Brittany, you're okay. Oh thank God." The woman whisked her off the ground and hugged her. The tiny hands grabbed her mother's hair and kissed her, then the woman broke into sobs. "Are you hurt?" She turned to the cop then to me accusingly. "Is she hurt?"

"This young lady saved your daughter's life. Some psycho had her out in the woods," the cop said.

"She's not hurt. I grabbed her away before the guy could do anything to her."

"You're a saint. A guardian angel." The dad had tears in his eyes. "How can we ever repay you?"

"No need," I said, feeling on the verge of tears myself. "If you'll excuse me, I'm exhausted."

"That's fine," the cop said, "but please stay in town so we can get you to identify the man. We want to catch this fiend."

"I will." I smiled, patted Brittany's soft hair and went to my room.

Once the hubbub had died down, I took my bag, got into my Jeep and drove further up 275. Then I remembered. I'd been sloppy, left a mangled body out in the woods. What were people going to think, that he'd been mauled by a Florida cougar? I supposed stranger things had happened. I didn't imagine the death of a child molester practically caught in the act would be scrutinized that thoroughly. But I'd have to remember to clean up after myself in the future.

I drove mile after mile of endless highway, all alone, in search of my destiny.

⊶⧉ Epilogue ⧉⊷

Several months later, I sat in a cyber café somewhere in North Carolina. The breathtaking panorama of Blue Ridge Mountains suited me just fine for the moment. I e-mailed from an anonymous hot mail account. I typed in the subject line, "Hi from an old friend."

"Hey Brendan. You'll be happy to hear I'm still alive, although, I don't have to tell you what that means. I'm going to take this opportunity to search out some of my family, see if there are any Favré relatives around who can give me some background on all this stuff and tell me what's going on. I'm not going to rush back to Tampa Bay any time soon, but I promise you'll see me again. Will you do me a favor and tell Michelle I'm okay? I really do love you, Brendan." I purposely didn't sign it, but he'd know who I was. And there was no way he could trace me through an anonymous account.

I ordered some breakfast: two eggs over easy, home fries and rye toast with hot coffee and ate it leisurely, thumbing through the address book I'd swiped from my mom.

One name stood out to me. Paulina Walsh and in parentheses 'Halfling.' What could that mean? I vowed that in the next few months I'd get in touch with my werecat roots and sort things out for myself.

I sat in an Adirondack chair overlooking the mountains and pondered the past month—the changes I'd gone through. I'd loved two guys and thrown them both away. I'd lost my parents and saved the life of a child. I looked at everything with a calm certainty now. No one could harm me. It seemed to me that all of this had happened for some reason. Fate was sweeping me toward some unknown destiny. I had no idea what at the moment, but I intended to find out.

About the Author

Sally Bosco writes young adult dark fiction. She's inexplicably drawn to the uncanny, the shades of gray between light and dark, and the area where your mind hovers as you're falling off to sleep. She loves writing young adult fiction because she strongly relates to teenage angst, the search for self-identity and the feelings of not fitting in.

Originally from Connecticut, she graduated from the University of Florida with a BA in Graphic Design and then went on to complete her MFA in Writing Popular Fiction at Seton Hill University. Her published novels include *Alt.Death.com*. In spite of her affinity for the dark and macabre, she lives in sunny Florida.

The Werecat Chronicles is the first book in a series.

Be sure to keep updated by following her blog and website at **http://sallybosco.com**.